Players Got Played

Also by ReChella

Scandalous

Players Got Played

ReChella

www.urbanbooks.net

Urban Books
10 Brennan Place
Deer Park, NY 11729

ISBN-13: 978-1-60162-020-0
ISBN-10: 1-60162-020-9

First Printing October 2007
Printed in the United States of America

10 9 8 7 6 5 4 3 2 1

This is a work of fiction. Any references or similarities to actual events, real people, living, or dead, or to real locales are intended to give the novel a sense of reality. Any similarity in other names, characters, places, and incidents is entirely coincidental.

Submit Wholesale Orders to:
Kensington Publishing Corp.
C/O Penguin Group (USA) Inc.
Attention: Order Processing
405 Murray Hill Parkway
East Rutherford, NJ 07073-2316
Phone: 1-800-526-0275
Fax: 1-800-227-9604

Acknowledgments

First and foremost, I thank God for life, love, and His one and only Son, Jesus Christ. Secondly, I thank Him for His mercy and grace. Love and thanks to my family for being supportive and understanding as I dedicated much of my time to sitting at the computer working this novel. Many thanks to Urban Books for the opportunity. And to the memories of Ms. Marie Clark, Ms. Catherine Price, Ms. Lucille Graham, and Ms. Minnie Clemons, I dedicate my strength of perseverance and determination. They were awesome moms during the first seventeen years of my existence. I will forever be grateful for the way they allowed God to use them in my life.

Chapter One

Parrish

"**C**ome on ladies, what are we waiting for? Let's get the first story started! I've been waiting too long as it is to hear all of this sexy ass dirt!" Myilana *(My-lane-uh)* hollered with enthusiasm from her seat on the sage-green sofa.

Dhelione *(Dee-lee-on)* plopped down playfully on the sofa next to her and said, "Damn, Myilana. Aren't you in a rush tonight? And who do you think you're fooling? You're not waiting to hear sexy dirt . . . your secretive little ass has got something real juicy for us, don't you? Who'd you fuck, the Mayor? Girrrl, if you did, I've only got two questions for you. How big is his dick? Is he as freaky as he looks? Do he know how to use that wide ass tongue he's always sliding across his top lip like he's searching for leftover ice cream juices? And do he eat the kitty with his eyes open, closed, or partially in between?"

Myilana gave Dhelione a devilish grin. "What the hell? That was four questions."

"So, who the hell's counting? Are you gonna answer them, or not?" Dhelione chuckled. "Oh, I forgot one. Did he sneak you inside his house, and maybe tie you up in one of those famous rooms we've heard about, and make you pretend like you were the maid while he fucked you?"

Myilana squinted her eyes and slowly shook her head at Dhelione. "You are one sick in the brains, freaky heifer. Do you know that?"

"Thank you." Dhelione reached her hand around and patted her own back. "Now did he or didn't he?"

Myilana laughed out loud. "Maybe. Ya'll won't know if it was him or not 'til we get started, now will you?" The two of them raised their wine glasses and sipped happily.

It was about to be on like a pot of neck-bones up in there. I could hardly wait. I knew the girls probably had some shit to tell that was so far out there it was almost unreal. Why? Because the shit I had to tell was unreal too. All week long I'd been on a countdown and now the day was finally here. Me and my four girlfriends had waited a whole damn year for this one weekend.

To the average Joe Blow it was just another Friday, Saturday, and Sunday in the slows of the country, but to us, it marked the anniversary when we celebrated flipping the script on our cheating ass husbands and giving them a secret dose of their own deceitful medicine. I say secret dose, because even though our men were being paid back for all of their lousy indiscretions, they sure as hell didn't know about it. We named the event our "private relaxation gathering" for the sake of all the nosy folks in town.

A small town in northern Mississippi by the name of Coldwater is where we call home. The Friday evening that kicked everything off was one of the most beautiful autumn evenings in October of '99. Light jazz oozed through the speakers of the big entertainment center that sat in one corner of the den, and plenty of food and drink was spread across the kitchen table. All of the club business was finally out of the way, so we were in full swing.

Myilana and Dhelione were the first to simmer down from all the dancing and jumping around. They'd already fallen into their usual spots on the oversized, plush sectional that curved along two of the den walls in the cozy, six-room cottage. Talk about a big comfortable sofa, that bad-boy was one of a kind. And in another corner, a large accent chair for two matched it.

The cottage, a country getaway house that the girls and I rented each year was meant to allow us to do just that, *getaway* from it all. Located in a secluded area just on the outskirts of town, the little place was equipped with a genuine wood-burning fireplace, three additional bedrooms, and exceptional bathroom facilities. Such a lovely place to get lost in time. The den, of course, being the largest room, was where we spent most of our stay, lounging and running our mouths 'til we ran out of ridiculous shit to say.

About two hours into the festivities, the night was already filled with enjoyment. All five of us were bright-eyed and sho'nuff geared-up to sip on some nice, bubbly *Dom Perignon* wine while blabbing all the dirty, hot details of our past year's secret rendezvous. Our tales were usually so steamy and untamed, they put the stories in *True Confessions* magazine to shame. It felt good knowing that five liberated sisters could get together for an entire weekend in unity and share some of our deepest, darkest, and most intimate secrets without worrying about a big mouth gossiper putting our business in the streets.

We left every care and stressful priority we owned at the house for our families to deal with during this occasion. Make no mistake, my girls and I spent most of our time tending to our families, but we considered these three days and three nights to be our very own "unwind and let our hair down" private time.

Not to brag, but the best description I can give for each of us would be vibrant, ambitious, refined, career-oriented, and to let our many gentlemen friends tell it, sassy and beautiful. We were sure as hell in a class all by ourselves. One of our golden rules was, "nobody other than the five of us already in the organization would ever be a part of it." The simple reason for that? We had too much at stake to risk on somebody we didn't know anything about. In our hometown our reputations were ideal; if the good ol' folks of Coldwater had only known the truth.

For years my girls and I played our game so well no one ever suspected a thing. We were bound by a set of rules that we never compromised. We stuck to those damn rules like paper to glue because we knew if we didn't, and somehow managed to slip-up there would be hell to pay. The kind of creeping we were doing called for discipline, so we squeezed discipline by the balls and took charge of it.

Our husbands couldn't even match our skills, but it sure wasn't from lack of them trying. They'd been doing their dirt long before we attempted to do anything about it. Call it an old cliché, but we got tired of getting fucked and started fucking. And when I say fucking, I mean, really, really fucking. Like most hopeful little wives who love their husbands and want the marriage to work in the beginning, we smiled, gritted our teeth, and took their *ho-hopping* gracefully in hopes it would one day stop. Guess what? It didn't. So, hell yes, things had to change. While their asses were out playing, if only they'd known they were getting played.

The so-called "players" didn't have a clue about the shit they were in for the night the girls and I got acquainted for the first time at a local social event. The event itself wasn't much to brag about and it damn sure wasn't entertaining, but we credit it for bringing us together and giving us the opportunity to become the best of friends.

All we did that night was drink as much champagne and wine as we could get our hands on and bitch about how bad our husbands were treating us. How the five of us ended up sitting together in the first place beats the hell out of me. But by the end of the night our need to vent encouraged us to get together again and vent some more, not to mention, just plain chill with each other. From that point on, we were inseparable. As time went on, we found that the circumstances surrounding each of us were too much alike to just be coincidence. We came to believe that fate had brought us together.

Though we probably could have done it forever, we eventually got tired of getting together and yakking non-stop about our sorry-ass situations at home with the hubbies. It wasn't long after, we came up with a plan, or game rather, to get with as many fine men as we could handle in our spare time and do as much inconsequential fucking as our pussies desired. That way we would have some different shit, more exciting shit, to talk about when we got together.

Our most highly regarded rule of the game was, *what went on in our presence, stayed in our presence, when we weren't in our presence.* So once we made it on the inside of that modest, but beautifully decorated cottage and locked the doors, there was no contact with the outside world. Five years running and none of us had ever broken that rule. Why in the hell we decided to break it on this particular day is unbeknownst to me. But I can say without a doubt, it was one of the biggest mistakes we ever made. Out of the five of us, I was considered the somewhat clueless one. Truth be told, that wasn't so. I never missed too many details about what was going on.

The fifth gathering, which was the gathering of all gatherings, is the one I remember most. That disastrous shit constantly plays in my head like it was yesterday. None of us saw it coming. It crept up slowly in disguise, but when it hit us, it crashed into us like a big ass 747 airplane. A tragedy that fucked our lives up for good!

"Okay, ladies. Myilana's itching to get the show on the road, so let's settle down a little, " Dhelione said softly. Her light voice with a hint of New York accent was barely heard. Don't get me wrong, she could sure enough get loud when she wanted to, but being naturally loud wasn't her thing.

Dhelione's brown skin, short tapered haircut, and model's figure always kept her ego on cloud nine. She considered herself to be a class-act, but without the snobbish or bitchy attitude. Even though she'd lived in the country her entire thirty-seven years like the rest of us, her accented speech would never have given it away. Neither of us completely embraced the downright country lingo that the south is so well known for, but Dhelione was a few steps ahead of everybody in that department.

By now, I was just as anxious to get the *story-telling*

started as Dhelione and Myilana. Full of food, still sipping from my wine glass, and slightly tipsy, I plopped down on the sofa near them. The three of us joined forces in rushing Renalia *(Ree-nal-yah)* and Emberly *(M-ber-lee)* to hurry and finish stuffing their faces. They were the only two still wandering the place aimlessly and gabbing on about nothing. They soon settled down in their favorite spots on the sofa with us, and as usual, we had the soft lamp-lights illuminating the atmosphere. Now it was a go.

"All right, who's got the keepsake box?" Renalia asked, glancing from place to place trying to lay eyes on the box.

The keepsake box was a small, handheld, oak chest that we put our names in and randomly pulled from to decide who'd kick off the story-telling. Renalia grabbed the box from the corner table and began shaking it.

"Okay, everybody's name is in, right? Do the honors, Emberly, darling?" Renalia held the chest in front of Emberly for her to pull the first name.

We eagerly waited to see who it was going to be.

"It's Myilana!" Emberly yelled excitedly, throwing the piece of paper in the air.

"All right, come on with it girl! I knew it was going to be you! I could feel it in my bones," Dhelione burst out.

The five of us slapped high-fives and began singing a taunting little jingle to hype Myilana. *"Myilana's got the hot seat . . . Myilana's got the hot seat . . . Myilana's got the hot seat . . . "*

Myilana stood up smiling and took a bow while she waited for one of us to ask the questions. Yours truly did the honors.

"Okay, Myilana, question one and two." I took a deep breath and let it rip. "How many men have you fucked, and how many rendezvous have you had since our last October '98 gathering?"

"Well, my dear, sweet, Parrish *(Pair-rish)*." Myilana gave me a grin like grinning was going out of style. "I've had twenty-four rendezvous, but guess what? Only one man. Why? 'Cause he was so hot and sexy, I needed all twenty-four times just to cool my *kitty-kat* down." She began flapping one hand in front of her face as if fanning the heat away.

"Woo!"

"All right . . . all right!"

"I heard that, girlfriend."

"Whoa! You go girl!" Each of us boosted Myilana with cheery compliments.

Our procedure was so routine it was almost ritualistic. It was corny as hell too, but it was fun to us.

"Shhhh, question number three." I interrupted everybody's cheering. "Myilana, without revealing his name, tell us about your lover and your love affair."

Aside from the soft jazz still playing, silence combed the room as Myilana began. It was part of the game to listen to the description of the man and try to guess who he was before she revealed him at the end of the story.

"First of all, I've known *of* him for quite some time, but we got better acquainted when he came into the finance company one Monday morning." Myilana sat her five-seven, one-hundred-twenty-pound frame straight up on the sofa and folded her legs Indian style. She looked like she was really fixing to get into it now.

"He's five years older than me, that would make him thirty-eight. Okay, that's the math for whoever's had too much wine to add it up," she said jokingly. "Anyway, he's one of those light-skinned brothers with hair everywhere—coal black hair. He wears a neat little mustache, full eyebrows, and a low haircut. I'm going to say he's about six-one. Oh, and he's slim, but not too slim. He's got a great chest, great abs, and his ass is to die for. The day he came into the finance company he was in the process of getting some information from the secretary, and I happened to walk out of my office on my way to see one of the other loan officers. This guy's ass, oh my goodness, was the first thing I caught sight of." Myilana's face lit up as she seemed to relive the incident while describing her guy.

The four of us listened attentively.

"Naturally, when the secretary saw me, she called me over and told me the customer needed to see a loan officer. As I walked up I was so distracted by his ass, I had to ask her to repeat herself. N-A gave me a warm smile and instantly extended his hand for a shake.

"Hold up, Myilana. N-A? What does N-A mean?" I asked, slightly frowning.

"Nice Ass, what else? That's my nickname for him 'til somebody guesses who he is or until I tell." Myilana ran her fingers through her long, black, layered hair and shook it out.

"Oh, my bad." I then shut my mouth.

"Anyway, as I was saying before I was interrupted by *Parrish the slow-poke*, I showed him to my office so we could discuss his financial needs. He wasted no time explaining why he wanted to use our company instead of the bank that he usually did business with. The entire time he was talking, I sat behind my desk mesmerized by his smooth, seductive voice. I was completely drawn in by his sexy eyes as they peered into mine. Each time he smiled he brightened the room. With all of his assets and the properties he owned, he definitely qualified for the loan, but by the time he was done talking I knew I wasn't going to approve it for him."

"Hold up, hold up." I interrupted again while at the same time tying my shoulder length wrap into a ponytail. "Why the hell not, Myilana?"

"Damn, Parrish, isn't it obvious, girlfriend?" Myilana sounded like I should've already known why she wasn't going to approve the loan.

"Hell, that's not a bad question," Renalia said, parking her big brown eyes on Myilana. "I wanna know why you didn't give it to him too."

"Not you too, Renalia," Myilana gasped in surprise. "Becauuuuse, by the time he was done talking, I was wet from just watching his luscious lips and absorbing his deep gaze. Hell, I was already trying to figure out how I was gonna fuck him without seeming so desperate. Ya'll know me, I like to play hard to get games. Besides, I don't mix business with pleasure, that's automatic termination from my job. They call it conflict of interest." Myilana's seriousness about her job showed as she leaned forward and picked up her wine glass from the center table.

"In other words, Myilana, ya'll can't *fuck'em and fund'em* at the same time. It's either one or the other, huh?" Dhelione asked, trying to hold a straight face. "Well, listen, can you maybe *fund'em* first, and after they pay-up in full, then *fuck'em*?" The second she dropped her wise crack, she exploded into laughter, taking us with her.

Once we got all the hilarity out we urged Myilana to get back to the story. She raised her hand in the air signaling silence.

"Okay, hush now, so ya'll won't miss anything. Like I said, I wasn't going to approve his loan, but I wasn't crazy enough to tell him that. I asked him to wait in my office for a few minutes while I had a word with one of the other loan officers. I walked down the hall to Bill Berkley's office and quickly filled him in on the new file, then made up some kind of excuse as to why I wouldn't be able to work the loan. Bill came back to my office with me and asked N-A to come with him so they could start processing the loan. It took about forty-five-minutes for them to finish. The attraction between me and this guy was so strong, I just knew he was gonna stop in to see me on his way out.

"A gentle knock sounded at my door. I asked the knocker to come in and there stood N-A. He closed the door behind him with this polite smile on his face, then told me he didn't want to leave without saying thank you. I told him his thank you wasn't necessary because I wasn't the one who worked his loan. By now I was relaxing back in my chair with my legs crossed trying to look sexy and be cool at the same time. He threw that same sweet ass stare on me from before and told me, 'Maybe you didn't work it, but you worked enough.'

"I stared back at him and asked what did that mean. He invited me to discuss it over dinner that upcoming Thursday night at 8:00 o'clock. Girrrrrrls, when he came closer to me and stood in front of my desk, I wanted to throw his ass on that floor and get me some right there. I could've licked him like a lollipop he looked so damn good. But ya'll know I had to contain myself, don't you? I mustered up this semi-serious look and told him in case he hadn't noticed I was wearing a wedding ring, which meant I was married.

"Without hesitation he went, 'I'm married too. I didn't ask you to marry me, I asked you to have dinner with me.' My smile probably clued him in that his answer was clever-n-cute.

"I pretended not to be interested and told him I didn't think it was a good idea. He said he respected my decision, but wanted permission to say one more thing before he left. The second I told him to go for it, he started going-on about how flawless my caramel skin is, how drop-dead gorgeous I am, and how appealing my southern professional accent is. If only he'd known, flattery was getting him everywhere. But I kept up my nonchalant act, thanked him for the compliments, and rose to let him out.

"As I held the door open, he walked so close to me while passing, I inhaled a big sniff of his cologne and almost had an orgasm right there in the middle of the floor. His cologne stayed with me the rest of the day. I wasn't surprised when he phoned me back a few hours later with the same proposal. I did a hell of a job flirting with him for about fifteen minutes over the phone, but in the end I still told him no." Myilana paused to refresh her wine and drink some. That gave the rest of us a few minutes to comment on the story, thus far.

Chapter Two

"Shiiiiiit, girl!" Emberly's motor-mouth zoomed ahead of everybody else. "An attraction that strong? I would've scooped him up on contact. The folks in the office would've been paging me, and my ass would've been outside in his car, or in my car, or in your car, or in some damn body's car, fucking!" She pointed around the room at each of us as fast as she was talking. Again, we broke into laughter.

Emberly was the youngest and thinnest of us, but ironically she was the one with the most mouth. And man-oh-man did she have a serious speeding problem with words. The first time I heard her talk on the night we met, I had to ask her to repeat herself three times before I finally caught what she was saying. Her speech wasn't the problem, just the pace of it. We challenged her more times than a few to slow the hell down, but she always laughed and told us to speed our brains the hell up, because it wasn't her fault we had to ride the short bus in high school.

She could've made a damn good living as one of those hill-billie auctioneers. It was hard to shut her up once she got started. She talked more shit and had more philosophies than one person should be allowed in a lifetime. We gave her props though, she could get a party started and keep it crunk to the max.

"Ya'll might as well holler yep yep, 'cause you know I'm not lying, don't you?" Emberly laughed. "Girrrrl, somebody would've had to call Curtis Marlston on me."

"Isn't that the Chief of Police here in Coldwater?" Renalia asked, stretching her legs out on the sofa.

"Hell yes!" Emberly shrieked, then suddenly stopped her laughter as if she was thinking about something important. "But the more I think about, there's not much he could've done either."

"Why do you say that? He isss the Chief of Police, girl." I giggled.

" 'Cause me and him did some bumping and grinding too!" Emberly fell into another laugh riot.

"Damn, girl! You've been fucking the chief of police, again? Please tell me not in the police car!" I hollered at her.

None of us could stop laughing long enough for Myilana to get back to the story. Emberly was so tickled, tears formed in her light-brown eyes. And her long, auburn-streaked hair trembled like leaves on a tree in high wind.

My smooth, russet face was turning red from the strain of the hard laugh. Thank goodness somebody slowed up and told Myilana to continue.

"Come on, let Myilana get back to the story. Ya'll need to put those damn wine glasses down and stop tripping," Dhelione said, struggling to control her own laughter.

"Dhelione's right, I'm gonna get back to the story." Myilana straightened up and cleared her throat. "Where'd I stop at?"

"You stopped at . . . aahhh, you stopped at," I stammered, snapping my fingers trying to recall. "You stopped at when he called you on the phone a few hours later and asked you about dinner again, but you still ended up telling him no."

"That's right, Parrish, he was very persistent, but I kept saying no." Myilana nodded at me. "And after a couple more days, and several more phone calls from him, I finally agreed to see him that Thursday night as he requested. Ya'll know how nosy most of the people in this little town of ours is. So he and I made plans to meet in Memphis at the Adams Mark Hotel out on Ridgeway.

"We had dinner in their fine dining restaurant, *Sacthmos*. Afterward, he ordered a bottle of chilled champagne to take up to the room with us. He was so courteous, and such a gentleman with his good looking ass. The cologne he wore intoxicated me more than the champagne did. I remembered it from that day in my office. It was *Aramis*.

"When we got on the elevator he pushed the sixth floor button. We stood side by side on our way up. He shined those gorgeous dark-brown eyes down on me and asked if I enjoyed dinner. I gazed back and told him it was nice. I guess he could sense how bad I wanted him, because he leaned over, took me in his arms and kissed me.

"His tongue was so hot and tantalizing. I squeezed him as tight as he squeezed me. We moaned as one. Our tongues wallowed in each other's mouths. We fell against the back wall of the elevator and rolled from side to side, hunching through our clothes. Thank goodness nobody else was in there with us. When the elevator stopped, we straightened up in a hurry and walked to the room holding hands in silence.

"As soon as he unlocked the door and we stepped on the inside the room, we were right back at it. We didn't even make it to the bed. The black fitted dress I was wore went one way, and my strapless bra went another. He stripped that shit off me so fast, I thought I was in the middle of a damn hurricane. The only thing he didn't take off was my thong. We plunged down on the floor kissing and rolling like we were trying to put out a fire—me wearing only my thong, and him still in his shirt and slacks.

"There were no words wasted. We couldn't get anything out except mumbling and loud breathing. It all happened so fast, I didn't even remember when he sat the champagne bottle down on the floor. All I know is in the middle of our tongue wrestling, he suddenly stopped and grabbed the champagne bottle, shook it briskly, then uncorked the top. It splashed all over us. As the foamy suds settled down, he began to slowly pour it over my body. I lay on my back looking up at him, thinking how gorgeous he was and how I was going to fuck the hell out of him.

"The bubbly brew chilled me in a keen, ticklish sort of way. Each drop splattered gently onto my skin, making me twitch with arousal and sensation. My reaction seemed to turn him on even more. I began to slowly gyrate while caressing the champagne all over my body, my breasts, stomach, and thighs. The way he was looking at me made me feel straight-up *scandalous*. He watched a few seconds longer, then slowly leaned down and began licking on me. As he glided his tongue back and forth, I scythed my hands through his soft short locks. He worked his way up and began suckling on one of my nipples, then the other.

"My spine tingled from top to bottom. His fingers drifted down and made their way to *Kitty-Kat* and roved around inside her. *Kitty-Kat* was hot and wet, she wanted some tongue action. I gapped my legs wide and made her available for his tasting pleasure. He eventually obliged her by going down and rendering taste after swipe after lick. He positioned his head directly between my legs, placed both of his hands under my ass, and squeezed my ass-cheeks firmly as he indulged.

"My pussy lay open in his face as he treated himself. His groans told me he was enjoying the eat as much as I was enjoying him eating it. Then he messed around and hit my G-spot and a stream of pre-cum trickled down but he didn't shy away. He sopped up all there was, while working on my clit until it stood stiff. He gently sucked it, dangled it with his tongue, and caressed it with his lips. My body began to tremble. I knew I was getting ready to have an orgasm. Out it came. I creamed his mouth with thick, rich cum. He slurped it like a sweet, velvety milkshake.

"As soon as I had my first orgasm I immediately wanted another one. I raised myself from the floor and sat upright, then grabbed his face in the palms of my hands and pulled him up to me. When his face reached my face, our tongues wrapped in each other. We kissed long and intense like before. I tasted the residue from my pussy juices all over his tongue, lips, and mouth. I quickly stripped the smooth, creased shirt off his fine body while we continuously licked and kissed all over each other.

"Together we hurriedly removed his pants and underwear. He picked up the champagne bottle and took a nice even swallow, then handed it to me. After I took a mouthful, I sat the bottle aside. As soon as I did, he grabbed me and re-engaged in our passionate kiss. We were stark naked with our bodies overheated, sitting in the middle of the hotel room floor engaged in steaming fore-play. There wasn't an area on my body he didn't kiss and taste. I was dying to taste him.

"I overpowered his embrace on me and steered my head down to his thick, veiny hard-on. We exchanged positions. He lay flat on his back on the floor and I turned my body toward the bottom of him with my head buried in his crotch. As I slowly teased the tip of his shaft with my tongue, he murmured something. I didn't quite understand what he said, but the second I felt his hand gripping the top of my head, I knew he wanted me to hook him up.

"I went deep down on his raging cock. So deep, I almost choked, but I quickly relaxed my throat and took it all in. I savored every suck of his dripping boner, massaging the roof of my mouth and the back of my throat with his mushroom shaped head. He fingered through my layers of hair as it kept falling down alongside my face, covering the look of pleasure I held while satisfying him.

"In the midst of his murmurs, he told me to turn my sweet, hot pussy back around so he could have more of it. I hurriedly swung my body around and lay *Kitty-Kat* right down on his face, all the while I didn't miss one suck of his rod. He reached his arms up over my hips and placed his hands atop my ass and squeezed my meaty cheeks yet again. I rolled *Kitty-Kat's* sweet slickness over his face.

"When I felt his tongue enter my cunt-hole I rolled

even harder. I was surprised he could breath. He was definitely wearing a face full of pussy. The way I plunged up and down on his face, it was obvious he liked eating it very much. I also liked being at the opposite end, working-it-out on his *delectable-dick*. I couldn't see his face, but as wet and slick as my pussy was, his face had to be well-glazed. The sixty-nine position never felt better. He's got a pair of the prettiest, finest legs and thighs I've ever seen on a man.

"As we continued indulging in the forbidden pleasures of each other's sexual delicacies, I felt another orgasm approaching. I also tasted the pre-cum from his dick increasing in my mouth. He was getting ready to shoot off. I sucked even harder and took in even more of his beautiful cock. I gently caressed and massaged his balls with my fingers while I awaited the arrival of his fine substance. He, in turn, sopped all around my asshole and licked it wet! He then began fingering me in my ass as he slid his way up to my clit once again. By that time he had figured out he couldn't go wrong with the clit.

"He gently sucked on it, and was about to get a repeat occurrence of the way I'd creamed his face during my first orgasm. Then it came. We cummed in unison. He erupted all over my neck and tits. I spurted into his mouth and he swallowed every little drip-drop of it.

"We disassembled our number sixty-nine position and smiled in gratification, but we still couldn't keep our hands off each other's fervent bodies. I anxiously waited for my strong, handsome prince to sweep me up, pour me into bed and make mad passionate love to me just like our oral performance had been so fulfilling. But the strangest thing happened. In all of our moving around and turning, he guided his mouth down to my feet. I heard these strange but pleasing sounds coming from him. It went something like, 'umm-mmmm. . . . ohhh, smaaacck, ummmm, ohhh, ummmm . . . umm.' Next thing I knew, he was ravishing my damn toes! Literally raping them!

"Ladies, he was sucking and eating my toes harder and more intense then when he was eating my pussy. I was like damn, is this for real? But, of course, I didn't say it out loud. He had the biggest *foot-fetish* I've ever seen. He slid his tongue in and out around my toes, then slurped on them like he was finishing a caramel, Slo-Poke sucker. Gripping both of my feet in his tender, manly hands and firmly massaging them, he munched away. He drooled from toe to toe, keeping me turned on every step of the way with his incredible hankering. He finally satisfied his longing to splurge over my feet and made his way back to my upper body. I'm not lying, when I saw into his eyes he looked like he was completely renewed from his orgasm after sucking my toes. It was almost as if that's how he replenished himself after splattering all over me before.

"When we kissed again, I was thirsty as hell to get his robust rod inside of me. I felt my way downward and grabbed hold of his erection, guiding it in. We began to fuck right there on the floor. In the same spot we'd been utilizing the whole time. I lay under his warm, brawny body with my legs wrapped around his lower back while he thrust in my tight pussy. He rolled his ass non-stop like he was twirling a Hoola Hoop.

"I stroked my pussy back at him and caressed his back with both hands. Around and around we went as our bodies slapped together in the same movement. His dick crammed my pussy-hole full, and I felt every muscle and crease in it against my soft, tissue-like walls. I worked my hands down from his back, grasping his ass-cheeks and rubbed over them while he and I gyrated simultaneously. I felt the muscles in his ass begin to shake and tremble. He bounced on me, and at the same time reached his mouth down to suckle my nipples. I was jealous because I didn't want my titties getting all the attention. I wanted to look into his eyes as we prepared to reach our peak again.

"I removed my hands from his ass-cheeks and placed them on the sides of his face, lifting his head from my tits so we could gaze into each other's eyes. His big brow and sexy eyes were even more spellbinding. He quickly kissed at random over my face, leaving a trail of wetness from place to place. But he never stopped stroking his ass. The very last kiss that he softly lay onto my forehead fucked my mind up all the way! It was something about the way he did it. His lips were barely touching my forehead, but at the same time I felt the tip of his tongue on my skin. The breathing from his nostrils gently blew over the top of my forehead and mesmerized me. There was even a tiny bit of wind in his kiss. I remember thinking to myself, *this man has got a forehead fetish too*.

"My heart rate increased and I began to feel a warm, tingly sensation all over. I became erratic and began talking all kinds of off the wall shit to him. Shit like, 'I wanna fuck you outside in the lobby. I wanna fuck you on top of this building. I wanna fuck you in my bed at my house. I don't care who finds out, I just wanna fuck you when I get ready to.' Then I made him promise me that whenever I got ready to do it, he would always be available for me. He promised me in a sensual whisper, then repeated his forehead kiss one last time. He listened to me blab out of control, and even agreed to some of the crazy shit I was rambling on about. Then finally I told him I was getting ready to cum again.

"Even though I was raving like a madwoman, and not to mention, out of breath from trying to keep up with his vigorous ass strokes, he kept his composure up 'til the moment he let it all out again. We shook like currents of electricity were running through our bodies. When that final one passed through and I saw the muscles in his chest, neck, and arms as he strained and buckled his body tightly. A big stream of milky juice flowed through both of us. I felt it trickling down the inside, then outside of my pussy.

"After our awesome ending, he held me in his arms on the floor and gently stroked through my hair, whispering how pretty and shiny it is and how much it turned him on. I was so caught up with him I didn't even realize how beautiful the hotel room was until after he and I had showered and tucked ourselves underneath the covers in bed. We cuddled and talked. It was like I'd known him forever." Myilana's face lit up like a Christmas tree as she spoke so tenderly about her lover and their first rendezvous.

The rest of us listened attentively as she neared the end of the story. By now, we could tell how infatuated she was with her unrevealed lover. Still, none of us had been able to guess who he was.

"Well, what more can I say about that night?" Myilana smiled, rubbing her hands together slowly. "Except . . . as he and I chatted, he ordered another bottle of chilled champagne and we treated ourselves all back over again. We overstayed about two hours, but it was all good. Wheew! It was the first time within the five years that we've been doing this shit, I actually fell head over heels for everything this one man made me feel. Believe me when I say, he did something amazing to me. I don't know what, but something. I can usually handle myself with men no matter how 'together' they think they are. But this guy did me so good, I can't even think about fucking another outside man, except him. If ya'll really want the truth . . . I barely wanna fuck the hubby." Myilana glanced around the room at each of us, waiting for somebody to say something.

Chapter Three

I was so caught up in all the explicit details Myilana had given us, my eyes were still bugging out. I shook my daze off and took a quick look at the other girls. Dhelione and Emberly appeared as captivated and filled with admiration as I was. Renalia, on the other hand, beheld this blank look.

Emberly commented ahead of everybody else again. "Myilanaaaa," she said with emphasis. "Girlfriend, I don't have but one thing to say. You need to hook me up with dude's digits 'cause he sound like he's something serious. I've been trying my damndest to figure out who he is, but I can't do it. Damn!"

"Paleeeease," Myilana replied, squinting her eyes at Emberly. "Honey, I'm gonna ride that horse for as long as he's galloping. And with no interferences. You're gonna have to find your own stallion, baby girl. This one belongs to me and his wife . . . in that order." The two of them giggled.

"I know that's right, Myilana," I said. "When you find a good one there's nothing wrong with holding on to him for a minute. At least, 'til it goes bad. I'm like Emberly though, I can't figure out who he is either."

"Neither can I." Dhelione looked at Myilana anxiously. "But I'm dying to know, so come on out with it, girl."

Myilana smiled. "Okay, okay. His—"

"Emberly, if Myilana doesn't give you his number you can get it from me." Renalia interrupted, sounding unpleasant. We turned our attention to her.

"I beg your pardon?" Emberly frowned.

Renalia's blank look was now worse. It matched her bitter tone of voice "You heard me. You can get his number from me if she doesn't want to give it to you."

Myilana drew a confused look similar to Emberly's.

"How did you get his number, Renalia?" Myilana asked softly, staring at her.

Renalia made no attempt to hide her bitterness. In fact, her reply was downright devious.

"Evidently, Mr. N-A, as you call him, has been spreading himself around pretty good. I've been fucking him for the past couple of months too. Ha, ha, what do you think about that?"

I gasped in surprise. So did everybody else. Myilana stared at Renalia like she'd just slapped her in the face with a hot skillet.

"You're kidding, right?" Myilana edged an unsure smile. "I mean, you're so not serious."

"I'm afraid not, darling," Renalia said unapologetically. "You and I have been riding the same stallion."

"Ain't this a bitch. Ya'll gotta' be shitting me." Dhelione put her hands over her open mouth, signifying *oops*. "Damn, what's his name?"

Myilana was too dismayed to answer. Renalia appeared just as disappointed, but she had no problem dropping Mr. Wonderful's name. "His name is Ashton

Drapers and he owns the day spa here in town . . . and the one in Senatobia, and the one in Batesville."

"I know Ashton," Dhelione said.

"I do too." Emberly grabbed some strawberries from the fruit tray on the center table and bit into one. "But I didn't know he owned any day spas. I thought that chain of day spas was owned and operated by a Caucasian family. The Latham's."

"They have been for the last four or five years," I answered her.

Maybe the shock of Renalia sleeping with the same guy had worn off Myilana, or she'd decided to play it as "no big deal." She calmly uttered, "Duhhh, ya'll don't remember me saying that's how I got acquainted with him? He came into the finance company for a loan."

"Oohh, that's why he wanted the loan? To purchase the spas?" Dhelione asked. "Well, if that's the case, why hasn't he changed the name of them since he's the new owner?"

"He said he wanted the setup to pretty much stay the same 'cause the business had been very successful over the years." Renalia tossed Myilana a snub look. "Isn't that right, Myilana?"

Myilana pitched the same look back at her. Their testy behavior was intensifying. Dhelione, Emberly, and I suspiciously eyed each other momentarily, before Dhelione questioned them about it.

"I know ya'll aren't tripping off this shit? I'll be the first to admit, Ashton is one fine ass piece of dick. And listening to Myilana's story, the brother's got it going on too. But hey, we're the high class divas running shit. We dish out attitude like this, not take it. We've got it going on, and we're gonna deal with this little slip up like the pros we are, right?"

Myilana didn't utter a word. Renalia didn't utter a word. The two of them seemed lost in thought. My heart raced, waiting for one of them to say something. I silently hoped that this trivial incident wouldn't tear so much as a snag in the long-standing friendship the five of us had managed to build. I crossed my fingers. I just knew one of them would agree with Dhelione in a minute. They didn't, so I spoke up, sounding as peaceful as I could.

"She's right, guys. I mean, if nothing else, let's at least be real about the situation. This was bound to happen sooner or later. There's no way on earth the five of us could have continued jumping in and out of secret relationships and not get tangled up with the same man at some point. Just think about it, we sex up different men down through the whole year, and don't tell each other who we're screwing 'til we come here. It's not like one of ya'll went and slept with the guy on purpose after he'd been revealed at a previous gathering. To be honest, I think we've done extremely well considering it's taken this long for some shit like this to happen."

"I agree. This kind of shit simply goes with the territory," Emberly said. "But it's nothing we haven't thought about at least one time in the past. Hell, I know I have."

"Dammit, Myilana and Renalia. Are ya'll just gonna sit there, looking from face to face like we're some aliens, and not say anything?" Dhelione demanded.

Renalia humped up her shoulders. "There's nothing to be said, Dhelione. I mean, damn, the facts are in. We've been fucking the same guy. His dick has been keeping both of us happy. What do ya'll want us to do? A jig in the middle of the floor?"

"Renalia." Myilana finally broke her silence. "It took

me quite a while to tell the story, at what point did you realize who I was talking about? I mean, did you know who he was in the beginning? The middle? Toward the end? When?"

"Your description sounded like him, but it wasn't enough for me to know for sure," Renalia answered. "Then later you mentioned the foot fetish and the seductive forehead kiss, I knew without a doubt. He did that shit to me so many times, whew. I thought I was gonna pass out from feeling too good."

"Why didn't you say something when you first figured it out?" Myilana's soft words were filled with emotion. I could've sworn she was holding back tears. She was tenderhearted that way, never involving herself with misunderstandings if she could keep from it.

"And miss hearing the unedited version of one of the most romantic stories of the year? No way." Renalia was now being sarcastic. "I wanted to hear evidence that he swept you away as much as he swept me away. 'Cause he really swept me away big time, darling."

"Well, did you hear what you wanted to hear? Or do I need to take another turn and fill everybody in on his and my second rendezvous? It was just as romantic, you know." Myilana bragged, sounding nothing like her usual easygoing self. I felt it was her way of responding to Renalia's obvious spitefulness. And at the same time dealing with the mishap without acting resentful.

Renalia, on the other hand, wasn't trying to veil her true feelings, at all. Her bitchy attitude was front and center for all to see. She leaned over and picked a handful of grapes from the tray while sneering at Myilana.

"Oh, I heard your story, and it was very . . . aahhh, how can I put this? Interesting? The two of you had a few nicely lit sparks, but please spare us on telling another back to back exaggeration about you and him. It couldn't have been that good between ya'll 'cause he's fucking me, isn't he?" She shot Myilana a cruel wink.

I was shocked at her bold, unfeeling remark. We all knew she could be a little rigid sometimes, but none of us expected anything to that degree. After she said it, I don't know who's eyes bugged out the most, Dhelione's, Emberly's, or mine. For a moment, we did nothing except look at her. Renalia making light of one of us? I never thought I'd see the day. It may seem a little hard to believe that five black chicks could be friends for that long, doing that kind of fucking around with so many different men, and not have the usual female drama like backstabbing, bitching, and straight up jealousy. We never did. Honest to goodness, we never went through shit like that. It was one of the many things that made our time together so enjoyable. And now it was being threatened by a bunch of unnecessary crap. At this point, I was willing to try anything to loosen the tensed atmosphere. I attempted to make a joke of it all.

Bursting into laughter, I said, "Renalia, if I didn't know any better I'd say you were insinuating that your affair with Ashton was more exciting and passionate than Myilana's." Oh how I hoped they'd follow my joking streak. Damn if my own antics didn't backfire in my face. Now I felt as airheaded as they thought me to be.

Renalia turned her nose up with this gratified smile. "Hey, I didn't say it, Parrish, you did. Thank you for having enough backbone to call a spade, a spade. You hit the nail on the head." She turned my whole meaning inside out. Her no nonsense attitude extracted more of the same from Myilana.

"Parrish may have said it, but as far as I can understand you're certainly not denying it," Myilana snapped.

"No, I'm not denying it. But I'm not confirming it either," Renalia replied. "I'm simply saying you probably didn't get a chance to make it all the way to the full fledged experience with Ashton the same way I did. You might wanna hear what it's like for the walls to catch on fire, and the ceiling to blow off the whole damn building while fucking him."

"Humph, what a joke." Myilana rolled her eyes. "Jealousy don't fit you, and exaggerating looks even worse. So you slept with Ashton, big damn deal. The small amount of action you probably had with him doesn't begin to compare with what he and I shared, but you know what? Out of sheer curiosity, I wanna hear about your little mediocre adventure. And I'm pretty sure the girls can't wait for you to drop it like it's hot. Go on, we won't even bother to pull from the keepsake box this go around."

The two of them sounded like high school girls about to catfight over some little musty ass boy. The shit was sure enough hitting the fan. Whatever Ashton had done to them, they were dick-whipped all the way. Neither of them took our advice to try and work the issue out sensibly. Maybe that's why the three of us were now listening silently instead of trying to convince them not to bicker.

"Jealous? Jealous?" Renalia grumbled. "You can't be serious, Myilana? For me to be jealous of the story you just told would be a waste of my *jealous* emotions. But you did slip one true fact through those resentful lips of yours. And that is, I'm definitely gonna drop it like it's hot. There's no other way for *my* story to be told, except hot. I'm talking about steam-n-cream. Girls, he put it on me like thick chocolate icing on a three-layer cake." She paused in the middle of her bragging as if waiting on the same kind of cheery props and woos we'd given Myilana in the beginning.

News Flash! The situation wasn't nearly the same as when the first story started. Too much confusion was happening now.

If she's waiting on me to say something, she's gonna come up short. I'm not getting back in that shit anymore. Humph, Dhelione and Emberly don't look like they're gonna be mouthing off anytime soon either. You're on your own, baby girl, I said silently.

Renalia didn't look too happy about us not complimenting her, but at this point she had to be smart enough to see our problem with it. If for no other reason, she should've remembered how she turned my innocent teasing into something it wasn't. The "letdown" expression her smirk had faded into made me feel bad, but I wasn't about to put my foot in my mouth again.

"So what's up, ladies?" She waved her hand in the air as if we couldn't already see her. "How about it, can I tell my story next?"

Nobody said anything. Then, out of nowhere, Myilana came at us. "Aw, come on, ya'll. Lighten up. We're supposed to be having fun. Tell her it's okay for her to go next. Say something."

"All right, dammit, I'll say something." Emberly spoke up with attitude. "What in the hell are you two trying to prove? The three of us have been sitting here for the past ten minutes or so listening to ya'll squabble back and forth like mammy hens over a rooster that's probably somewhere fucking some other heifer as we speak. Dicks come a dime a dozen and ya'll are about to let one dick fuck up everything. This is exactly the kind of childish shit men get off on seeing females do. Five years ago, we swore to rule over every dick we allowed in the pussy. We swore to make them as vulnerable as they've been making us all these years, or have you two forgotten about that? I don't know about anybody else, but I don't wanna hear this guy's fucking name anymore. N-A . . . A-D, or whatever the fuck it is, too much drama comes with it."

Emberly was irritated and didn't mind saying so. She was also right on the money. Dhelione and I didn't hesitate in agreeing with her.

"Here, here." Dhelione raised her glass.

"Couldn't have said it better myself." I took my glass from the table and raised it too.

Renalia slumped her head down, looking embarrassed as a fool now. And Myilana's eyes was stuck in one spot on the floor. The good thing was they both looked regretful for acting so juvenile.

"You're right, Emberly," Myilana uttered pitifully. "And I'm sorry. I don't know what came over me. Damn . . . he's not even my husband." A tear hit her cheek without a doubt this time.

"Mine either," Renalia mumbled just loud enough for us to hear. "Look, I'm sorry too, ya'll. I know I've been tripping and I'm really, really sorry about it."

Now I was smiling. Hearing them say that was music to my ears. Emberly's angry outburst obviously popped a light or two on in their heads.

"Renalia, I'm especially sorry to you." Myilana's apology was so genuine, I felt it. Her tears made me want to cry. "I did let a little jealousy get the best of me. Forgive me?"

"Only if you forgive me for mine," Renalia replied softly. They scooted closer to each other and hugged.

"Awww . . . group hug. Come on ya'll." Emberly

grinned, joining in the hug and gesturing for Dhelione and I to come.

After our big hug, all of us were sniffling like foolish cry babies. But leave it to Emberly to pull a three-sixty turn around.

"Is it the wine or are we really this emotional?" she whined. "Shit, I haven't cried like this since that episode on *Good Times* when James got killed in the car wreck. Then after the funeral, Florida threw the glass bowl down on the floor and screamed 'damn, damn, damn!'" Emberly was serious as suicide. Her face said so.

The rest of us were already falling over laughing at her crazy statement, which had nothing whatsoever to do with our situation.

"What in the hell is the matter with ya'll?" she asked, staring from one of us to the other. "I don't see what's funny, I'm serious as a heart attack about *Good Times*. That shit had me crying half the night." She didn't laugh right away, but she eventually let it out.

Chapter Four

The laugh did us good. Afterward, we agreed to kill the unnecessary drama, and get back to the real business. Myilana even suggested that Renalia go ahead and tell her story about Ashton. At first, Dhelione, Emberly, and I were against it, but Myilana made us realize how unfair it was to ask Renalia not to share her story just because of the circumstances.

Renalia assured us that she was okay with not telling if it was going to make things uncomfortable in any way. "Look, guys, let's just pull from the keepsake box and see who's next, okay?" She held the box up. "I told you, I'm fine with leaving that part of my year out. He's not the only guy I slept with anyway. I've got a lot of juicy stuff to tell."

"Fine. This is what we'll do," Dhelione said. "You go ahead and tell the story about Ashton now. So when we start up again tomorrow, it'll already be behind us. I agree with Myilana. If you don't tell us about your thing with him, it'll be like we're making you shut up to keep peace over something that we shouldn't have to keep peace over in the first place. As long as we're not sleeping with each other's husbands, then the other dicks don't matter, right ya'll?"

"Right!"

"Damn right!" Our vote was unanimous.

"Okay, okay. Where do I begin?" Renalia glued her eyes to the ceiling for a moment, thinking.

"Come the hell on, girl," Emberly told her. "You're acting like my Grandma when she's trying to remember where she hid some money in the house fifty-five years ago."

"All right, all right. I'll start with the first time he and I did it . . . which was in a small, secret room in the back of his spa," Renalia said.

"Ya'll did it with people still in the spa getting services?" I spat that question out with not so much as one thought going into it.

"Girl, it was after hours." Renalia shook her head at me. "The place was closed for the night, Parrish. Nobody was there except him and me."

"Oh." I cringed, feeling a little dumb. But my next question contained plenty of thought. "So how was your first time with Mr. Ashton Drapers?"

Emberly sighed, and chucked a grape at me. "Maybe if you be quiet she can go on and get to that, *blondie the black girl*. Go ahead, Renalia," Emberly told her.

Renalia was still shaking her head at me and grinning. "It was like fireworks on the fourth of July." She paused. "Forget that. It was like when the United States bombed the hell out of Hussein's ass in Iraq!" Her enthusiasm kicked in almost immediately.

"Was it girl?"

"I heard that!"

"Aw yeah!"

Now we felt comfortable enough to cheer Renalia on just as we'd done Myilana when she began her story. Myilana, with plenty of showmanship, was leading the cheering squad. She appeared to be as happy as she was when we first arrived at the cottage. Maybe we needed our heads examined for deciding to go back down the same road that lead to the troubles in the first place, but now it was done. I felt pretty confident that the foolishness was gone and we were all good as new. It had to be, because our enthusiasm quickly linked up with Renalia's, and we were once again laughing in unison as she began telling her story.

"Anyway, I was the only one getting services that time of night. He took me into the little room and asked me to have a seat on the sofa. I don't know what Ashton had in the atmosphere in that room, but the smell put a spell on me. I mean, it was like an invisible scented aphrodisiac had been let loose in the air. The second I sat down on the sofa I just wanted to strip off everything. So I did. In fact, he was still standing at the door when I started taking it all off.

"At first, I began rubbing over my breasts real slow with both hands. My shirt was still on, but I quickly unbuttoned it and put it down on the sofa. I wasn't wearing a bra, so my big twins immediately came toppling out. I then stood up in front of the sofa and began caressing them seductively for him. My nipples were beginning to harden and my pussy was beginning to throb.

"He was gawking me down, but at that point he hadn't said anything. I asked him did he want some. He smiled and told me I didn't waste any time. I told him wasting time was for people who didn't know what they wanted. I knew exactly what I wanted and meant to get it. He walked over and stood in front of me, then leaned down and blew one of those sweet kisses in the middle of my forehead. He then grabbed my right breast with one hand and took over the caressing. He squeezed it firmly. He leaned his head further down and began dangling his tongue over my stiff nipple. I still had on my skirt, underwear, and pumps. I attempted to unzip my skirt and pull it down, but he grabbed my hands and whispered for me to keep it on. I knew then he wanted to do it sneaky and dirty after that. A let's-do-it-quick-and-cheap-style thing. Ya'll know what I'm talking about.

"Anyway, since he'd indicated he liked dirty games, I decided to play a few cards from my own dirty deck. I slowly lifted his head up from my breast, shifted our positions, and pushed him down on the sofa. He sat looking up at me as I stood in front of him. I hustled out of my pumps and stepped up on the sofa with my legs on opposites sides of him. My fitted skirt wasn't very long at all; it hung midway down my thighs. He enjoyed two eyefuls of succulent thighs.

"He gripped both of my legs in his hands and rubbed from my ankles all the way up to the top of my thighs. That was one of those times I wished to be taller than five-six, so my legs would've been longer for his hands to glide up and down. Still the same, I widened my thighs for him and began a gyrating tease that was too shameful. Sort of like a lap-dance, only in this case it was a face-dance.

"The twang between my legs was like *whoa*, and then some Mya shit. Ya'll know that song by *Mya*? *My Love is Like Whoa*. Anyway, I worked it and worked it while, slowly pulling my skirt up and exposing my hi-cut underwear and round cheeks. I then eased down and rested my front part on his lips. He began gently biting at my panties and kissing me down there. He slid his hands further up the back of my thighs and grasped both of my ass-cheeks and squeezed so tight it almost hurt. As he squeezed, I gyrated more intensely in his face, pressing my pussy to his mouth every now and again.

"I guess I got a little carried away, because I pressed so hard that he had no choice but to lay his head down on the back of the sofa and let me work it like I wanted to. I felt the warm air coming through his nostrils and mouth as he breathed on my stuff. Now he was biting more vigorously at my puss. My panties absorbed his mouth's wetness. The way he was breathing so heavily on my hot cat tickled all the way up my spine.

"Next thing I knew I had closed my eyes, and spread open rolling on his mouth like a dick was there. I soon felt his hand pulling the crotch of my panties to one side, then two fingers slid up in my pussy-hole. He was double finger-fucking me. As soon as he realized how good he was making me feel he added another finger. A triple finger fuck. It wouldn't have mattered to me if he had quadrupled the fingers. My stuff is not all loose like that, but he could've rammed the whole damn hand up there if he'd wanted to. That's how good it felt. He went ahead and stuck with the three fingers, gliding in and out.

"After a brief time, he pulled his fingers out and began nibbling at my panties again. I knew he wanted his luscious lips and tongue to do some real pussy tasting without any more interference from the panties. So this time I reached down myself and pulled the wet crotch of my hi-cuts to one side and held them there. That gave him a straight shot to my steaming flesh. His tongue sprang out and he instantly began licking me through and through. I rolled nonstop. He licked

nonstop. His uumming and oouuing told me it was
tasting good to him. He suddenly firmed his grip on
my ass-cheeks and squeezed tighter while pressing my
pussy closer to his mouth and sticking his tongue
where his fingers had not too long ago played.

"Feeling his tongue ramble inside my soft entrance
made me want to cum in his mouth. He moved his
tongue from place to place until he came across that
one spot inside that made me lose all self control. I
didn't know what spot it was, but I did know when he
touched it I almost twisted his neck off, rolling and
reeling myself to orgaz-paradise. With his tongue working overtime, he tingled that spot, tickled that spot,
licked that spot, slurped that spot, and tantalized that
spot. But when he sucked that spot I let go of the At-
lantic Ocean. Oouuu, gosh, it was good! He'd made me
do it so good.

"He then hurriedly pulled me down from over his
face and helped me lay on my back on the sofa. As I
lay there, my body was still trembling from the extreme orgasm. He quickly took off his white tee, jeans,
and shoes, then tugged out of his underwear. Now he
was buck-bare. After that, he reached down and began
taking off my skirt and panties. He'd obviously decided that he wanted me buck-bare along with him. At
a second's notice, he dived down into my toes. Stroking them, kissing them, caressing them, and dribbling
little wet salivalets from his mouth onto them. I could
tell he was about to get off just doing that, but I still
wanted to taste the flavor of his lovely dick before he
ran his river as I had already done.

"He didn't look like he was going to let go of my toes
anytime soon, so I had no choice but to get a little aggressive. I had to flip the script in order to suck the
dick. I gradually took charge as he carried on with my

toes. After a bit of moving and swerving around with minimal help from him, I was now on top with my head right over his scrumptious looking cock. He lay under me still going at it on my toes. He loved devouring him some toes and pussy. I clutched his dick and stroked it lightly for a few seconds. Then I took my time and kissed on the tip of it, in front of it, underneath it, and on each side of it. I did all of that just before I slipped it through my lips and glided it down the walls of my warm, tender mouth. I jawed his mushroom shaped head for the sheer pleasure of it.

"He began to moan in enjoyment and roll his ass as if he was fucking inside of my pussy, but he still didn't turn those toes loose. He rolled harder, just as I had done earlier when I'd almost dislocated his neck. I received his aggressive rolls and made my jaws flexible enough so that he could move inside my mouth as he damn well pleased. I even clasped my jaws together from time to time and gave him clear passage through to my throat. The dick was a good ten inches. It was definitely a mouthful, but I licked it like a lollypop and slurped it like a slushy. His savvy secretions leaked out and tickled my taste buds while trickling down outside my mouth.

"It was getting better and better to both of us, but at that point I desired to feel him licking up in my cunt all over again. I pulled my toes away from him and backed my jelly ass up over his face for him to dig in once more. There it was hanging over his face waiting to be eaten hearty one more time. It was still just as wet and juicy as ever. He was just as apt to consume it as ever too. Gobble, gobble . . . he jumped right into the pussy and smacked away. His hands rested firmly atop each of my cheeks and every so often he gripped me downward.

"Evidently, he desired to do his cumming while fucking rather than eating, because just as I tasted the pre-juices begin to seep from his tip-opening, making way for him to cum, he slid his hands off my ass-cheeks and up my back to my head, then began lifting my mouth off his dick. I felt what he was trying to do, so I raised my head upward. After I'd sat up, he then quickly gripped the sides of my hips and directed my pussy over his dick. Since I was already sitting on top of his bare crotch, I grasped his dick, placed it at my entrance and stuck it inside of me in a flash. I screeched out in pleasure as it went in all hard and hot. I then hastily twisted around and looked back at him. He had slid upward and propped his head up on the arm of the sofa. From there he still gripped my thighs tightly—his sweaty palms all heated up.

"I saw how he was peering down at my juicy ass-cheeks as he began to roll under me. I put my left foot down on the floor for better support, while my right leg hugged the right side of his pelvis real tight. The slow teasing cheek-roll I started made him yell out in pleasure. My cheeks were gradually moving in and out, back and forth, around and around. He moaned, he whimpered, and I continued gyrating. I moaned and whimpered, too. My pussy sucked up his dick each time he thrust up in me. We gradually increased the pace.

"Our stroking became so intense, I felt my ass-cheeks flopping and flapping excessively. His stone-solid cock hammered the walls of my cunt repeatedly. He was under me operating overtime. I pussy-pounded on him as if that was the last I'd ever get. But I stopped occasionally to buckle down and long-stroke it. In other words, to slowly scruubb the pussy on the dick.

"I stretched the leg on the floor out wider to open my pussy-lips even more, then leaned back on him as I stroked on and on. My cat-split was open wide and cocked up in the air, rolling with the light atmospheric wind slightly whisking through it. He saw how good I could work my pussy all by myself, so he let go of my hips and steered his hands between my underarms, grabbing both titties from each side. He rubbed them up and down and squeezed them as they bounced all around. Then it came. The cum came rupturing out of him into me, and mine flowed out too.

"He growled and shivered, while giving my tits an unbelievably strong squeeze. I moaned in tune with his growl. Together we made such sweet melodies with our gratification cries. I leaned my back all the way down on his chest and lay on top of him for a few minutes as we chatted. I could feel the cum running out of my pussy onto my ass, just as he probably felt it dripping from there into his hairy crotch area.

"That little room of his had everything a person could want. It was very nicely decorated too. He told me he'd decorated it himself. He also said he had the only key to the room and no one else was allowed in there without his permission, not even his wife. He swore she had never been inside of it. That certainly told me something. It told me the room was his 'in a rush' fucking room. It also told me I wasn't the first one who'd been in there and damn sure wasn't going to be the last. Did I care? Hell no! He had it going on and I was in love after fucking him only one time.

"I eventually tore myself away from him to go tinkle. To my surprise his bathroom was just as lovely as the rest of the room. There were big decorative towels, matching bathroom accessories and shower curtain. He even had a damn half-size jacuzzi-tub in there, ya'll. I could hardly believe my eyes. By the time I finished peeing, I'd decided to take a quick shower and clean myself up real good before leaving for home. He killed that noise real quick.

"As the water from the shower flowed down on me, I heard the stereo system crank up. Ya'll better know it was old school too. *Keith Sweat. A right and a wrong way to love somebody*. The next thing I knew, Ashton was bombarding the bathroom door, hopping into the shower with me. I didn't protest. He grabbed me from the back and swung me around facing him. We fell into a invigorating kiss. Smacking, licking, and greedily munching. The water continuously streamed down on us, splattering all over. He'd become just as wet as I was.

"When we retracted from the kiss, he immediately reached for the soap, then lathered it all over his body while smiling at me. I leaned back on the shower wall and watched attentively as he was becoming more and more soapy and sexy. His big beautiful eyes melted me. They revealed to me he wasn't sorry for anything that had happened between us, and only wanted more of the same.

"When he was done playing with the soap and enticing me, he took my arms and raised them straight over my head against the wall and pressed his abdomen into mine. My breasts sprouted straight out and the water drops dripped off my nipples as they rose to attention. My hair was in for a good drenching, but oh well. We kissed again and he stuck his tongue out on my neck, then glided it down my body inch by inch, licking through the soapy water until he made it to my stomach. He dabbled in and out and around my navel with his brisk tongue.

"I placed my hands on top of his shoulders and caressed them. He soon rose back up and palmed both of my round slippery titties in his hands, then doggedly sucked on them, one then the other. The water still ran warm and tantalizing on our bodies. He groaned. I walled my eyes around in satisfaction as he reached one of his hands down and rammed his middle finger up in my pussy. It was good, but it wasn't enough.

"The hankering to fuck had once again recurred for both of us. He eventually pulled his lone finger out of me. Whoa! What a high nature, and I felt it rising right between my upper thighs as he leaned into me. His erection had grown full stretch. I gripped it and placed it further between my legs to cuddle it. I begged for him to hurry up and fuck me. He secured his hands underneath my ass-cheeks and picked me up. I wrapped my legs around him, cross-locking my feet at his buttocks. My pussy was then open to let his manhood penetrate inside.

"I remained with my back plastered against the wall as he held me up and pushed his cock in, slippery and wet. He instantly began humping. He maintained himself so strong and rigid as he held me up on the wall and pumped fiercely. The muscles in his arms and chest sprouted out, displaying his mighty strength. He whispered in my ear that he wanted to fuck me doggy-style. No sooner than he said it, he abruptly let me down and I swirled my ass around to him in a 'bent-over' position.

"We faced the stream of water as he re-entered his slippery dick into my pussy and began thrusting. I opened my legs as wide as the jacuzzi floor allowed me to, and then I arched my fluffy cheeks high and stiff as he banged me. Swish swash, the water splashed along with the slapping of our soaking wet skin. Oohhh, man . . . what a fuck!" Renalia suddenly yelled. Her face and body language said she was nearly re-living the shower-fuck right there on the sofa.

Before Emberly beat me to it, I was anxious to let my comments fly first. "Damn, this guy is a regular Stud-Romeo, isn't he?" I said, smiling.

"For real," Dhelione agreed. "I need to meet somebody like him, so I can serve my toes up on a silver platter. I love it when a man sucks my toes. That shit drives me crazy. Plus, it makes me feel like the queen that I am."

"Forget the damn toes!" Emberly's Speedy-Gonzales mouth burst into laughter. "Two good hits in a row?! Don't sound like Mr. Drapers knows how to miss! I'm almost not angry at him anymore. And I damn sure ain't mad at ya'll! Neither one of you!"

Myilana's smile was just as grand as each of ours when she gave Renalia props. "That was awesome, Renalia. You guys really had a hot time. You go girl."

Chapter Five

Now the proof was in the pudding. We truly had it going on once again. Just like back in the day, there was no drama. Renalia had told her story, and Myilana hadn't flinched negatively one time. I knew because I'd shot a few nosy glances Myilana's way from time to time while the story was in progress, just to be on the safe side. We yakked on about nothing for quite some time, then a few bathroom breaks took us away from our lounging.

Once we were all back in our spots, Dhelione grabbed the keepsake box. "Okay, everybody ready for another round?" she asked excitedly.

"Let the games begin." I was practically jumping up and down in my seat.

"All right then! I'll pull it, Dhelione?" Myilana said, reaching over to dig out the next name.

"Good. You make sure you pull Parrish's name out of there, girl. If she's the one telling the story she can't ask anymore of those hair-brain ass questions of hers." Dhelione laughed.

I pitched her an eye-roll. "Ha, ha, ha, that's not funny."

"Damn right it's not funny," Emberly replied hastily. "Now you see how we feel when you be coming up with all that coo-coo shit. Ha, ha, ha."

"Ya'll can cut all the yang-yang out! Guess who's up?" Myilana hollered, looking at the unfolded piece of paper in her hand.

"Who is it, girl?" I asked.

"It is—"

"Hold up, hold up!" Renalia cut in. "I've got something to say before you do that, Myilana."

Myilana nodded "okay" with a big smile. "What's up?"

Renalia had interrupted her, but for some reason seemed hesitant about whatever it was she wanted to say. "My bad . . . I didn't mean there's something I wanna say. I meant there's something I wanna ask you."

"Okay, shoot," Myilana told her innocently with excitement.

"Did you ever go into the little room?"

"Huh?" Myilana's puzzlement was contagious. After hearing the question, my frown became as deep as hers. So did Dhelione's and Emberly's.

"It's no big deal, Myilana," Renalia said, holding a smile that suddenly didn't look so real anymore. "I'm just curious to know if he ever took you in the little room, that's all."

For a minute, I didn't have a clue what Renalia was talking about. A light must have popped on for Myilana like it did for me.

"Oh, you mean, Ashton?" Myilana screeched, sounding surprised. "Where'd that come from, girl? We're about to move on to the next story."

Myilana's question was reasonable. I wanted to know where it came from too. The part of our conversation about Ashton had been over for quite a while. We had touched base on several topics since then. It was surprising when Renalia brought it back up out of the blue.

"Yeah, I mean Ashton," Renalia answered sharply. Her smile was becoming more fake by the minute. It practically looked pasted on with bad glue at this point.

Myilana shrugged her shoulders. "Well . . . I think he took me in there a few times."

"A few times?" Renalia snapped. Her smile completely faded now. "What do you mean a few times? As tight as you claim ya'll were, surely you remember how many times he took you in the room."

"I don't know. Maybe he took me in there once or twice." Myilana remained calm, but reluctant. "Is it really . . . important? It's over and done with."

"You're the one making a big deal out of it. Like it's some kind of top secret question. Damn, just tell me," Renalia ordered rudely.

More shit was on the verge of being stirred back up, which meant it was about to get stinking up in there again.

"Did I miss something?" Myilana snapped back, sounding insulted. "What's your problem, girl?"

Renalia's angry backlash caught us all by surprise. I for one didn't see it coming.

"Wench, don't throw that innocent look at me," Renalia snarled. "We all know you've been trying to cover up your real feelings. Your *jealous*, real feelings."

Myilana peered in disbelief. "Why are you doing this? I can't believe you're tripping about this stuff all over again."

"Please, honey. I'm not tripping about anything. I'm just being honest." Renalia now held the bitchiest expression of the evening on her face. "The whole time I was telling my *hot* story you were about to implode with envy, and you know it. Those fake ass compliments you gave me wasn't about nothing. You just made them up to keep from being so obvious. Why don't you tell everybody how jealous you really are?"

A chameleon can hide her colors for only a while, then eventually she's got to show them all in full detail. It's her nature. Renalia was beginning to remind me of a chameleon. She hid her real feelings at first, and now they were out for everybody to see. I didn't want to believe that jealousy and spite were a part of her nature, but there she was accusing Myilana of something she was doing herself. Her motives were as transparent as daylight.

"Somebody pinch me 'cause I'm dreaming. Or better yet, I'm having a nightmare," Emberly spoke in Myilana's place.

Myilana's mouth had dropped open. She was too stunned to respond immediately.

"Where the fuck did all that come from?" Emberly demanded. "Seem like to me, you're the only one who's jealous, Renalia. And to top it off, you're in denial about it. Why did you bring this shit up again? If Myilana was pretending, at least she was doing it to keep the peace. That's more than I can say for your selfish ass."

"What?" Renalia shot Emberly a "I know you didn't" look.

Emberly pitched the same look back at her. "What, hell. I don't stutter when I talk. You heard me loud and clear, wench."

To say that Emberly was pissed would've been putting it lightly. But like always, she wasn't afraid to call it like she saw it.

"Aw, hell, not again," I exclaimed. "Stop it! Just stop it, ya'll! Renalia, why are you trying to blame Myilana for something you're doing? I'm sorry to be the one to tell you, hun, but like Emberly said, you're the one who's starting this shit back up. You're the one with the problem, so just stop it."

I couldn't believe it was happening all over again. We had misread Renalia's hidden motive from the beginning. She'd been faking her true feelings about laying the crap to rest all along. Damn, she was good. But the real question now was, how were we going to get past this second incident with her being so hell-bent on proving how much better her relationship was with Ashton?

With all the commotion going on, I didn't realize right away that Dhelione was the only one in the room who hadn't commented on the issue yet. Her pissed-off look said it all.

"What's up, Dhelione?" I turned my attention to her for a moment. "You okay?"

She looked at me, slowly nodding her head in disgust. "Hell no, I'm not okay. This is nothing but bullshit, and I refuse to sit here and listen to any more of it."

"Are you going to blame me too?" Renalia whined at Dhelione.

"Don't nobody have to confirm the blame for you, Renalia. You know as well as we do, you started this shit again." Dhelione sprung to her feet angrily. "Let me ask you a question since you so damn confident about your man, Ashton. If he had a choice to be with you or Myilana, which one do you think he'd choose? Huh, huh, which one?"

"What kind of bullshit question is that?" Renalia retorted, not too happy with Dhelione's hostility.

"That question has about as much bullshit in it as your childish-ass attitude over some nigga you hardly know. And depending on your answer, we'll find out just how far gone in stupidity you really are. What are you waiting for? Answer me," Dhelione demanded. Like Emberly, Dhelione's temper had taken over.

Renalia didn't say anything. She rolled her eyes as if she could care less. My guess was she didn't want to answer because she knew she was going to look even more stupid than she already had. How could she have answered a question like that with real confidence? We already knew the majority of men say what's convenient, not what's true. She was married to one like that. All of us were.

"Too bad that bastard can't answer for himself." Emberly quickly spoke out of turn again.

"Who says he can't?" Myilana murmured softly. All eyes landed on her.

"Excuse me?" Dhelione slightly frowned.

"I said, who says he—"

"Oh, I heard what you said." Dhelione assured her. "But what I wanna know is . . . what do you mean?"

Myilana sighed. "Where better to get an answer to your question than straight from the horse's mouth? I mean, how can anyone other than Ashton answer it for you?"

"Like if he did have a chance to answer, he'd be honest about it." Dhelione plopped back down on the sofa. "Hell, that's nonsense anyway, Myilana. What would ya'll do, ask him through mental telepathy?"

"No, we'd ask him in person . . . in everybody's presence." Myilana carefully eyed each of us as we sat listening.

"Here? At the cottage?" Dhelione threw Myilana a look that said she'd lost her ever-loving mind. "Damn, girl, you need to take a nap and sleep that alcohol off. You are seriously talking crazy as hell. Ashton, up in here? Paleese."

"Why not?" Myilana whispered innocently.

"Don't be asking me a crazy-ass question like that, hell, you know the rules," Dhelione replied. "Once we're inside this cottage, we're in. No communication with anybody."

"Dhelione, we made that rule. We can do whatever we want," Myilana reminded her.

"That's right, we did. And that rule was established for a reason. To protect our asses." Dhelione's voice grew with intensity. "If what we talk about in here somehow leaked out into this lifeless ass, pleasure forsaken town, it could destroy our families. Not to mention our reputations, you know that. So stop talking like a damn fool, girl."

"We're in control, that's not gonna happen," Myilana said, not giving up so easily. "He's one man. Besides, it's not like he don't already know he's been messing around on the side. Think about it, why would he talk? He has just as much to lose as any of us."

Dhelione gazed at Myilana deeply for a moment before she answered. "You're serious, aren't you? That man know about yours, his, and Renalia's business, he doesn't know shit about the rest of ours. In my opinion, it would do plenty of harm for him to come here just to prove some ridiculous shit that he's gonna lie about anyway."

Myilana sat back on the sofa and crossed her legs as if she'd given up now. "Okay, fine. But you know as well as I do it wouldn't be a big deal for him to jet by here a few short minutes."

"Don't be trying to get an attitude with me. I thought you were the one with the sense. I guess both of ya'll batting crazy-for-crazy alongside each other." Dhelione gestured her hand at Renalia. "Trying to blame me for—"

"I'm not trying to blame you for anything." Myilana cut Dhelione short . "I had put this mess aside. I'm not the one who brought it back up again. You asked Renalia a question, and I simply thought you'd like to hear the answer from the one person who can give it to you."

"Oh that's some shit, and you know it. You just want a shot at boosting your own ego." Dhelione squinted her eyes. "And what makes you so certain he'd choose you anyway?"

"I didn't say he would choose me. Hell, I don't know what he would say. But one thing for sure, we'd all find out together."

"This is ridicu—"

"I agree." Renalia jumped in the middle of Dhelione's words.

"Thank you." Dhelione gave her a quick nod. "I didn't expect *you* to agree with me, but at least you're talking with some sense now."

"No, darling. I agree with Myilana," Renalia clarified herself.

"What?" Dhelione gasped. "Oh, hell, I don't know why I'm surprised to hear that coming from you."

For the first time since Renalia had revived the chaos, she appeared more peaceful. I had to admit, I was glad to see the hellish look on her face soften a little. Nevertheless, she still disregarded Dhelione's comment and went on to say what she wanted to say.

"Maybe you shouldn't be surprised at what I have to say, but I'm still gonna say it anyhow. I'm with Myilana. What could it hurt for him to drop in here a few minutes? Shit, it might even make things better. Ashton's got a family and a reputation just like we do. A wife of fifteen-years and three teenage children. He goes to church on Sunday, hell, he's even on the deacon board, I think."

No doubt, Renalia had her own selfish reasons for agreeing with Myilana on the subject of Ashton coming over, but at least she was agreeing on something.

"I don't care if he's the pastor of the—"

"Excuse me for interrupting you, Dhelione, I've got something to say," I politely eased in the conversation. "I might get hung up by my toes, but I don't think it's a bad idea. Who knows, it could possibly steer things in a better direction. Once he's face to face with both of them, they'll see how full of shit he really is. Then this mess will be dead and buried for good."

I barley finished my input when Dhelione gave me this shocked look, then hastily turned to Emberly and said, "Do you hear this shit?"

Emberly wasted no time voicing her opinion. "Hell, yes, I hear it! And I can't wait to meet this hairy bastard face to face! As much peace as he's disturbed, the first thing I'm gonna do is make him strip and inspect his dick! I'm about to be a rich bitch 'cause after he's naked I'm gonna slice his gold-dick off and sell it to the highest bidder! What the hell are you waiting for? Get to calling, Myilana! Time is money. My money."

As upset as we knew Dheilone was, none of us could

hold back our laughter after hearing one of Emberly's weird and crazy monologues.

"Damn, Emberly. You're gonna jack the man's dick?" I fell over, laughing.

"And then sell it?" Myilana screamed, giggling as hard as I was.

Renalia couldn't keep her tickle-box from turning over either. "Now that's some serious shit to say . . . even for you, Emberly."

"Ha, ha, ha, he, he, he . . ." Emberly yelped. " Laugh all ya'll want, but after I box that shit up and sell it on ebay, we'll see who's begging for some of the profits!"

Dhelione stared us down for several minutes before saying anything. "I don't believe this! Have ya'll gone mad? Yeah, that's it, you're all insane!"

"Hell, no, I'm not insane." Emberly wiped the fun-tears from her eyes with the back of her hand. "Not yet, anyway. Let me break it down and tell you the real deal about the thing. If I don't hurry up and get me some of that dick that's got Renalia and Myilana crazy, I just might become insane!"

"It does sound tempting, doesn't it?" I agreed with Emberly. "No offense Myilana and Renalia, but the last thing we need is another one of us sprung on dude like ya'll are."

By now Emberly was hitting the *Dom Perignon* bottle heavy, and had slipped even further into her laugh riot, mouthing off big-time. "Hey, Myilana, you and Renalia may be a little upset with each other right now, but that's fixing to be over. When Ashton gets here, I'm gonna work his ass out! Then ya'll will be mad at *me* instead of each other. Ha, ha, ha, he he he . . ."

I knew it wouldn't be long before Emberly's antics drew laughter out of Dhelione. Reluctant laughter, but at least some laughter.

"This is insane! This is insane! This is insane!" Dhelione squealed, covering her mouth with both hands, trying to control her laughing. "Damn, this isn't going to work, ya'll, it isn't!"

"Who said anything about him working? Hell, I'm the one who'll be doing the working!" Emberly was pulling out all the stops with her comic-relief.

Before long, each of us were making wild suggestions on how to sneak Ashton into the cottage, and what to do after we got him in. Yes, Dhelione too.

Chapter Six

Our laughter once again sounded like the joyful hours before the same dark cloud rolled in for the second time. Deep down, I knew we were still trudging on perilous territory no matter how much giggling we partook in. When I saw how Renalia and Myilana conveniently put away their trivial dispute about Ashton, it almost spooked me. But for the time being, I didn't let my skeptical feelings rain on the happy parade. I pushed the eerieness as far south in my stomach as it would go, and jumped up to break open a freshly chilled bottle of wine for everybody.

"Wait a minute! Wait a minute!" I disrupted all the noise. "While we're babbling on and on shouldn't somebody be calling this negro before it gets too late?"

"See there! See! That's a negative sign, dammit," Dhelione exclaimed, thrusting her hand to her forehead.

"It's a sign all right. A sign we're loosing our damn memory," Emberly yawned on her way down from cloud-funny.

"We did forget to call, didn't we?" Renalia asked calmly. "How could we forget to call him?"

"What time is it?" Myilana looked at the clock on the wall. "11:45."

"That's all? I thought we'd been at this a lot longer than three hours," Dhelione said, twisting to a different position on the sofa.

"Well, the only question now is which one of you girls wanna make the call?" I took a fleeting look from Myilana to Renalia.

"Renalia can call," Myilana replied.

"It was your idea, Myilana, why don't you call?" Renalia was being considerate? Whoop-de-doo!

"Damn, since ya'll can't make up your minds, give me the phone I'll call," Emberly chuckled.

"No, she's gonna call, right Renalia?" Myilana was almost insisting.

Renalia got up from the sofa and walked toward the hall. "If you say so."

A few minutes later she strolled back in the den with her cell phone. After she'd made the call she lay her phone on the center table.

Dhelione let out a deep sigh and said, "We're really gonna do this, aren't we? I mean, let him in on our secrets. Hell, pretty much let him in the club. 'Cause ya'll know he's gonna ask questions . . . and somebody's gonna have to answer them."

"I didn't look at it like that, but I guess you're right." Myilana slowly nodded at Dhelione. "If it really makes you that uncomfortable, Dhelione, it's not too late to change our minds you know. I mean, she can call him back right now and cance—"

"No I can't!" Renalia cut in, rejecting Myilana's notion before she could get it out all the way.

Renalia was simply in rare form on this night. Her

mood was swinging back and forth like a bi-polar victim. I'd already taken into consideration her well-known insensitivity, but it still wasn't enough to answer for her newly found odd behavior.

"Damn, relax girl," Dhelione told her, sounding aggravated. "He's coming. If you don't mind, we were taking a minute to let this shit soak in. Is that okay with you? The cost of changing one of our main rules is on the line. And guess what, if it goes bad . . . even your ass has got to pay."

Renalia was so good at rolling her eyes, why smirk too? I translated her smirk as saying she didn't give a damn about any cost or anybody's reconsideration, she just wanted what she wanted.

To take the focus off Renalia's insensitivity, I tried offering a more positive viewpoint. "I wouldn't say we changed the rule, Dhelione. How about we modified it a little."

"Well, if you ask me, we should've done this a long time ago." Emberly threw in her comical opinion. "Let's be real about it. Ya'll are my girls and everything, and believe me, I've looked forward to this party every year since we started the club. But tell the truth, haven't ya'll thought about inviting some crispy-clean, newly picked dick up in here?"

"Emberly, now—"

"Emberly, hell." She snatched my response before I could give it. "Save it Parrish. I already know we get more than our share of screwing all year, especially me. Hell, I get more rod than any female ought to have in one lifetime. But when we get to telling all of these steamy ass stories, don't ya'll wish you could pull a man out of the de-freezer, or refrigerator, or something?"

Nobody replied right away, we eyed each other for a

few seconds. Then the replies poured out almost in unison.

"Oh, yeah."

"Hell, yes."

"No doubt."

All except Renalia's. Hers came last and leery. "Aren't ya'll missing the point? Ashton is coming over here to straighten out something important . . . not to fuck all of you."

"That includes you too," Emberly said bluntly. "Why don't you calm your ass down, and make up your mind if you wanna be happy or sad, peaceful or mad. Choose one emotion and stop changing back and forth like you possessed. Keep on, I'm gonna call a priest so he can exorcism your ass."

Renalia hated being scored on and laughed at. Too late, it was done now. As impossible as she was being, we had to laugh to keep from crying. We couldn't have resisted another one of Emberly's crazy comments anyhow.

"To answer your question about inviting guys over, Emberly." Dhelione talked through tightened teeth, looking fed-up with Renalia's ignorance. "If this town weren't so small I don't think we would've deprived ourselves of some hot handsomes all this time. I know I wouldn't have, but I can only speak for myself."

"Ya'll don't remember, do you?" I glanced around. "We briefly touched base on this same subject once before. I think it was during our second gathering."

"Hell, yes, I remember," Myilana said. "And we dismissed it as fast as we brought it up."

"Sure did." Dhelione reached for her glass, then raised it in the air. "Well, I guess it's high time for some new challenges. I can't believe I'm saying this, but let's toast to new beginnings."

One by one, our glasses went up. "To new beginnings."

"To new beginnings." Emberly swallowed a big gulp, then said, "And to how fucking long is it gonna take Ashton's ass to get here? I'm ready to get to work on that hairy dick he's got!"

Myilana laughed so loud I thought I heard an echo, but she didn't laugh as loud as Emberly.

"Why'd you call it hairy?" Myilana asked, teary-eyed from the tickle.

"Hell, you're the one who told us he's hairy all over. I'm just going by what you said." No doubt, Emberly knew she was going to irritate Renalia with that comment, which was probably why she'd made it. The fact that Myilana laughed too, only increased Renalia's already furious look. She didn't say a word.

I wasn't a fan of making her angrier, but she had gone too far, too many times. Telling her best friends that a guy wasn't coming to fuck us was unnecessary; we already knew that. She of all people knew how Emberly liked to make playful remarks that were never meant to be taken seriously. She also knew that nobody could silence Emberly when she wanted to speak, especially not by way of temper tantrum.

Emberly eventually smoothed out her scornful comment. "Ya'll know I'm just joking around, right? I mean, I'm not gonna rape the man or anything. But on a serious note, how are we gonna play this out? The last thing we need is division and misunderstanding when he gets here. We've already had enough of that shit for one day. I'm not trying to look like a fool in front of a fine man."

Dhelione set her eyes directly on Renalia after hearing that. "In other words, Renalia, can you at least pretend not to be so uptight and sprung when he gets here?"

"I'm not the only one in this. What about Myilana? Have you forgotten she's in it too?" Renalia was back to her more sincere looking state now.

"No, I haven't forgotten, but she's not the one taking every little thing about Ashton personal, and getting bent out of shape," Dhelione replied.

"Look, I'm cool. Why would I act uptight or bent out of shape, he's only a man?" Renalia's pleading eyes were almost convincing.

"Hell if I know," Emberly said. "I've been asking myself that same thing about you all night and still don't have an answer."

"Renalia, you and Myilana need to agree that no matter what Ashton says, ya'll won't let it come between you." I was serious as suicide when I told them that. "Can ya'll at least try to get a understanding before the guy gets here?"

The three of us waited for their reply. Moments of silence passed as they gazed at each other, then finally Myilana said, "I have no intentions on letting this situation cause any more problems than it already has. So yeah, I'm in agreement with you, Parrish, about it not coming between us. I refuse to waste anymore emotions on somebody else's husband."

"Damn skippy!" Emberly shrieked, then cleared her throat loudly, signaling Renalia.

"Oh, ahh, yeah . . . I'm not gonna waste anymore emotions either. Whatever happens, happens." Renalia's hesitation didn't sound convincing. I knew that and I was sure the others knew it too.

"What's that supposed to mean? Whatever happens, happens," Dhelione asked her.

"Look, what do ya'll want me to say? I agreed that

we're not gonna let it come between us, damn." Now she was snapping at folks again.

I sighed deeply. "We know you said it, but do you mean it? 'Cause it doesn't sound too convincing, Renalia."

"Well, Parrish, would you prefer I say exactly what Myilana said? I mean, since ya'll have obviously decided she's right about everything."

"That's a damn lie and you kno—"

Ding Dong. Saved by the doorbell just as Emberly was fixing to lay into Renalia.

"It's him, ya'll," Dhelione whispered.

"Hold up, an idea just hit me." I thrust my hands up for everybody to stay still and listen.

"Aw hell, Parrish. This is not the time for any of your blondering ideas. Get it, blond-ering," Emberly sniggered.

I ignored her wannabe cute remark and quickly continued. "Renalia, the only thing you told Ashton was that you were at a gathering with some girlfriends and wanted him to drop by for a while, right?"

"Right."

"So he doesn't know who the friends are, does he?" I talked as fast as I could.

"No."

"Good. That means he doesn't know that Myilana's here, so we can—"

"So we can have a little fun with his ass. You don't have to say another word, Parrish, I know exactly what you're talking about." Dhelione took the words out of my mouth. "Quick, Myilana, take your wine glass and hide in the hallway. You'll still be able to hear everything from there."

"Aw, come on, ya'll. Isn't this a little unfair?" Myilana said, heading toward the hallway.

"Hell, no, it's not unfair. Serves him right." Emberly was all for the idea. "Whatever bullshit he tries to feed us now, we'll have an ace in the hole waiting for him."

"Not bad, Parrish." Renalia pitched me a soft smile. "I like it."

The downside to her sudden "I like it" was that her behavior had been so unpredictable, I didn't know whether having her approval was good or bad.

"Are ya'll sure we need to do this?" Myilana barely raised her voice from the entrance of the hallway.

"Can you hear us pretty good from where you are?" Dhelione asked her.

"Yeah, but you might wanna turn the stereo down another notch," Myilana replied.

"Okay, we'll turn it down," Emberly spoke for Dhelione. "Now sit your ass down on the floor and be quiet. We got this."

Myilana let out a faint laugh.

"Listen carefully, ya'll," I cautioned them once more. "Don't let Myilana's name slip 'til we've gotten all the info we want, okay?"

"Parrish, we know what to do," Emberly gestured me to the door with her hand. "We're gonna wing it. Now get the damn door before the brother thinks we're crazy up in here."

"Renalia's gonna get the door, not me." I sat back and crossed my legs.

The doorbell sounded again.

"I don't give a damn who's getting it, just open it," Emberly demanded.

Renalia dashed over and opened the door. In came the man of the hour wearing brown slacks, a black shirt, and a very appealing smile. She introduced him, and we greeted him in a friendly manner. After joking and jiving with him a short while, it became clear why

Renalia and Myilana were so captivated by his charming personality. He was smooth as silk, and fine as hell.

Twenty-minutes or more went by, and Emberly had managed to keep from saying anything too off-the-wall to him. Just when I thought we were home-free of whatever silliness she had waiting, boom, the first one shot out of her mouth without warning.

"Mr. Drapers . . . Mr. Drapers," she chanted. "You need to listen carefully 'cause I'm not saying this but one time, okay?"

"Okay, I'm listening." Ashton gave her his undivided attention.

"It isn't safe for you to be coming up in here looking and smelling as good as you are. I'll be damned if you ain't in serious danger of ending up on a milk carton, my brother. Your fine ass might get kidnapped and put under all kinds of sex-periments." Emberly held back her laughter as she babbled on.

"Wow, you talk fast. Really, really fast. I'm not sure, but I think I caught most of what you said," Ashton replied cheerfully. "Who would wanna kidnap me and put me under these . . . sex-periments?" he joked along with her.

"Damn sure ain't the aliens. You're looking at her. Me!" Emberly exploded into laughter. "I better calm the hell down. Shiiiit, I'm about to grab your fine ass with your woman sitting right next to you."

It was good to see that Ashton had such a jolly sense of humor. He plowed a smooth, magnetic laugh through the room, and at the same time maintained his cool modesty. Another good thing was Renalia didn't appear to be offended by Emberly's fresh comments. She laughed along with us. Afterward, she warned Ashton that Emberly was the royal jester of our group, and there was never a way to tell what would come out of her mouth. He agreed that with her around we shouldn't ever have a dull moment.

"So you ladies get together from time to time and just chill out all by yourselves, huh? I mean, just leave the rest of the world behind for a whole weekend?" He was starting to ask questions now.

"Yeah, what's wrong with that?" Renalia asked him.

"Oh, nothing," he quickly replied. "I think it's a great idea. Plenty of wine, and food, and good ol' jazz. Plus, way out in the middle of nowhere? There's no danger in anybody disturbing you either."

"That sounds more like a question instead of an observation." Renalia leaned closer to him and cuddled.

"Yeah, well, isn't something missing. I mean . . . maybe a little company?" He all but whispered.

"Oh you mean, men?" Emberly taking over the conversation was no surprise. "Hell, women can have plenty of fun on a weekend trip without men coming along, don't you know that?"

"I heard that!" Ashton raised his voice with excitement. "Aw, it's that kind of party, huh? Damn, girl, I didn't know you got down like that!" he beamed at Renalia.

Renalia widened her eyes at him with the quickness. "Like what?"

"You know, like that!" he laughed, glancing around at each of us naughtily.

As bad as I wanted to put him in his place, Emberly beat me to it. She stood up from her seat and parked her brown gazers on Renalia and said," Tell me this negro ain't suggesting what it sounds like he's suggesting?"

"I wish I could, but I think he is," Renalia replied.

"Aw, hell no." Emberly was now looking directly at Ashton. "You about to get straight-up checked, negro."

Ashton gave Emberly this innocent frightened look, and asked her, "What? What did I say?"

"Pretty boy, let's get something straight." Emberly pointed her finger at him with this half-grin on her face. "The only thing a woman can do for me is point me in the direction of a man. I don't know what kind of fucked up fantasies you got on your damn mind, but this ain't Fantasy Land where you can get four for one. If there was even the slightest chance of you fucking somebody up in here tonight, you better believe it would only be one at a time. You got that, nigga? One at a time."

He lifted his hands in surrendering position. "Oh, my bad. You thought I was serious? I was only kidding Mrs. Emberly. I couldn't resist, I just had to throw that in." He returned her grin.

Emberly shot him a suspicious eye as she eased back down in her seat. "Sure you were kidding," she chuckled. "You probably thought you were getting ready to be the luckiest man in Coldwater tonight. I'll be the first to admit, I'm a freaky ass bitch, but let's not go overboard."

"Yeah, Ashton. How would you feel if you and some of your best buddies got held-up together just kicking it, and somebody dropped in and accused ya'll of getting your freak on together?" I raised my eyebrows at him.

He was still beaming. "No joke, I was kidding for real, ya'll. Tell them," he said, pointing at Dhelione.

"How would she know you were kidding?" I asked.

Dhelione smiled. "'Cause he had already winked his eye at me a few times before he said anything, crazy girl."

"Oh, is that what he was doing when he was flicker-

ing his eye in your direction? Hell, I thought he'd gotten something in it." I thrust my hand to my chest.

Maybe he was joking, but I still believed there was a
little wishful thinking on his part. That's every man's
fucked up fantasy. Ask Charlie Sheen.

Chapter Seven

"Ladies, let's enlighten Ashton on the purpose of our little club, so he can stop assuming shit," Emberly giggled.

It was all gravy after that. We swore him to the highest level of secrecy, then filled him in on the purpose of our organization as he shared wine with us. Before long, he was commending us on being so creative and liberated with our choices. Whether we'd planned it or not, Ashton now knew what we knew about our business. Maybe not detail for detail, but enough. There was no turning back. He was part of the gang.

"All right, Ashton, my brother," Emberly puffed out a deep breath. "Now you know all about our shit. It's time we heard something about you."

"There's not much to tell about me, not really." He furrowed his brows and took a swallow of wine from his glass. "I mean . . . I don't have anything going on as exciting as ya'll."

We bombarded him with responses, one after the other.

"Bullshit!"

"Stop lying!"

"You're wrong for that."

After our unified attack, he couldn't help but smile widely and pretend he was going to give in. "All right, all right, what do you wanna know? But I'm still warning you, there's nothing I have to say as thrilling as what ya'll got going on."

"Let us be the judge of that," Renalia told him.

Dhelione didn't waste any time getting to the nitty-gritty. She point blank asked, "Are you fucking anybody other than your wife and Renalia at the present time?"

He pitched Dhelione a "did I hear you right" look, and grumbled, "Damn, is that a trick question or something?"

Dhelione exhaled impatiently. "How in the hell can you answer a question with another question, Ashton?"

"Oh, come on now," he whined. "My lady of the hour is sitting right here next to me. What's up?"

"Don't you mean your *flavor for the minute*?" Emberly quickly corrected him. "Renalia's not crazy, and shame on you for implying she is."

He boggled his head from side to side. "Hey, wait a minute. I didn't imply that she's crazy. I was—"

"You might as well have," Renalia cut him short. "If you're gonna sit here and try to convince us that you're not fucking anybody except your wife and me, then you're not only insulting my intelligence, you're insulting all of ours. We know better."

Wow! I was damn proud of Renalia for once again sounding like the old Renalia, who was on her girlfriend's side. If only he'd known what he was in for. We were about to grill him like he was on enemy territory in Iraq.

"So you see, Ashton, don't try to hold back on us. We know the tricks of the trade, you feel me?" I hit him with a speck of my input. "We just finished telling you all of our cloak-n-dagger shit. You need to come better than that before we have to turn you over to Emberly for some good old-fashioned, tied-up torture."

Emberly gave him a slow enticing wink. "And I'm gonna torture your fine ass real good. When I'm done, you'll barely be able to see the bruises on your body," she purred sensually. "Is that okay with you, Renalia?"

"Sure is. You have my full cooperation. Just promise me you won't bring out the kerosene-soaked fire-whip 'til last. " Renalia grinned mischievously.

"I promise." Emberly slid her tongue across her top lip as she peered in his eyes.

"You're outnumbered, so come on with it, Ashton," Dhelione told him. "Maybe you can give us some pointers."

"Trust me when I say . . . ya'll are some scary ass, freaky females, especially you," he nodded at Emberly. "I doubt very seriously if I can give ya'll pointers on anything. In fact, the longer I hang around here the more I think I'm gonna learn. And what the fuck do you do with a kerosene-soaked, fire-whip?" He was now looking puzzled.

"Forget the whip. Answer the damn question." Renalia slightly elbowed him in the side. "It's no big deal, Ashton. We just told you the main reason we have this club is to fuck around on our husbands."

"Okay . . . yeah, I'm talking to another hottie. And . . . she's real sweet," he hesitated terribly.

"Now, see, was that so hard?" Renalia patted his knee.

Even with everything we had revealed to him about us, I could still understand him not wanting to spill his guts with one of the women he was screwing sitting right next to him. He would just have to get over it.

"That's it, real sweet?" Dhelione frowned. "How sweet is real sweet?"

"Yeah, how sweet is real sweet?" I repeated her question.

He broadened his smile. "Real sweet is . . . real sweet. I mean, what else can I really say?"

"You can give more detail for one thing," I told him.

"Aw, come on, ya'll," he began whining again. "I can't be disrespecting my girl sitting right here next to me. It's not considerate."

"Look, I told you it's okay," Renalia said without hesitating. "I've already got a husband and I'm not thinking about leaving him. Not to mention, you've got a wife. If I recall correctly, the first time you and I did our thing, you told me straight off the bat you only wanted fun, nothing serious. So we know we're only in this for the fun, right?"

"Don't forget the pleasure of it, girlfriend," Emberly jumped in before Ashton answered. "We're in it for the pleasure too."

That girl never ran out of shit to say.

Ashton nodded yes, raising his glass and took a big swallow. "All right then!" he roared. "Maybe I *am* in the mood for some fun and games, so what do you wanna know?"

He damn sure didn't have to ask twice. Dhelione hit him with the next question instantly.

"On a scale of one to ten, how would you rate your real sweet hottie, as you call her?" Dhelione's face lit up as she and I caught momentary eye contact while waiting for his answer.

In the brief moment that her and my eyes met, I just knew she was thinking what I was thinking, which was, *Please let Myilana still be listening 'cause the moment of truth or lie is about to be told.*

Without making too much disturbance, I eased into the kitchen and pretended to get something out of the refrigerator. On the way back to my seat, I stole a peek at Myilana, still sitting in the hallway with her back against the wall. She threw me an "okay" hand sign and nod. I was happy that she didn't appear too worn out or upset from the slight overlapse of time we'd used to wear him down. It would've been a crime to quit now that we were so close to reaching our goal.

Ashton was in the process of spilling his answer to Dhelione's question, but not before repeating it as if he didn't hear it right the first time.

"How do I rate her? Well, what can I say? She's a fine woman." He gave each of us a quick once over from head to toe, ending with Renalia. "Just like ya'll. And believe me, ya'll fine as hell!"

Putting emphasis on the fact that we were fine was a clever move for him.

"Is she a down-to-earth chick, or one of those high and mighty heifers?" I added a second part to the question.

"To be honest . . . she kinda reminds me of ya'll." He seemed to be doing a little too much pondering and examining us, all of a sudden.

Oh, shit! I hoped it was my imagination, and he wasn't about to figure Myilana for our friend.

"Like us? How so?" I asked, trying not to sound paranoid.

"Well, she's very classy for one thing. Very beautiful, and open-minded too."

"Oh really." Emberly took over. "Open-minded enough to be in an organization like ours, you think?"

"I don't know," he replied. "I can't really answer that one, but she does like to have fun."

Renalia listened without interrupting. But after a while, I guess she decided we weren't asking the right questions fast enough, so she took over. We sat quietly as she interrogated him nonstop. "How long have you known her?"

"Ummm, about a year."

"How long have you been fucking her?"

"About a year."

"Is she married?"

"Yes."

"Does she live around here?"

"Actually, she does. She lives here in town." He co-operated nicely until Renalia asked him one of the key questions of the night.

"Oh, she lives here in town?" Renalia faked a big smile. "As small as this town is if we don't know her we probably know *of* her. What's her name?"

That's where his answering slowed up and his smile shrunk. He peered at Renalia like she had said a bad word. "Come on now. You know I can't tell you that."

"Why not?" Renalia complained. "It's not like we're gonna tell anybody. Right girls?"

"That's right."

"Why would we?"

"It'll be our little secret." We answered back to back.

"So tell us who this *real sweet* mystery lady is?" Renalia's pleading look should have done the trick on him, but it didn't.

I could tell by the look in his eyes, we were wasting our time trying to get a name out of him. He grasped

Renalia's hand and locked their fingers together, then gazed back at her.

"Hey . . . I can't give up her name. And I wouldn't do that to you either." He was smooth as milk chocolate.

After the small award winning performance he delivered, we knew better than to pressure him any further on the name thing.

"Why don't we talk about us, baby?" he said to Renalia. "I'm here with you, not with somebody else." He leaned over and lavished a slow kiss on her lips.

"All right! All right!" Emberly hollered. "Cut that shit out! Hell, we can't do it so ya'll can't either."

"I know that's right." I clapped my hands together loudly for them to break it up. "Mr. Drapers, if you don't have three extra men sticking somewhere in your back pocket, you need to slow your roll."

Ashton and Renalia retracted from the kiss and began smiling. That nigga was on fire with his cute ass. Almost made me wanna fuck him and become *crazy woman* number three. I was beginning to understand the "caught-up" shit the girls were going through with him.

"Okay, Ashton. I've got one more question," Dhelione said.

"I can do one more," he agreed. "But that'll be it, right?"

"That'll be it, I promise." Dhelione assured him. "Here it goes. If you had to make a choice between Renalia and whoever this mystery lady is, who would you choose?"

"Aw, that's easy as pi—"

"Careful now!" Dhelione cut him off. "You better give it some careful thought before you blurt out how easy the answer is, because once you've said it, that's it. You can't take it back. And please keep in mind, Ashton, one of our rules is complete honesty about whatever."

"Yeah, we try our damndest not to condemn each other. That is, unless one of us happens to stumble across some irrational behavior from time to time, and has to be put back in her place." I seized momentary eye contact with Renalia after making my cynical statement. She knew exactly what I meant by her behavior being so funky lately.

"What she's trying to say is, we don't judge," Dhelione said, looking serious enough that it should've convinced Ashton not to lie. "We pride ourselves on always trying to be objective. So whatever you say, Renalia's not gonna take it personal. And even though she's our best friend, we won't take it personal either. That's assuming you choose the mystery lady, of course."

Ashton nodded yes, then said, "Can I choose both of them?"

"Hell no," Emberly answered in a flash. "Haven't we already talked about that freaky shit? And don't think we don't know you're stalling for time again. Oh, come on, don't mess up your good track record. You were doing so well."

"All right," he said playfully, reaching his hand up and running his fingers through Renalia's hair. "Mystery lady may damn well have it going on, but if I had to leave with somebody, you know it would be you." He then leaned over and lavished a slow tantalizing kiss on Renalia's lips once again.

I could almost see the smoke from their mouths circulating in the air.

"Hey! I thought we told ya'll to put a pause on that shit," Dhelione screeched. "And Ashton . . . that was a line if I ever heard one. Let's give this award winning actor a hand ladies."

Emberly, Dhelione, and I began clapping.

He tried his best to sell us an offended look. "Hey, that wasn't a line."

"Oh, please." I laughed like hell. "Not only was it a line, it wasn't even an original one. If your *real sweet* mystery lady had been sitting here with you instead of Renalia, you would've told her the exact same thing."

"Ain't it the truth," Emberly declared along with me.

Ashton was now clutching Renalia's hand and laughing too, but he still wouldn't admit he'd given us a line.

"That wasn't a line, that was the truth." His most sincere look, as handsome as he was, still couldn't pull the wool over our eyes. "Why do ya'll think I'm putting a line on her? Aren't we past that now?"

So what, he'd agreed to answer our questions. I knew all along he wasn't going to risk blowing his *right now* thing with Renalia. Especially since he knew there was no way for his so-called mystery lady to know what he'd said. No doubt the girls knew that too.

Surprisingly, Renalia didn't seem too thrilled over him choosing her. I thought she would've been turning cartwheels by now. But instead, she leveled a rather disappointed look at him.

"Yeah, we're supposed to be past it, but I guess men are just gonna be men," she said. "It's not really your fault, so we don't blame you. Those are your natural instincts." She wrapped her hands around his jaws like he was a little child, then pecked a quick kiss on his jaw. There was an enormous amount of gentleness in her eyes, like she'd suddenly turned into Mother Theresa or somebody.

What was up with this girl tonight? Emberly had already warned her about the possibility of us calling for an exorcism if she didn't make her mind up what mood she wanted to be in. Of all the moods I'd witnessed from her throughout the evening, this one was brand new. It was much more tolerant than her peaceful mood, divine almost. Yeah, right.

Chapter Eight

With the exception of all her peculiar behavior, she did speak logically to Ashton about his answer. I guess that was what counted the most. But she didn't stop there. She exhaled a slow breath and gently spoke again. "You see, Ashton, me and the girls know you would've said differently if the situation had been different. You know . . . if the other lady in your life had been here instead of me."

"Look, baby—"

"Shhh." Renalia lay her index finger on his lips, silencing him. "Don't speak . . . just give me a hug, okay?" She put her arms around him and he embraced her back.

While they hugged, she shot her thumb up. That was our cue to bring Myilana in. I wasted no time initiating the first hint.

"Dhelione, do you think Myi is awake?" I asked loudly.

"Probably not," Dhelione replied. "If she was she'd probably come back up here and join us."

Emberly couldn't wait to get in where she fit in. The gratifying look was all over her face. "I don't know ya'll, she's been back there asleep for quite a while. Maybe one of us needs to go check on her."

"She's probably okay, just sleeping that headache off she was complaining about." Renalia now joined the charade.

Ashton looked totally puzzled as he listened to us. "Is somebody else here?" he asked in a low tone.

"Just our other girlfriend, but you don't have to talk low, she's asleep." Renalia's nonchalant answer left a question mark on his face.

"Oh, okay." He smiled softly. "Ya'll didn't tell me there were other members in your club."

"There aren't any other members, just her. She had a headache earlier, so she went in the back bedroom to sleep it off." Renalia locked her hand in his and leaned against his shoulder.

Seconds later, Myilana strolled through the hall entrance, stretching and yawning as if she was just waking up. For a minute, I figured she was pretending, just to add that extra touch to her performance. But then I thought about how long she'd been waiting in the hallway, she probably needed to be stretching and yawning for real.

"Ohhhh . . . what a nap," she uttered softly. "I tell you girls, I feel a lot better now." She stood at the end of the sofa where I sat, instantly seizing eye contact with Ashton. "Why didn't ya'll wake me up and tell me we had company?" She slapped her hand on her hip playfully. "Hello there."

Ashton looked like he'd seen the ghost of *Halloween Past*. His eyes widened tremendously, peering at her in complete silence. I thought he was going to pass out any minute. He couldn't even return her greeting right away.

Emberly snapped him out of his trance. "Ashton! Didn't you hear our friend, Myi, speak to you, brother? You don't look so good. Say something to her."

He took a brisk head shake and said, "Oh, ahh . . . hi. I mean . . . hello." His ass was straight up busted. All of that stuttering and shit made me want to burst into laughter so bad I didn't know what to do, but I held it in.

Myilana widened her smile, maintaining the intense stare she had with him. "Are you all right? You look a little flushed?" she was almost whispering.

"Uhh . . . yeah, yeah. I'm fine." He was so damn nervous there was no way he was fine.

The four of us watched closely. He didn't take his eyes off of Myilana's the whole time.

I asked myself silently, *Shit, has he forgotten Renalia's still sitting next to him?* Emberly and Dhelione appeared to be getting the biggest kick of all from the floor show, but I couldn't take it anymore. I had to say something to try and help relieve the awkward moment.

"Oh, Myilana, let me introduce you to our newest club member." I pointed to Ashton. "This is Ashton Drapers, Renalia's friend."

Myilana plopped down on the sofa next to me with her bright, enchanting smile and said, "Nice to meet you." She purposely kept him in agony by not acknowledging that they already knew each other.

Ashton's thoughts must have been zipping around like a ricocheting bullet because his mouth wasn't working at the moment. Finally, he yanked his hand from Renalia's and slumped his head over cowardly, boggling it from side to side.

"Aww damn. Damn, damn," he grunted. While his head was down in distress, the five of us quickly exchanged grins without him seeing.

"Aww damn?" Renalia repeated his words. "What do you mean by that, Ashton? Is something—"

"Come off it," he murmured. "You know what I'm talking about. All of ya'll know." He eyeballed each of us, ending with Myilana. "How are you, Myilana?"

Myilana puckered her brows. "Excuse me? Didn't I speak to you when I came in? Am I missing something?" She was dead serious about keeping that charade going 'til it couldn't go anymore. So I figured it wouldn't hurt for me to throw one last brick on the load.

"I don't mean to sound crazy, but do ya'll know each other, Myi?" My phony question put the icing on the cake.

Myilana not answering right away gave Renalia time to ease in more of her dramatics. "Do—you—and —Myi . . . know each other, Ashton?" she stammered.

By now he appeared to be much more composed. He even sounded better.

"Ya'll called her Myi, short for Myilana. That's why I didn't catch the name earlier." He partially smiled, then parked his eyes back on Myilana. "Yeah, we know each other." Blushing all over the place, he seemed proud to say so.

Myilana smirked playfully. "Why'd you tell? I wasn't gonna let on."

After hearing both admissions, Renalia had no choice but to continue acting out her *clueless* part. Her eyes traveled from Ashton to Myilana.

"Wait a minute! What in the hell is going on?" She sprang to her feet, pretending to be angry. At least, I assumed she was pretending. It was hard to tell with her.

Ashton looked up at Renalia peacefully and said, "Stop it. You already know I know her, that's what this is all about. Ya'll planned it. Ya'll called me over here to play with me like some kind of damn joy stick. Tell me you didn't?" He slowly stood up, glancing at us one by one. "Is anybody gonna answer me or what?"

"Or what," Emberly replied nonchalantly. "Ashton, my man, your ass just got served!" She clapped her hands and bellowed out a laugh.

The rest of us, except Ashton, clapped along with her, laughing to the top of our voices. He stood in that one spot halfway smiling, shaking his head from side to side slowly.

"Damn, Ashton. You should have seen your face when Myilana walked in the room. Look like you'd seen a whole damn gang of ghosts," Dhelione shrieked.

"No he didn't! He looked like he wanted to *be* a damn ghost, so he could vanish up out of here!" Emberly screamed.

"Okay, Okay! Stop ya'll." Renalia waved her hand in the air as she plunged back down on the sofa tickled as we were. "Myilana, you wanna do it back over since we know his answer was bullshit?"

"Nahh, I'm cool with it," Myilana replied peacefully. She seemed okay with the outcome even though Ashton's answer wasn't in her favor.

"You sure about that, Myi?" I double checked to be on the safe side.

"Yeah, I'm sure. What's done is done." She waved her hand once to let it go.

Ashton eased back down on the sofa, looking a little offended. "Wait a minute now! Ya'll do see me still in the room, don't you?" He raised his voice. "Ya'll are sitting here talking about me like I'm gone."

"Are we lying on you?" I asked bluntly.

"What?" He tossed me a baffled look.

"Are we lying on you?" I repeated my question. "You know as well as we do we're not lying. That bullshit answer you gave us when you chose Renalia sucks. And—"

"Now hold on. Let's not be too hasty, Parrish," Dhelione interrupted me. "Maybe he meant what he said. Maybe he does prefer Renalia. Do you, Ashton?"

"Do I what?" He really put on a puzzled look now.

"Do you stand by your decision in choosing Renalia instead of that damn *mystery lady* you told us about?" Dhelione yakked on with no pity, knowing the tough spot the poor guy was already in. She was only making it worse for him.

I didn't know exactly when he decided to do away with our "got him" games, but when he did, he hit us with a big ass homerun answer.

"First of all, there is no mystery lady," he insisted. "Myilana is the woman I was talking about. And if ya'll really have been playing this lover's game the way you say you have, then you should know I wasn't about to throw all my aces on the damn table at one time. Matter of fact, would either of you have answered the question any different than I did?"

"We don't have to answer that 'cause it's *not* one of us," Renalia laughed. "It's you. Don't try to change your shoes just 'cause you stepped in a big ol' pile of cow shit. Nobody in here can wear your size anyway."

"Ha, ha, ha, ha, ha, now that's funny," I screamed. "Ashton, we already knew about you, Myilana, and Renalia's little love circle when you first got here. Like you said, that's one of the reasons we invited you. We were dying to find out what you'd say if you had to choose between the two of them. Can't say we were surprised. Damn, you men are so predictable."

"Okay, ya'll, that's enough of this shit," Emberly yawned. "It's boring now. There's nothing else to talk about, we've covered it all. What time is it? I've been messing around with ya'lls' asses so long it's probably too late for me to call my man over for some hot sex tonight."

"When did we decide we were gonna call more men over?" Dhelione sounded surprised.

"The second that one walked through the door," Emberly replied, pointing at Ashton. "Hell, there's no need in taking one lonely baby step. We might as well go the whole nine yards."

"Amen." Myilana lazily flung her hand up once. "No need in turning back now."

"Dhelione, you knew if Ashton came here to meet Renalia, we'd all want some action for the weekend. That goes without saying, duhh," I mumbled.

"Damn right it does. See, even *blondie the black girl* knew that. I'm so proud of you, Parrish." Emberly winked at me, slouching over on the sofa sleepily.

"I didn't know, but I guess I do now." Dhelione being the naïve one for a change was funny.

"I'm sleepy as hell, ya'll." Emberly suddenly sat straight up on the sofa, shaking her drowsiness off. "Which means I'm fixing to take my ass to bed. It's painfully clear nobody's getting any sex tonight except Renalia."

"I know that's right," Myilana chuckled. "We may as well take a cold shower and save our Mandingo invitations for a Saturday party."

"I'm with you Myilana, I'm getting sleepy too." I had started to yawn now. "Let's get up early in the morning and see how fast we can put a little something together. I'm sure we won't have a problem getting a few fellas to join us."

The minute I made my statement, Ashton set his eyes straight on Myilana. I could tell he wanted so badly to say something to her. But what? He'd already been sneaking a stare here and there when Renalia wasn't paying any attention. I'd only seen Myilana make eye to eye contact with him twice, but even with those two times a person would've had to be Ray Charles not to see the strong attraction between them. If I noticed it, Dhelione and Emberly had to have noticed it. I crossed my fingers, hoping Renalia didn't notice it.

Judging by Ashton's new disturbed expression and sudden reserved talking, I felt he regretted the choice he'd made. The connection between him and Renalia simply wasn't as powerful as the veiled one between him and Myilana. And the amazing thing about that was, he hadn't even kissed or touched Myilana like he'd done with Renalia.

I wished a hundred times he would keep his eyes on Renalia, so nothing unpleasant would happen. For a few minutes, I constantly repeated in my head, *please don't let Renalia notice, please don't let Renalia notice.* Then all of a sudden Ashton broke my concentration with the wrong shit to say at the really, really wrong time.

"So ya'll are gonna have a party tomorrow, huh?" he asked Myilana, staring at her like he was five seconds away from throwing her on the floor and fucking her right there in front of us. "I know you're not inviting another guy, are you?"

"Excuse me?" Myilana frowned, looking insulted.

"Tell me you didn't just ask me if I'm gonna move on and start fucking somebody else, now that you're with Renalia? I know that's not what you just asked me, right?"

That shit revived everybody, including Renalia. If she hadn't noticed the sparks between Ashton and Myilana before, she damn well was about to now. Ultra high intensity was loaded in Myilana's peer while waiting for him to answer her question. A question he was about to regret having asked.

Though Ashton's gloomy eyes didn't leave Myilana's questioning ones, he didn't reply immediately. This really put me on nervous edge. *Damn, what are they fixing to do, kiss?* I wondered.

"Hello, hello!" I had to shout at them to break up their fiery ass stare. "I believe she asked you a question, Ashton."

He still didn't say anything.

"He doesn't have to answer, I'll answer for him," Dhelione said, coming to the rescue. "Hell yessss. That's exactly what he's asking you, Myi. He doesn't want you to get with another guy even after he sat here and kicked you to the curb!"

Dhelione laughed behind her little tease, but Ashton didn't think it was funny at all. He wasted no time speaking after that.

"Hey, that's not true. I didn't kick you to no curb." He never took his eyes out of Myilana's. "I didn't even know you were here," he uttered an almost whisper to her.

The plus in all of this was Myilana got a chance to see how sincere he was through his eyes telling her that he wished he could turn back the hands of time and choose her. That was damn sure what his eyes were telling me. But unfortunately, they were probably telling Renalia the same thing. That's where we were shit out of luck when she all of a sudden went off.

"You've got to be fucking kidding me!" Renalia screamed viciously. "You think you can keep both of us on pussy patrol?"

Her outburst confirmed for me that she'd read his eyes the same as I had.

"Hold up, you've got it wrong, Renalia. That's not what I'm saying at all," Ashton defended himself.

"Well, just what in the hell are you saying? According to what I heard, you're sitting right next to me, and questioning Myilana about who she's gonna be fucking tomorrow. Me and Myi are friends, Ashton. And our friendship is thicker than a dick."

Did I hear that right, coming from Renalia? Evidently so, because Myilana began cheering her by chanting, "Say that, say that. Tell him like it is, girl."

He looked almost too wounded to bear. "I'm sorry if you—"

"Sorry isn't good enough, Ashton," Renalia cut him off in mid-sentence. "Myilana and I agreed that whoever you chose would be the one. You can't fuck both of us! The only reason it went on as long as it did was because we didn't know!"

Now that was the Renalia I knew and loved, telling the brother the importance of our sisterhood with no holds barred.

No doubt Myilana was cheering for her because she knew it was the right thing to do, but I could see straight though her gloomy eyes and saddened spirit. She felt just as strongly about Ashton as he'd been showing her through his eyes. Still, the Myilana I knew was not going to go back on the agreement she'd made, no matter how strongly she felt about him. That was way more than we could say for Renalia lately. She may have been telling Ashton the truth about our friendship being thicker than a dick, but she was doing it way too loud. My eardrums were about to burst. I was so glad when Myilana eased in and took over.

"Listen, Ashton. We never got into any details about our relationships throughout the year. Then once we're here at the retreat, we let it all out," Myilana explained peacefully. "That's why we didn't know both of us were seeing you until tonight."

"Yeah, this is the first time something like this has ever happened." Renalia had settled down a smidgen.

"And the last time too." Emberly sighed. "We are seriously revising some rules for next year. I don't wanna see nobody else getting caught up like this again."

Ashton seemed to accept the explanation they gave him fairly well. Especially, since things had gotten so serious now.

"Okay, I can understand that," he said to Renalia. "I'm sorry if I offended you, all right?"

"All right."

Then he turned to Myilana. "And I'm sorry if I offended you too."

Myilana shook her head, smiling softly. "Apology accepted. No harm done."

Her accepting his apology was as genuine as her disappointment for the way it was ending between them. The wall Myilana put up was pretty thick, but I still saw past it to her hurt feelings. *Damn, Myi, don't cry. You look like you're gonna cry.* I wondered if Dhelione and Emberly saw too.

"Thank goodness!" I said aloud, hoping to break the awkwardness of the sad moment. "I'm outta here. I'll see ya'll good folks in the morning." I was now on my way to the back to shower and hit the sack. Myilana came right behind me. Then Dhelione, then Emberly.

Chapter Nine

Emberly

After going to bed at 2:00 A.M., I sure as hell didn't plan on getting up too early the next morning. But we'd made an agreement to get up about 9:00 o'clock and start making preparations for our little extended gathering. The only one of us who already knew the exact man she was going to invite was Renalia. Naturally, that man was Ashton. The rest of us had plenty of options, but most of the guys that we were fucking were married. So we didn't know which ones would be able to ditch their wives, or other women, or whatever plans they'd already made for the day, and come on such short notice.

Needless to say, after each of us made a few phone calls apiece we were in business. We got our confirmed dates for the evening. Around noon we began sprucing the place up a little, then prepared the kitchen table pretty much like we'd done when we first made it to the cottage that Friday night. Fresh cut vegetables, a variety of clean crisp fruits, sliced meats, and garnishments galore were at our fingertips.

The party was on once again, only this time it was ten strong instead of just five. For me, the best part of all was knowing at some point before the night was over it was going to be "get my sex on" time. One by one the men arrived, and one by one we briefly filled them in on the fine points of our club like we'd done with Ashton the night before. It was no surprise to us when every one of the whorish bastards grinned naughtily at the idea of what we told them.

The ten of us eventually scattered around in the den and kitchen. The place was overflowing with music, chatter, laughter, drinking, and a bit of snacking from time to time. As much fun as I was having with everybody, I hated to skip out, but just the thought of having an explosive orgasm or two ran chills down my spine. Shit, my body had been craving some hot, sizzling sex all night. I felt like I'd been deprived long enough.

I yelled *sayonara* to the girls on my way out, then dragged my black handsome Mandingo straight to the back bedroom that I'd slept in. All I could think about was how we'd made the best decision ever to invite some fine ass men to our annual gathering. I stood in that room with my "man for the minute," staring him down right before I sprinted over and slapped a kiss on his thick, luscious lips.

"Do you know how long I've been waiting for some of you?" I whispered between tongue lashes.

His mouth was warm and succulent. I could practically taste the Dom Perignon left on his lips.

"Ummm, umm," he hummed as he embraced me tightly while we kissed. A candle on each nightstand allowed a little light in the mauvish colored bedroom.

The night before I'd dreamed of that very moment with him, or some other guy if he couldn't come. It didn't matter to me. I just wanted a real man to give it to me like I needed it.

"Ohhh, baby, you feel so good," he whispered between kisses. "I could hardly wait to get here and see you after you called me." He overpowered my tiny lips with his full, manly lips and sucked my tongue with an escalating hunger.

I clawed his back through the dark blue silky shirt he wore.

"Ummm. You like my tongue?" I mumbled during a short pause from the kiss.

"Ohh baby I—"

"Shut up!" I shouted, cutting him off. My sudden aggressive tone not only caught him by surprise, it seemed to frightened the hell out of him too. I had his undivided attention. "I know all about you. You're nothing but a black ass criminal." I curled my lips and grasped hold of his chin with one hand, firmly squeezing his lower jaws.

The grip on his jaw was so tight, my fingertips imbedded in his skin. It had to sting a little, but he didn't complain. He only stood there like a scared ass little boy, looking as if he thought I'd snapped and lost my mind or something. He'd teased me many times in the past about being a super-duper, fast-talking motor mouth. So this time I purposely said what I wanted to say to him real slow; slow enough that the words were practically dripping off my lips like sorghum molasses in the winter time.

"Do you think I'm gonna fuck a black ass criminal like you? Huh, huh? Do you?" I got all up in his face. He should've felt the wind seeping through my narrowed mouth onto his, because I felt the back draft.

Only the tip of my lips touched his lips. At this point, I had taken complete charge of him and the situation.

"I—"

"I, I?" My controlling temperament wouldn't let him get a word in edgewise. "What's the matter? Cat got your tongue? Or did you loose it down my damn throat?" I quickly swiped my tongue across his lips leaving a dampness behind. "Back up against that wall and assume the position. Now!" I ordered him.

He backed up and leaned against the wall without uttering a word. I stood and watched.

"Are you deaf?" I barked. "I said assume the damn position!"

Still, like a scared little boy, he spread his legs and raised his brown muscular arms while plastered against the wall, peering at me. His neat head of black hair and smooth facial profile peeked from beneath the dancing shadows of the soft flame-lit room. The man I'd just ordered to stretch out along the wall was none other than the chief of police of Coldwater, Curtis Marlston. And damn, did Curtis have a serious obsession with role playing during sex.

In many of our first rendezvous he'd told me how being chief of police gave him the authority and power to discipline others, but several fucks later I found out he had entirely different desires in the bedroom. I came to know how he desperately wanted to be overpowered and disciplined by someone else. It damn sure didn't take long for me to let him know that I was the right woman for the job. I'd always gotten off on having the complete power to control my men, so this was right up my alley. Under my expert tutelage, Curtis soon learned exactly how to play his role. He enjoyed every minute of the high intensity I brought to the table. And to the bathroom, and to the floor, and to the bedroom, and to everywhere else we decided to fuck.

I almost laughed out loud when I ordered him to back up on that wall. He stuck to it like glue, waiting for my next command. I grabbed his blackjack stick off the bed and strolled back over in front of him.

"Now that I've got you just where I want you . . . Chief." Slap! Slap! I smacked the blackjack in the center of my hand time after time. "I'm gonna make sure you get just what you deserve. Justice. You've been a bad boy, haven't you?" Slap! I smacked the blackjack in my hand again. "Haven't you?!" I then poked the stick in the middle of his chest and held it there.

"Yes," he answered quickly in his deep voice.

"Corrupt cops get no sympathy from me." I slid the stick from his chest slowly down to his stomach until it reached his crotch, then circled it on top of his increasingly stout dick. "What's that?" I poked at it. "Answer me dammit!"

"It's my penis," he replied nervously, still pretending to be a scared little boy.

"It's your penis . . . what!"

"It's my penis, Mrs. Em." Curtis freely gave me the respect I insisted on having. His eyes said he wanted to fuck 'til we conjured up a tornado. Like always, he was really loving my "take charge" talent.

"Oh really. Well, I'll see about that for myself." I reached down and snatched a handful of his cock through his navy slacks. He jerked from the firm grasp.

"Umph," he sound out.

I began to rub and gently squeeze him down there. "It feels hard. It feels big. It feels long. It feels like it wants to get out." My tantalizing became more fierce. "I guess I could take your word for it, but I think I'll do a strip search instead. Take it off! Take it all off, Chief!" I moved my hand away to let him undress.

He lowered his arms from against the wall and did as he was told. I patiently watched 'til he had stripped down all the way.

"What are you going to do with me, Mrs. Em?" he asked with a pretend tremble in his voice.

I took my time, giving him my version of an intimidating smirk, then said, "Whatever the fuck I want to. Don't you know dirty cops get the worst kind of punishment? Now turn around and face the wall."

He slowly turned his back to me and pinned his chest, and one side of his face against the wall, then gradually raised his arms over his head. My eyes searched over his solid brown body, admiring his stocky built ass. I darted over to the dresser for my bottle of baby oil, then reclaimed my spot right behind him. Taking my time, I squirted the oil all over his neck and back, then tossed the bottle and began caressing the oil onto his skin.

As I rubbed, the greasy oil dripped off his arms and trickled down his backside onto his thick buttocks, leaving them to gleam in the dim light. I rubbed my hands over every inch of his body until it was completely drenched and sleek in oil.

"Spread those damn thighs wider so I can get a better view of my handywork," I told him.

He did as instructed. I leaned the front of my body into his back, clutched his slick ass cheeks with both hands and we began twirling our bodies together. He followed my lead. The thin red dress I wore was the only thing between his fervent moist skin and mine.

"Do exactly what I say, and I promise to hurt you real good," I whispered in his ear while playing around it with my tongue. "Don't say a word unless I tell you to." I began dragging my mouth and face over his warm slippery shoulders.

"Yes, ma'am." He trembled, enjoying my commanding touch all the way.

I suddenly yanked one of his arms down and bent it behind his back in handcuff position. "Walk to the bed and lay face down. Come on, do it in a hurry." I clutched his wrist tightly as he fell down on the bed and stretched out just like he'd done against the wall. Smack! Smack! Smack! Smack!

"Ohhhh, ohhhh, ouuuu, ouuuhh!" he yelled out fiercely as I slapped his rigid ass-cheeks over and over with the blackjack. Smack! Smack! "Oouuuhh!" *Pain and pleasure*, he exemplified both emotions at once.

Pain, because I was wearing his ass out with no holding back and no pity. Pleasure, because each time I hit him it intensified his arousal, causing his dick to grow harder and harder, making him want to fuck even more. I knew this because he'd told me so many times before. The chief got a ferocious hard-on from getting his ass slapped with a blackjack, and believe me, I knew how to give him just what he wanted, the way he wanted it.

"What's my name, boy!" I demanded. Smack! Smack! "What's my name! Answer me!" The more I whipped him the more I became excited too. I knew he was going to fuck my brains out after his disciplinary pain kicked in.

Smack! Smack! Smack! The meaty flesh on his hind-quarters slightly jiggled each time I whacked him.

"Ohhhhh, ohhhhhhhh!" He roared, jerking his thick ass in and out.

As hard as I was hitting him, the very imprint of the stick should have embedded in his skin, but it didn't.

"Did you hear me? Huh? I said what's my name, boy!" I was really feeling it now. My nipples had popped up and their print was showing through my silk dress.

"Mrs. Em!" he exclaimed. "You're Mrs. Em!"

"That's right. And what punishment do you deserve for breaking the law?"

The tone of his voice had deepened a lot more when he answered me this time. "Whup my ass! Oh, baby! Oh, Mrs. Em, whup my ass!" he growled. I threw myself on top of his rear end, dress and all.

"What else, Chief?" I lowered my tone, gliding myself over his oily body. "What else do you deserve?"

When he felt my softness fall on top of him, he instantly reacted by reaching one hand down and grasping my hip. He didn't get permission, so I couldn't have him doing that, could I?

"Hey, you can't touch me! I didn't tell you it was okay to touch me!" I shrieked, raising my voice again.

"I'm sorry," he whimpered. "I'm sorry."

I quickly took his hand and instructed him to turn over on his back. He liked the way I manhandled him. He'd told me before he thought it was incredible the way I shoved him around being so petite.

"Sorry isn't going to cut it. You violated a direct order. And now . . . well, now I've got to handcuff your hard-headed ass."

"Okay, okay! Handcuff me! And then whup my ass!" he cried out, turning onto his back and raising his arms over his head to be handcuffed.

"Don't tell me what to do!" I snapped. "I'll whup your ass, all right. Just wait! Just wait one damn minute!" I clacked the handcuffs on him, then got out of my panties as fast as I could.

I stood straight up in the bed astraddle him still wearing my dress, then lowered myself down on his long brown erection, which was sticking straight up in the air with a slight left slant.

"I'm going to whup your dick!" I yelled. "Huh? How about that? You're going to get a dick whupping!"

The tip of his humongous rod had barely entered me and I flew into a passionate frenzy. I wiggled and rolled until it was all the way inside. I felt his patch of hairy hairs that surrounded the trunk of his penis scratching on me down there. *Oohh, it's so good* , I thought as my eyes boggled around the same as my wiggling hips.

"Ohhhh! Ohhhh!" I screeched, reeling in a circular motion on top of him.

Although he was locked in metal cuffs with his hands over his head, he stroked and rolled upward as hard as I did. Curtis was a strong man with a strong muscular penis. If he had put his mind to it, he probably could've lifted my tiny ass up in the air with his dick alone. I had to laugh about that my damn self.

"Ohhhh! Ouuuhh!" he growled, tilting his head forward and looking down at me ride him.

I took hold of my dress tail and hoisted it up in the air, giving him a clear view of how my pussy was pumping on his cock. I enjoyed riding him like a prized bull rider. The cottage wasn't all that big. I figured Curtis and I had probably drawn the attention of everybody in the front—even over the music and their chattering. It didn't matter one damn bit to me though because I had to get mine. And from the looks and sound of Curtis's non-stop excitement, it didn't matter to him either if they heard. We galloped and bellowed all the way to the finish line without holding anything back.

"Wheew! Woo!" I puffed. "What a workout, Chief! You're a real live lion, tiger, and stallion rolled up in one."

The extreme workout brought about two big smiles. One on Curtis's face and one on mine.

"Baby, if I'm all that, you're a damn good rider." He beamed. "I take it that means you're satisfied, right?"

At the end of our many sex encounters, he never failed to ask me if I was satisfied. He had a thing about making sure I was just as fulfilled as he, which I thought was considerate.

"Aw, you never forget to ask, do you?" I leaned down and smacked a kiss on his jaw. "For now I am. We'll have seconds and thirds later, okay?"

"Sounds good to me." He nodded, his arms still cuffed over his head. "Are you about ready to unlock me?"

After I unlocked him, we took a few minutes to prepare ourselves to go out and rejoin the others.

"Ready?" I asked, walking back in the room from using the bath facilities. I had to put an entirely different set of clothes on. The red silk dress I'd worn earlier was too oiled-up to wear again.

"Almost." He winked at me, bending over to put his shoe on. "As soon as I finish this."

I leaned against the wall in front of him, waiting while thinking, *that might've been a quickie, but it damn sure was a goodie.*

Curtis had a wife of twenty-five years, three grown children, he was Chief of Police, and he could fuck my brains out and satisfy me. Those four things were all I needed to know about him.

He, in turn, knew only the basics about my private life. He didn't want his home life messed up over a *backseat bounce* any more than I wanted mine messed up. Not that mine wasn't already fucked-up with my husband's many years of cheating. But that's another whole story.

The thing I liked most about Curtis was no matter how much time passed between our hooking up with each other, we always managed to successfully pick up where we left off. There weren't any commitments or obligations between us, which was more than I could say for one or two of the obsessive guys I'd fucked on impulse in the past. Needy guys worrying the hell out of me later because I'd given them a quick *cum-along-with-mine*. That kind of shit got on my nerves. Curtis and I didn't have that kind of drama. We simply had a great time whenever we did get together.

We didn't bug the hell out of each other, trying to force it when it didn't fit. Our total amount of times together were maybe nine or ten, and each one was well worth it. I knew he was probably screwing somebody else other than me and his wife, or maybe even several somebody else's. He damn-well better have known I was too. He was the kind of guy you always keep around as spare-ware.

We had that thing on lock. The way he and I did it was how the game was supposed to be played. Not like the "off the wall" shit Renalia and Myilana were on the verge of getting twisted up in over one man. Their trivial crap had thrown me in a blue-funk for a while on Friday night. But after hearing Curtis brag so much about how impressed he was with our club, I hoped to soon regain the same kind of confidence I'd had the four years before this one bad incident happened to us.

Curtis told me he understood why we'd given it so much serious thought before allowing anyone else to join us at the cottage. A slip of the tongue by the wrong person and we would've been ruined. I didn't think we had that type of thing to worry about with the ones who'd shown up for this first invite. By the looks of those players, including Curtis, they had reputation on top of reputation to protect.

Everybody up in that joint was married with families and lives they didn't want damaged. The girls and I, after much discussion, ultimately made the choice to turn the heat up on our little social venture, and I had to admit, having all those prominent heavyweights in the house made me even more confident that nothing we did would ever leave the premises. At least, by way of them it wouldn't.

I was glad to be content about our guests. I only wished my thoughts concerning Renalia, Myilana, and Ashton had been as comforting. I tried like hell to bury my skepticism, but the way things had gone down with them kept nagging at me. They'd supposedly come to an agreement and put everything to rest. Hogwash. Several reasons made me feel that things weren't as settled as they should've been.

One reason was when Myilana first began telling her story, she stressed how Ashton had fucked her so good she couldn't think about screwing another man aside from her husband, and the only reason she was still screwing him was because she was married to him. The second reason was the obvious attraction between her and Ashton. The kind of fiery desire going on between the two of them was too strong for anybody to ignore. I'd seen the sparks the second Myilana walked into the room from hiding in the hallway the night before.

After Ashton got over the initial shock of her being there, the expression on his face was so damn extreme when he looked at her, it made my liver quiver. If I could see it, there was no way Dhelione and Parrish missed it. I knew them too well. They just hadn't said anything about it yet.

I'd even noticed how Ashton was struggling hard to avoid direct eye contact with Myilana while the ten of us were scattered around laughing and mingling. Myilana was doing the same thing. She tried her damndest not to look at him or say much to him either. When the two of them did exchange a few words, it was so intense that Blind Willie Johnson could have picked up the passion vibes.

Renalia no doubt knew that Ashton really wanted to be with Myilana, and he was only going along with the decision they'd agreed on for the sake of peace, which was the best reason of all to go along with it. Enough animosity had already been created between two best friends. The only thing the rest of us could do was keep our fingers crossed that none of the under-surface drama backfired. Especially since Renalia had been playing Dr. Jekyll and Mrs. Hyde most of the weekend. I kept telling myself maybe somebody had cloned her and dropped the bad copy off for us to deal with. That was the only sense I could make of her sudden crazy ass behavior.

Chapter Ten

Parrish

"Look who decided to come back and join us," I said to Emberly and Curtis as they walked into the den from their backroom rendezvous. "So Chief . . . have you and your officers been keeping our fair town safe? Have ya'll been fighting crime and *whupping ass* like the big city boys?" I purposely put emphasis on "whupping ass" because everybody in the front room was still tickled about the rowdy commotion we'd heard from Emberly and him earlier.

If it had been one of us Emberly wouldn't have waited 'til we finished our business and came out of the back. She would've knocked on the bedroom door and made fun immediately. The whole scenario was in good humor though. Everybody felt the laughter, even the out of control sexmates themselves.

Curtis proudly answered my question with a fat smile on his face. "Not much crime around here, you know that. Hell, it's barely 1800 people in this itsy bitsy place."

How right he was about tiny Coldwater. Yet the most important thing was most people loved the peace and quiet the small town offered and didn't mind calling it home. There were maybe a handful of people who always claimed they felt confined by the limited business opportunities and small amount of entertainment the town offered. But their complaints were only talk since they never made any attempts to move somewhere else.

Twenty-five minutes south of Memphis, Tennessee, and two hours north of Jackson, Mississippi is the area where Coldwater claims its spot on the map. Interstate-55 and Highway-51 are the two main routes of entering our slow, but steadily growing town. Each route leads to the one and only traffic light that hangs smack dab in the middle of town. Folks living in Coldwater have a well-known saying for outsiders and visitors that dates back as far as the history of the town. The saying goes, "When passing through town, you better not blink or you just might miss it."

If coming in from the north on Highway-51 there's a family-owned Big Star Supermarket that incomers will see. If coming in from the south on Highway-51 there's a tall cotton gin. Either way 51 highway gives visitors the opportunity to see where all the happening happens, and that's Town Square. The circle of sightseeing begins and ends all too quickly in Town Square, but the good residents still have immediate access to most of life's necessities, such as, Coldwater Branch Bank, a pharmacy, clothes cleaners, and a Fred's Dollar Store sitting on one side of the street, while a modest banquet hall, laundromat, auto parts store, and mortgage company sits on the opposite side of the street.

After finishing the Central Street cruise, there's the option to visit the nearby day spa, owned and operated by the one and only Ashton Drapers. With the exception of the post office, city hall, several churches, and a few other locally owned business, the autumn season always does a beautiful job of decorating the entire town with tan grass and two-toned, brownish-red leaves. The leaves customarily fall from the trees and scatter all over the place during their due shedding time of year. The five of us had chosen the autumn season to have our little soirée because we believed it to be the prettiest and coziest. Emberly was the only one who argued for another time during the summer months. She was out voted four to one. Now that there were five handsome men at the cottage with us, helping make things cozier, it was official we'd chosen the right time of year.

I laughed and joked with Curtis and Emberly about their loud sex'capade, but if the truth were told, I wanted my man to scoop me up and haul me off to one of the back bedrooms so we could get our groove on just like they had done, just maybe not as loud. I wasn't the only one with jokes for Curtis. Ashton eased one in after everybody had laughed the cushion out of mine.

"Whoa man! Are you still up and about?" he asked him. "I mean, can you walk straight and shit? We heard some serious azzz whupping going on back there."

Ha ha ha ha! Ha ha ha ha! Haaah ha ha! Everybody laughed as Curtis sat down in the oversized chair. Emberly plopped down next to him. They were tickled to pieces with the rest of us.

Dhelione's tall dark date, Mitchell, hit Curtis up next. "So ya'll are into that kinky shit, huh? I hear you, man. I wouldn't mind getting my ass whupped either, as long as one of these fine ass ladies gave it to me." He eyed Dhelione lustfully as she sat on his lap.

Mitchell struck me as a guy eager for fun and games, and anything else he could get his hands on that wore panties and a skirt. Not like Eric, Myilana's slender-build, bright-skinned, mellow man. Eric was a bit more on the quiet side. And he sure seemed to love him some Myilana. He'd been all up in her face since the minute he walked through the door. Ashton didn't look happy about it either.

The most surprising guest of all was probably my hook-up for the evening, Zeke McCall, better known as Reverend Z. McCall. Pastor of one of the largest, well-known churches in a town just five miles South of Coldwater called Senatobia, Zeke needed no introduction. Anybody who didn't know him personally, without a doubt, knew *of* him. He strode around the cottage like he was at one of his own family reunions. That's just how comfortable he and the guys had become with each other in those few short hours. The incredible thing was none of them had ever spent any time together before being introduced that day. Maybe they figured there was no need in pretending since each of them knew what the other was there for.

In the beginning, I was skeptical about asking Zeke to come, fearing he'd be concerned about people he didn't know, knowing who he was. That didn't seem to bother him one way or the other. After I thought about it, I realized I didn't have anything to worry about because he'd told me more times than a few, "Yeah, I'm a *man of God*, but I'm also a *man of flesh*." Charming as hell, wasn't he?

The longer he and I sat on the sofa rubbing against each other, the more I wanted him to get into my panties. If that wasn't enough, his debonair ass started layering a bunch of sweet talk on me real thick, like triple fudge pie.

"You know, you are by far one of the most beautiful women I've ever laid eyes on," he whispered in my ear while squeezing my hand.

I wrapped myself in his strong arms and whispered back, "Flattery will get you everywhere, my handsome Mr. McCall."

"Excuse me, ya'll!" Mitchell suddenly raised his voice, grabbing my attention along with everybody else's.

"Cut it out Mitchell, you're terrible," Dhelione giggled, trying to cover his mouth with her hand to keep him quiet.

I rarely heard that kind of silly giggling from Dhelione unless she was about smashed. Her wine drinking had caught up with her. She wasn't the only one, everybody was doing quite a bit of drinking. It was just a matter of time before we were smashed along with her.

"What's up, man? Lay it down for us, we're listening," Eric replied to Mitchell."

Mitchell moved Dhelione's hand from over his mouth and said, "I think we need to give it up for these five awesome sisters. They definitely got their shit together." He raised his glass for a toast. "Pulling off an outstanding party like this . . . right here in our little ol' town under everybody's noses, and nobody knows shit. I don't have to remind you fellas how nosey the folks around here are. But the ladies still did their thing with class."

"Here, here." Eric raised his glass. "I second that."

Then Zeke, Curtis, and Ashton raised their glasses.

"Ya'll definitely got some humongous guts hiding

somewhere in your panties. Cheers!" Curtis chuckled, winking at Emberly.

Cheers! The men turned their glasses up to drink.

The five of us sat and watched, smiling. But not for long. Emberly had to have a say. "Hold on a minute now. Ladies, please raise your glasses, if you will?"

Each of us raised a glass.

"Okay, *Mrs. Em*, what would you like to say?" Renalia replied, teasing Emberly about the name we'd heard Curtis yelling when he and Emberly were doing their thing.

"Watch yourself, Renalia. The only person I've given permission to call me that is big pappa over here." Emberly squinted her eyes at Renalia, then turned her attention back to us. "Anyway, ladies, here's to the five *lucky* men who dropped everything on such short notice to come over and join our little soirée. And to a whole night of fucking and fun! Oops, I mean fucking fun!" She could've kept her fake "slip of the tongue" oops, because we knew she meant exactly what she'd said in the beginning.

"Aw now, you know you said it right the first time, girl." I told her, then drank to the toast.

By now my heartbeat had left my chest and moved down to my coochie, and my coochie was thumping something awful. Plus, I was getting tired of sneaking-a-peek at Ashton as he continuously sneaked-a-peek at Myilana. He couldn't keep his eyes off her if his life depended on it. Eric kissed Myilana on her neck a few times while they were chatting quietly among themselves, and damn if the look on Ashton's face wasn't pure anger. I thought he was going to jump up any minute and knock the hell out of Eric. I don't know how Renalia missed that one. I guess she was a lot more teed up than the rest of us, which was a good thing. She didn't need to be alert to see all of that anyhow, it was only going to cause trouble.

On the flip side of the coin, Myilana was doing the same as Ashton. She was still working hard to keep her eyes off him, and on Eric. That whole longing eye contact thing between the two of them had been going on too long. It was driving me crazy by now. I hated to keep paying so much attention to them, but I felt I needed to be a step ahead of things in case Renalia finally picked up on it. Then things would get out of hand again.

After so long, I couldn't take anymore. I grabbed the first opportunity for Zeke and I to get the hell out of dodge.

"Hey, you, come with me. I've got something to show you," I whispered in his ear seductively, then raised up from the sofa to go in the back.

Zeke rose and followed me without uttering a word. Moments later we found ourselves tangled in a passionate embrace in the bedroom next to the one that Emberly and Curtis had been *whupping-up* on each other in earlier.

As we pretended to slow dance around the floor, Zeke began singing softly in my ear. "How sweet it is to be loved by you. Awww, baaaby. How sweet it is to be loved by you."

Not only could he preach up a storm, he could sing up one too. He had sang to me on several occasions before, and believe me, he knew more R&B songs than he did gospel ones. The church I attended and the church he pastored often fellowshipped. That was how he and I ended up going out on our first date. Each time our church visited his church, or the other way around, I always noticed how he stared me down throughout the entire service. For me to know he was looking at me, I guess I had to be looking at him too, right? He was bold as hell though, staring from the pulpit. I knew it was only a matter of time before he made a move on me. I was waiting on him when he did.

Tall, tempting, and tasty were the words that popped into my mind when I saw him. A yellow-jack, but not too yellow, just right. A sister couldn't help but clutch onto his love-handles when being intimate, but for the most part his body wasn't bad for a forty-six-year-old preacher with teenage kids. I didn't know if it was Mrs. Clairol or Dark-n-Lovely, but one of those brands helped to hide the gray in his "so high" fro. In looks, Zeke beat my ugly ass husband by 100 miles.

The only thing I didn't like about Zeke was the fact that he was a bonafide sheister. He couldn't hide it. Those beady little black eyes of his gave it away. True enough, he was good in bed, and I enjoyed the time we spent together, but I didn't trust his ass far as I could throw him. Just like with my husband, I didn't trust him either. As a matter of fact, Zeke and my husband had the same kind of cold, ruthless eyes. My husband and I had been together since high school, and my only weakness was I genuinely loved him in spite of his shitty ways.

Maybe that was one of the reasons I was so attracted to Zeke. In some ways he reminded me of my shiny, baldheaded husband. Not in looks, but by his character. Of course, my husband couldn't carry a tune in a bucket the way Zeke could. Zeke was about to sing me into eroticism with that Marvin Gaye song.

"How sweet it is to be loved by youuu . . ." He

clutched one of my hands and suddenly twirled me around once, then reeled me back into his arms like a ballerina.

"Serenade me if you will . . . you romantic devil you," I complimented him, smiling naughtily.

"Shucks, baby, you ain't heard nothing yet." He swayed me down and dipped me, then started singing a whole new tune. "There's a right and wrong way to love somebody." Keith Sweat's golden oldie. And Zeke was tearing it up. "You may be young, but you're ready . . . ready for love. Don't play no silly games with me baabby'a'a'a. No, no, no, no, it just ain't my thang."

As much base as Zeke's voice carried he could mimic to perfection just about any male singer, even if the singer's voice carried a higher pitch. Zeke had mad skills, and not just vocal skills, tongue skills too. He swooped me up and lay me on the bed and began pulling my clothes off in a hot flash. My denim skirt hit the floor. My tan top followed. Off with my beige bikini set, then he parted my legs and went straight for the gushy pussy and gushy it was. I was seeping like a loose faucet. He dangled his tongue around in my sweet nectar until he forced a pussy wiggle from me. Then he worked the tongue up and down, in and out, like it was a strong dildo.

"Ummm, you're so good, baby," he mumbled, licking away. "You get sweeter every time I taste you. It oughta be a crime for anything to be this good."

By now he had kneeled down at the foot of the bed and pulled me toward the edge and was working my pussy overtime.

"Oohhh, daddy. You know how to do it to me," I purred in pleasure, picking up the pace of my once slow wiggle that he'd interrupted when he dragged me to the foot of the bed. "Oohh daddy . . . you know it doesn't take much of your talented tongue. Keep it coming." I slid down even further until my ass was hanging completely off the edge and my upper body and back remained on the bed.

Zeke held tightly to the bottom of my ass as I went ahead and swirled it for him. He squeezed my backside and slapped my rotating cheeks repeatedly. Slap! Slap!

"It's coming, Daddy. Ohh, ohh, it's coming." My pet name for him during sex was daddy. He liked to hear me say it. "Oohhh, Daddy." My cum finally came and left me breathless.

My body shivered like an electrifying bolt of lighting was passing through. Zeke quickly slid my ass back up on the bed and began kissing around in my stomach area, from there up to my breasts. He squeezed them in the center of his wide palms, teasing my nipples, one then the other. He opened wide and sucked his mouth full of one breast. I was definitely feeling that titty sucking thing. It was setting my stuff on fire all back over again, and he knew it.

"Come on Daddy. You know you can't play around with those titties too long without filling me up with the big twelve-inch," I murmured, lifting myself up and reaching down to unbutton his black shirt.

He pulled himself away from my tits and began to help me unbutton his shirt. Moments later his black shirt, black slacks, and briefs were stacked on the floor near my clothes. When I said twelve-inch, I didn't exaggerate one bit. Zeke's humongous dick was *one* of the biggest I'd ever encountered, if not *the* biggest. His dick was every bit of twelve inches, and damn did he know how to work it. He stood over me butt-naked with a look of hunger in his eyes. His erection stuck out nearly halfway across the room.

I quickly flipped over to stand on my knees and hands, then hoisted my ass directly in the air in front of him. He palmed my ass-cheeks and eased his dick inside me promptly. I felt his huge hardness all the way up in my stomach. He began slow, gentle thrusts at first. It was good. Those slow strokes thrashing up against my insides forced me to spread my ass open wider. I parted my knees away from each other as far as they would go, and arched my back stiffly, then pressed my ass into his crotch preparing to take harder thrusts in my pussy.

"Oouuu, Daddy, that's it. Ram that dick in my pussy. Ram it. Ram it," I moaned, my eyes circling randomly.

Zeke could fuck me so good. The generous length of his dick was an added bonus. He could eat pussy really good too, but if I'd had a choice it would've been the dick. It didn't get any better than a huge brown cock in my opinion. My pussy was arched just right for the way he was wearing it out. He spread his legs apart and slumped down slightly to keep his thrusts straight and even. He knew how to find that perfect spot to work in. He rolled and humped while I kept the pussy arched upright for him to have his way.

"Oouuhh . . . oouuhh, baby girl. I'm about to do it in you. It's coming!" he growled.

"Me too, Daddy," I shrieked. And with that his thick nectar exploded into my pussy, distributing it all inside of me, then he eased it out greasy.

I was still clutching the bed covers tight in my hands as the after affects of the orgasm cascaded through my body. He huffed and panted a few seconds, then leaned over on my back and squeezed his hands full of my titties. His sweaty chest rubbed against my back, and he squeezed my tits like they were round balloons filled with water. After the massive cumming we'd just experienced, his hard-on was still full stretch. It was twitching and shaking back and forth between my legs, then he suddenly grabbed it and began cramming it into my ass-hole, anal.

That was another part of sex that really got him excited. He liked giving it to me in the rear and I liked getting it there too. I have to admit, I wasn't crazy about it in the beginning, but it grew on me and I eventually began to enjoy it. The only reason I'd agreed to do it in the first place was because I felt it was the least I could do for him since there wasn't a chance in hell of me sucking his dick. He knew that too. Of all the years I'd been married, I had never sucked my husband's dick, and I damn sure wasn't going to suck somebody else's husband's.

The girls always made fun of me because I refused to do it, telling me I didn't know what I was missing. Ask me if I cared. I didn't believe in oral sex, and every man I'd ever fucked knew I didn't. If for some reason a guy had a problem with it, then Mr. Tired-ass could take a walk no love lost. Zeke accepted my rule with no complaints. Regardless of not doing it, I considered myself an excellent sex kitten. The only thing getting past my lips was a tongue, some food, and some damn medicine. Yuck! My motto was, *no dicks pass these lips*.

As big as Zeke's dick was, he would have choked me to death. I had to admit, I was glad that me not sucking him didn't stop him from licking my sweet goodies. He was thrilled that I let him fuck me in the ass. He'd told me that his wife wouldn't even consider letting him do it to her in the behind. Maybe she thought his dick was way too big for something like that. It might've been too big for her, but the way he knocked against my rectum walls uncontrollably felt soooo hard and good. The slippery cum and juices he and I had let off earlier made it slick enough to thrash in and out of my ass without any problems.

"Come on Daddy, fuck that ass. Fuck it as hard as you can," I groaned, enjoying the jiggling of his balls against my rear.

As good as if felt to me, I knew I wasn't going to cum from him doing it to me back there, but I still wanted him to get another good one off because he'd tongued and sucked me so good earlier. He thrust harder and kept his tight hold on my breasts. His grunts became louder and his body began shaking continuously as he stroked. I knew he was getting ready to climax soon. He was in the zone now. There was nothing going to stop him from getting rid of that nut.

"Come on, Daddy, let it all out," I whispered.

"I am, baby girl, I am." He spurted as much cum in my asshole as he'd blown in my pussy, then he yanked it out and plopped down on the bed, breathing hard and looking up at the ceiling.

I fell down on my back alongside him, not breathing nearly as heavy as he. His long, hard rod finally began to shrink down to a chunk of thick meat—even in its limp state it was very sizeable.

"Damn, baby, I sure do wish my wife could work my stuff the way you do. I'm telling you, you can seriously back that ass up and roll it ferris wheel-style." His heavy breathing was now to a minimum. Before I knew it, he'd dozed off to sleep.

When he woke up about twenty minutes later I was already showered and dressed. As soon as he finished showering and clothed up, we poured ourselves some wine and reclaimed our seats in the den with every-body else, except for Dhelione and Mitchell. Emberly told me they'd skipped out, heading for one of the rooms shortly after Zeke and I left. They must have been awfully quiet because I didn't hear a peep coming from either one of the other bedrooms when Zeke and I were back there.

Chapter Eleven

To my surprise Eric took his nose out of Myilana's face long enough to hit Zeke with a playful tease. "Preacher maan, preacher maan! How do you be, my brother?"

"Aw, my brother, I'm holding it down like new money! Believe that," Zeke replied enthusiastically.

"Let that be the reason then. You're my hero for sho." Eric grinned with envy. "You the man. You the man."

Eric no doubt was giving Zeke props for getting his groove on the way guys do when they're joking about sex. But the longing look on Eric's face said he wanted terribly to get his groove on with Myilana too. Myilana, on the other hand, didn't remotely look like she was considering having sex with him. Then again, what did I know? I couldn't read their minds, I was judging by facial expressions.

A sudden angry outburst from Renalia captured everybody's attention. "Fixing to go? What do you mean you're fixing to go!" she barked at Ashton, who was turning red, trying to quiet her down.

"Hey, hey. Calm down, baby," he said in a low, annoyed tone. "You don't have to get loud about it. That's unnecessary. Just calm down."

"Calm down nothing! I just asked you to go in the back with me . . . and you suddenly gotta be somewhere!" Renalia stuttered angrily. "What? Are you scared to go in the bedroom and get some pussy? You haven't had any problems dragging me to your bed before, or anywhere else we've fucked. Why now?" She jumped to her feet and stood in front of Ashton with her hand on her hip.

"Hey, come on. Why are you acting like this?" Ashton pleaded softly, looking up at her, trying to hide his embarrassment. "This is nonsense. Let's talk about this in private. Don't spoil everybody else's fun, Renalia."

Renalia stood silently, staring at him with evil eyes I hadn't seen since early Friday night before he'd come over for his first visit.

Emberly, Myilana, and I snagged eye contact with each other when the outburst first happened. Eric, Curtis, and Zeke listened quietly with looks of surprise.

Renalia finally replied to Ashton's plea. "Talk about it in private? Really? Well, if we're gonna talk about it in private shouldn't Myilana come with us?" Renalia took a fleeting look at Myilana, then back to Ashton.

Oh shit, here we go, I told myself silently. My worst fear had come to pass. My heart started beating a mile a minute. I even crossed my fingers, as if that childish shit was going to help. No doubt about it, Renalia now knew what I already knew. Otherwise, why would she include Myilana's name in her and Ashton's conversation. I shot off at the mouth before I realized what I'd done, knowing I already knew the answer to my own question.

"Myilana? What does Myi have to do with you and Ashton's business, Renalia?" I asked patiently.

My question gave Myilana just enough time to look as puzzled as the rest of us while waiting to hear an answer. But before we could get one, Ashton jumped in, repeating my same question to Renalia. "Yeah, what does Myilana have to do with this?" He frowned.

"Oohh, please! Give me a little credit, ya'll! I may have been born at night, but it wasn't last night," Renalia shouted with disgust. "This shit has plenty to do with Myilana. In fact, it's all about Myilana. What, Ashton? You didn't think I noticed the fucked up eye-sex you and her been having all day?"

I almost pissed in my pants. Knowing in secret about the little unfortunate snag was one thing, but to hear it loud and clear in the open? I wasn't ready. None of us were. All of the screwed up faces said so.

"What? Ashton gasped. "You're kidding me, right? I mean, you really got to be kidding."

"Yeah, she's got to be kidding!" Myilana jumped in, raising her voice with a set of mad ass frowns equal to Renalia's evil eyes.

"Hell no, I'm not kidding." Renalia peered back at her. "Anybody in this room with eyes knows exactly what I'm talking about. And Parrish, you and Emberly know too, whether ya'll admit it or not. So don't even try to front." She now glanced angrily from Emberly to me.

"Excuse me, but I'm sitting right here in front of you, Renalia. You don't have to talk to Parrish or Emberly about anything, you can talk directly to me." Myilana wasn't bullshitting about this thing anymore.

Oh shit, oh shit, I couldn't stop repeating those words in my head. I didn't want this to be happening, especially since it had escalated to a far more serious level. Zeke and the other men were dumbfounded as hell, but that didn't stop Renalia from throwing more kindling onto the fire. She was taking this shit as far as it would go.

"Listen, bitch! I don't have to say shit to you! Fucking slut!" Renalia barked, looking like she was two seconds away from clawing Myilana to death.

"Renalia?" I gasped in shock. I didn't want to believe what my ears had heard.

The shit was personal now. And about to get physical. Bitch? Slut?

Myilana sprung to her feet without hesitation. "Bring it on, bitch!" she shouted. "You wanna act like a ghetto ho, I'll treat your ass like one! Your ass is mine!"

Renalia took a step towards Myilana, ready to scrap. She didn't have a snowball's chance in hell because Emberly and I were on our feet, standing between them before anybody could say, *this ain't happening.* Ashton was up a second after.

"Renalia, please don't do this," Emberly pleaded. "What in the hell is wrong with you? Are you that damn dick whipped?" She then turned to Ashton and said, "And as for you, I've been joking around all this time, but on the real, what in the hell are you packing in them damn jeans? You've fucked this situation up bad."

The question sounded humorous coming from Emberly, but her expression was nowhere close to looking funny. I didn't know what to think or do. It didn't matter anyhow because it wasn't going to help. Things were too far gone at this point.

Renalia cut back into the conversation, as heated as ever. "What's wrong with me, Em? There's nothing wrong with me!" she barked. "Ya'll know what's up, ya'll ain't crazy. Don't try to make it seem like I'm crazy either, 'cause I'm not."

Without warning, Myilana changed sentiments on us. Her anger had subsided within the short amount of time that the others were running off at the mouth. She'd never been a difficult person to deal with; this meekness was only a reflection of her true personality. She looked at Renalia momentarily before saying anything.

"You're supposed to be my friend, Renalia. I love you." She sighed gently. "How can you let this thing keep going on and on like it is? Calling me all these unnecessary names. Provoking me. This isn't us. This isn't the way our friendship works." Myilana's anger was now transformed to hurt. Hurt that didn't affect Renalia in the least.

Renalia exhaled loudly while crossing her arms and said, "Kiss my ass, wench." She had no remorse whatsoever.

Myilana didn't say anything back to her, tears rushed to the surface of her eyes.

Cold and heartless were the only words to describe Renaila at this point. *This heifer has lost her mind,* I stood there, yet again, trying to figure out who in the hell this awful villain was that Renalia had turned into.

Ashton took a few steps forward and raised his hands in front of him, cuing us to pause. "Hold up, hold up. Please stop, ya'll," he said glumly. All eyes turned to him. "Look, this is my fault and I'm sorry. I never should have let things play out like this. Please, Renalia. Sit down for a few minutes . . . and let me make it right?" He hesitated, sounding cautious. There was much regret in his voice.

Renalia rolled her eyes at him, but quietly stepped

back and eased down on the sofa, crossing her legs with a nonchalant attitude.

Ashton then turned to the rest of us. "Please, will ya'll have a seat too, so I can straighten this out?" he asked politely.

As Emberly, Myilana, and I took our seats, Dhelione came stumbling into the den, stuffing the back of her top in her pants. She'd obviously gotten dressed in a hurry and was still finishing the job.

"What in the hell is going on in here? Are you people insane? We heard cussing and arguing way back in the room." Dhelione glanced around at each of us with aggravation all over her face. "What's going on?"

"Please, Dhelione," Ashton said quickly. "If you will, just calm down. I'm getting ready to straighten this whole mess out right now."

"Somebody better straighten something out. I thought this shit between the three of ya'll was dead and buried." Dhelione dropped down on the sofa like somebody had shoved her, that's how mad she was.

Mitchell strolled in and sat down alongside her, looking as confused as the other men. The nine of us were now silent, waiting to hear whatever it was Ashton felt he needed to say. He took a seat on the edge of the sofa near Renalia.

"Look, Fella's. Ya'll are probably wondering what the hell's up, 'cause you don't know the story behind this little mix up." Ashton spoke evenly as he addressed the men. "If it's okay with the ladies, I wanna hook ya'll up with some real info on this thing." He glanced from one of us to the other, waiting to hear if it was okay for him to fill the guys in.

"What the hell, tell them," I said quickly, wanting him to get on with it.

"Yeah, tell them," Emberly agreed. "Otherwise

they'll be as lost as blind bats in hell with no fire burning, and can't see a thing."

"I don't care what you do, just hurry up and do
something," Dhelione snapped, reaching for some wine
from the center table for her and Mitchell.

Ashton set his eyes on Myilana, waiting for her yay
or nay. "It's fine with me," she murmured softly. "No
point in hearing the end if they don't know the beginning."

He then turned to Renalia. "How about it?" he asked
her.

"I don't care," she replied bitterly. If she had responded any other way I would've been shocked.

Ashton thanked her for cooperating, then proceeded
to fill the guys in on his Friday night arrival after he'd
been questioned by us without knowing Myilana was
at the cottage. The guys smirked "macho style" when
they heard he'd been sleeping with both Renalia and
Myilana. All except Eric, of course. He didn't look like
he was going to be laughing anytime soon. At the end
of the story, naturally, the men sided with Ashton.
They were so strongly opinionated about the incident,
they pretty much took over the conversation.

"Aw, now, come on, ladies. Ya'll know that was some
messed up shit to do. Tricking my man," Zeke griped.
"Any red-blooded man, or woman, would've said the
same thing he said under that kind of pressure and
ya'll know it. That was no way for the business to go
down."

"I'm telling you straight up, if it had been me, I'm not
gonna even front," Mitchell chuckled. "With girlfriend
sitting right in front of me? The answer is obvious, for
real." He stood up and slapped five with Curtis.

Everyone of them, except Eric, had voiced their real
opinions, but in a humorous way. Eric pasted a fake

smile on his face, looking more disappointed than anything. After all, he was somewhat caught in the middle of a three-way lovers' quarrel, and as far as I knew, he hadn't slept with anybody yet. I was curious to hear his take on the whole situation.

"So Eric," I raised my voice to get his attention. "You're mighty quiet. I don't believe you've told us what you think about all of this. How about it?" My question silenced everyone. They obviously wanted to hear what he thought too.

Myilana stared at him curiously as he shook his head in slow motion, then said, "Look, I'm cool, ya'll. I mean, I'm not gonna lie, this shit definitely caught a brother by surprise. But hell, it's the name of the game, right? Like Zeke said, it could've happened to any of us. I'm down for whatever." He turned to Myilana and smiled.

Myilana smiled back at him and humbly whispered, "Thanks."

"All right!" Zeke raised his voice impatiently. "Now that all that's water under the bridge, what was the big damn deal anyhow? Both of ya'll was screwing the brother. Maybe it's just me, but what's the problem? Why didn't it stay in the past like it already was? I mean, if that's what ya'll decided, how'd it all come back up again? And what about this eye-looking, or eye-sex, or whatever the hell you're being accused of, man?" Zeke parked his eyes on Ashton after asking more damn questions than the game show host on *Jeopardy*.

Ashton bravely gazed back at him. "I hear you, man. And that's what I'm about to settle, on the real." He inhaled a deep breath, then let it out smoothly. "Ladies, ya'll were right last night, I wasn't telling the truth about shit. I was lying through my teeth. You see, my mouth was saying one thing, but my heart was saying something different. It was never my intention to upset anybody, or cause any trouble." He shrugged his shoulders, then turned to Renalia. "Especially toward you. I mean, that's why I said what I said about being with you instead of somebody else. I was way out of line for not being on the up and up with you about who I really wanted to kick it with. Truth is . . . I'm crazy about, Myilana. Damn, there it is. I said it."

As soon as Ashton let those words out of his mouth, Renalia's chest snatched my attention. I could've sworn her heart was going to come through her skin at any minute. It began pounding so fast, I could literally see it hammering through her tight, thin blouse. Her appearance was more fierce than when she first flew off into an angry fit. Looking at her was like watching a demon transform to his worst state. But she didn't mumble one damn word. That fucked me up, because I didn't know what she was going to do next.

Nobody else said anything either, so Ashton turned to Myilana and continued talking. "Believe me I know your situation," he told her softly. "And I know my situation. Neither of us have room for anything like this right now, but my heart feels what it feels."

Though Ashton was looking directly at Myilana, she was staring down at one spot on the floor. Maybe she couldn't bear to look into his eyes at this heart stirring moment. Emberly and Dhelione didn't take their eyes off Renalia and neither did I. That told me they saw the same kind of crazy shit about her I was seeing. By now she looked like she was about to implode; wickedness to the five-hundredth power. Her face was as tight and swollen as her chest. Still, nobody said anything. I think we were trying to figure out what Ashton's confession meant, and what he expected Myilana to do. I know I was.

Ashton spoke again. This time the shit he had to say was much deeper than before. "Myilana if you wanna know the truth, look at me? Please, just look at me, baby."

Myilana slowly raised her head and their eyes met like two beautiful rays of sunlight, melting into each other. He continued. "I think I've fallen in love with you. No. I know I've fallen in love with you. And I can't sit here anymore, watching you with somebody else."

What the hell? This can't be. It's a dream. Yeah, that's it. It's gotta be a dream. I kept silent, but it wasn't easy. I wanted to jump up screaming for everybody to wake up. That's how unbelievable things had become.

The passion in Ashton's tone when he told Myilana he loved her was magnetic. I wasn't the one who needed convincing, but there was no doubt in my mind he really loved her and wanted to be with her. Genuineness was in his every action. Not to mention he had freely announced it to every soul in the room. We were all eyewitnesses. After I got over the initial shock, the bottom of my mouth dropped down in my chest. In the midst of all the sex and lust, somebody had managed to find a real *forbidden love?*

By now tears were dripping down my cheeks faster than I could wipe them. This dilemma had climaxed into a heartwarming sentiment. But I wouldn't have wanted to be in either of their shoes for shit. A quick fuck here and there was one thing, but falling in love, longing to be with each other all the time, and already having their own families? My sympathy was with them.

Chapter Twelve

A real romantic story for a change, something more than sex, sex, and more sex. And the man was brave enough to speak his feelings first, in front of other men. That was a rare occurrence in our parts. Regardless of all the negative comments the other men were probably getting ready to hit Ashton with, he'd decided to take a stand and be honest. He had my vote, hands down. I was about to hyperventilate, waiting to hear what the other men were gonna say to him. Just so happened, Zeke and the guys weren't as negative as I imagined. With the exception of Eric, they seemed moved by Ashton's affectionate display the same as we girls were. How about that? If only I could've seen something conclusive in Eric's blank appearance.

Myilana finally broke her long running silence. "I love you too," she said gently, her eyes still glued to his.

Their feelings were nothing I didn't already know in

the back of my mind. Their body language had been screaming it all along and now it was confirmed.

Eric smiled mildly, shaking his head slowly as if thinking this wasn't really happening. Renalia was the one who jolted everybody back to reality with her loud, obnoxious ass.

"What the fuck is this!" she demanded, jumping to her feet. "The rules of this club are about fucking, not falling in love!" Renalia took fleeting looks from Ashton to Myilana, then pointed at Myilana in a disrespectful way. "Love? Love? Ashton, you're gonna actually sit here and admit you love this fucking whore?"

"All right, bitch! That's the last time you're gonna call me out of my name and get away with it!" Myilana hopped out of her seat, heading straight for Renalia. "You want some of me? You can have all you want!"

I was so sick and tired of Renalia's bad attitude, I wanted Myilana to knock some sense into her ass. I didn't move a muscle this time and stayed right in my seat. Ashton, on the other hand, jumped up and stood between them.

Dhelione was sweating bullets. She leaped to her feet and raised her voice. "I've had it! This shit ends right here! Right now! I've sat and listened to the explanations, the outbursts, the name calling, and I'm sick of all of it!" She shoved her finger in Renalia's face. "And as for you? You're fucking possessed, Demonesha. You're the reason for all of this shit. Constantly spitting out sluts, bitches, and whores? Hell, if Myilana's all that, the four of us are too, dumb ass."

"Fucking A!" Emberly agreed. "All of us do the same kind of shit. If you're saying it to her, you're saying it to your own ass too!"

Renalia shrugged her shoulders, slowly eyeing each

of us. "Ooh, wait a minute now. Wait one minute. What is this, gang up on Renalia hour?" She lowered her voice to a pitiful hum. "Are ya'll gonna take her side? I guess nobody heard her call me a bitch, what about that?"

"Cut that kiddie shit out, Renalia," Emberly told her. "You started name calling the moment the first angry word came out of your mouth. Hell, I'm surprised Myilana waited this long to cuss your ass back. I would've done it way before now."

"You know it's true." Dhelione's eyes should have melted Renalia as fired up with anger as they appeared. "You're wrong and you know you're wrong. I'm not taking anybody's side, I'm just telling it like it is."

"Believe that. I'm not taking anybody's side either." Emberly nodded, preparing to shoot off at the mouth nonstop. "Now that we know the real deal, the best thing to do is calm the fuck down and kick the drama to the curb. The man said he loves the woman, the woman said she loves the man. Ain't shit you, or nobody else up in here can do about it, Renalia. So leave it be. We come out here once a year for fun and R and R. Hell, if I want drama, I'll keep my black ass at home with my crazy ass husband and all of my jacked up in laws."

Renalia briefly peered from Emberly to Dhelione. "I don't even believe the shit I'm hearing," she whined. "Ya'll are completely dismissing the basis of this issue."

"Which is?" Dhelione asked the question, but didn't look like she really wanted an answer to it. I wasn't the only one fed up with Renalia. Everybody was.

"Which is simple?" Renalia replied. "Ya'll somehow managed to forget the way she's been sitting here disrespecting me since the minute Ashton walked through the damn door."

"Renalia, have you even been in the same room with the rest of us? Or has it just been your body we've been seeing, and your mind has been somewhere else?" My question popped out without my permission. That was becoming a habit of mine. "Damn, girl. Ashton just explained all of that shit. He openly admitted he loves her in front of everybody. And she openly said she feels the same. Hello. What part didn't you get?"

By the time I finished my remark to Renalia, she looked like she was about to cry. Maybe that's why she didn't respond right away. Dhelione softened up after seeing Renalia's sudden display of hurt.

"Listen, Renalia. I'm not approving of the way all this stuff went down, but let's face it, it's some complicated shit to deal with. I know we're supposed to be having fun, no strings attached but be honest for a minute. Nobody can really control their heart or emotions if they start to care for a person, can they? Sometimes it just happens. All of us agreed on the same rules a long time ago to keep stuff like this from happening. It just goes to show, even the most well thought out plans don't work when human feelings are involved." Dhelione put her hand on Renalia's shoulder and softly stroked it. "Come on, you know as well as I do, no matter how hard we try we can't always suppress the way we feel about somebody. If we could would we still be with those cheating negros of ours?"

Renalia seemed to be taking in Dhelione's reasoning. But Emberly was the one who responded. "Sho ya right. I would've left that bastard of mine a long time ago, or cut his ass up or something." She paused in thought, then picked up where she left off. "Or maybe I would've chopped his shit off like that fed up white lady did to her husband up north. What was her name? Lorena Bobbit, wasn't it? As if chopping his dick off wasn't bad enough, she jumped in her car, hit the highway doing about eighty and slung his shit out on the interstate. Did they ever find his shit?" Emberly was now in one of her laughing moments. But the "chopping off dicks" topic didn't get any laughs from the men. And I wasn't sure we'd won over Renalia, so I wasn't about to laugh just yet.

When Emberly realized nobody was laughing along with her, she stopped cold.

"Damn, ya'll! Loosen up a little. Stop acting like we're at a funeral." She nudged Curtis in his side with her elbow. He smiled modestly, and kept sipping his wine.

Myilana eased into the conversation. "Excuse me, but I have to . . . no, I need to say something," she hesitated, sounding sincere. "Look, Renalia, I'm sorry. I am truly sorry for not being straight with you from the beginning. I should have told you how I felt about Ashton when you asked me, but I was gonna try to ignore my feelings, hoping they'd go away. At least, go away 'til this weekend was over. Plus, I didn't think he felt the same after I found out he'd been seeing you. The way I saw it, there was no reason to say anything. And as far as eye-sex, or whatever you called it, that's not true. I wasn't playing any deliberate eye games with him to disrespect you. To be honest, I was trying like hell not to even look at him, but obviously it didn't work out too well, did it?" Myilana exhaled. The genuinity we all witnessed from her should have been enough to change Renalia's blank look.

Myilana didn't stop there. "Please, Renalia. I don't know where we go from here, but I hope it's forward . . . as friends. We've been too close, too long. I don't wanna lose your friendship. You have to believe me when I tell you, this wasn't planned. It wasn't malicious intent."

Renalia finally came out of silence. "So now that you've admitted you have feelings for him . . . oh excuse me, you love him, how does it make you feel to know he was fucking me while he was fucking you?" Renalia's willful smirk left no doubt that she was still hell bent on keeping the shit alive.

Myilana inhaled, then said, "I'm not gonna lie, it hurt. It hurt a lot. Even before now. But during the whole time we've been seeing each other, Ashton and I hadn't admitted any of this to each other. No way I was gonna be the first to say it. And well, I can't speak for him."

Ashton had already taken his seat. He spoke for himself. "I didn't want things to get complicated, so I ignored what I felt too. That was the normal and simplest way to do things."

Both Renalia and Myilana looked down at Ashton when he answered, then Myilana turned her attention back to Renalia and said, "So I guess to fully answer your question, I would have to say that Ashton hadn't made any commitments to me, nor I to him. What sense would it have made anyway? We're both married. It still doesn't make any sense now, but it has happened and we have to deal with it."

"Better ya'll than me." Emberly shot off again. "I'm for love and all, but this kind of shit makes life too complicated. "Stirs up shit so stinking, you'll think the dead was walking the earth."

"You ain't never lied about that, girlfriend," I agreed with Emberly.

Dhelione plopped down on the sofa, leaving Renalia and Myilana facing each other by themselves.

"Cut the damn jokes 'til this shit is over, ya'll," Dhe-lione pouted, massaging the sides of her head with her fingertips as if she had a headache. "I didn't come here to be in therapy all weekend."

Emberly shot Dhelione a eye roll and said, "Excuse the hell out of me, Sue Johanson."

The men laughed. Myilana laughed. I laughed. Even Dhelione let an involuntary laugh slip. But guess who didn't laugh? Renalia.

"Go ahead with what ya'll were saying, Myi." Dhe-lione waved her hand.

"I'm pretty much done," Myilana replied. "Like I said, I didn't expect anything more than a good time from Ashton back then, despite what I felt. And obviously, he didn't either 'cause he was seeing you at the same time, Renalia."

"And now?" Renalia puckered her brows.

"And now, what?" Myilana frowned.

"And now what do you expect from him?" Renalia asked her. "You say *back then* you didn't expect anything but a good time. What do you expect now?"

Myilana slowly shook her head in thought. My guess? She was being careful not to say anything to offend Renalia and set her loud ass mouth off again. The delay gave Emberly a chance to butt in like usual.

"My first guess would be, she expects him to stop fucking all the outside women except her. That means you too, honey." Emberly clapped once playfully.

Ashton intervened, staring straight at Myilana. They had that deep eye-gaze shit on lock. He told her, "You don't have to answer that, I will. She should expect the truth from me because that's what I'm asking of her, right now." He stood up and held his hand out for My-ilana to take it. She did. He squeezed tightly from what I could see. Something went all the way through me when they touched.

"Is that a fact?" Renalia curled her lips while giving Ashton this nasty look. "Well, I guess I know the real reason you ran out of here last night and wouldn't fuck me, huh?"

Myilana gasped, and instantly spoke gently to Ashton, "You didn't sleep with her las—"

"No." He tenderly interrupted her. "I couldn't do it. Not after finding out the truth." Only a hint of the pleasing smiles they were trying to suppress emerged on their faces.

Renalia couldn't stand it when she realized she'd given Myilana one more reason to believe Ashton's sudden love story. She swiftly dived back into the conversation.

"Anyway! Correct me if I'm wrong, but Myilana, didn't you tell me and the girls you hadn't been seeing anybody else since the time you started seeing Ashton?"

"Yes," Myilana replied.

"Where'd he come from?" Renalia pointed at Eric. "Did you pull him out of a magic hat?"

Myilana looked at Eric in puzzlement. "Who, Eric? Me and Eric go way back. We've been friends for a while, but not intimate in a long time."

This bitch ain't giving up, is she? My thoughts were about to jump out of my brain. I never thought I'd feel this way, but I was beginning to dislike Renalia.

Myilana's way of answering said she was about fed up too. "Look, Renalia, if you're trying to prove I lied about sleeping with somebody else while being with Ashton, you're wasting your time. It didn't happen. Eric can vouch for that. This is the first time he and I have hung out since forever. But even if I was sleeping with him, or anybody else for that matter, it wouldn't have been any of Ashton's business. He was sleeping with you, remember? No boundaries were established."

What more could Renalia want to hear? She was never going to be satisfied because she was jealous, plain and simple. I refused to take her nitpicking anymore.

"Myilana, stop," I raised my voice. "You don't have to answer anymore questions, this is childish. And Renalia, if you aren't satisfied with the way things turned out, too bad. What do you wanna hear? They've answered every question you've asked. Just drop it, or Zeke and I are leaving." I meant every damn word of it. No way I was sitting through any more of her crap.

The weekend was almost over, and it was going to end in ruins if somebody didn't take a stand and shut Renalia's whining ass up. It would've been too simple for her to just accept my ultimatum without striking back with some of her own smart ass words.

Renalia had gone from unpredictable to impossible. She shot me one of her evil looks and said, "You're right. You're absolutely right. The purpose of being here is to have a good time. Hell, we're all married. Nobody was supposed to make any kind of serious commitments, so why'd they break the rules?" She pointed at Ashton and Myilana. "You know what, Parrish? I don't care why they broke them. All I care about is I'm not gonna break them. I'm here to have fun. I'm full of wine, I'm horny, and I wanna fuck. So how about it Erand or Eric or whatever the hell your name is? If you wanna have some fun, follow me?" She began walking toward the hallway.

"Hell, yes!" Eric roared, leaping out of his seat to

follow her. Without another word, he grabbed a bottle of wine and they disappeared into the back.

Maybe it was over now. The logical thing for them to do was hook up, since they were the only two solos. Ashton and Myilana didn't appear to have a problem with the idea. They sat down on the sofa near each other, smiling blissfully. Emberly jumped up, dashed to the kitchen and returned with a fresh bottle of wine, then stood in front of them.

"Ashton, Myi, get your glasses," she told them. When she was done filling their glasses, she turned to Zeke. "A few 'bye-bye-to-the-drama' words for the couple, if you will, brother Zeke?"

Zeke stretched a smile across his face and chanted, "Sho ya right! Sho ya right! Drama's over! Let the party start fresh!" Everybody clapped loudly and laughed. We were happy as hell for the garbage to be gone.

"Oh, oh! I almost forgot!" Zeke raised his hands, gesturing us to quiet down and listen. "I wouldn't worry too much about your friend, ladies. My man, Eric's gonna give her what she needs and she'll be as good as new. Fellas we know what the little girls need when they start acting the way she was acting, don't we? A good, hard—"

"Cut it out!" I punched Zeke on his shoulder playfully. He grabbed me and kissed me.

Emberly, Dhelione, and Myilana "booed" Zeke's chauvinistic remark, while the men "bravo'd." All of us laughed and chattered on continuously while refreshing our wine. The party was on again since the hellraiser was out of the way. Nobody had noticed that the music had played out, probably long ago, and wasn't set to replay. I put on a new disc. It was all good once more.

Chapter Thirteen

I figured Myilana and Ashton would be heading straight to the back to get their groove on now that they were free to do so. But they looked happy as ever, having the opportunity to enjoy each other without all the secrecy. Not twenty minutes into the refurbished party, Zeke had gotten full of wine, switched the music to straight up "old blues," and all kinds of outrageous outbursts were flying through his lips.

"Aww, yeah! Now this is what I call a party! Come on, baby! Let's show them how to do this thang!" He snatched me up on the floor to dance with him.

When B.B. King's, *I Never Make A Move Too Soon*, came on, Zeke tore the floor up, dancing *old-school style*. The rest of us were dancing along with him, trying to jam to that old shit too. It was fun. Reminded me of my grandma, drinking beer with her other grandma friends, frying fish, and boogying back in the day, when I was a young girl.

"Go ahead, Zeke, sing that song!" Emberly screeched,

tears dripping down her cheeks from laughing at him so hard.

Zeke never missed a lyric. "Three days of snow in Birmingham . . . thought you would wonder where I am. Landlord said you moved away . . . and left me all yo' bills to pay. Lookout, baby! You might've made yo' move too soon!" When I say Zeke was sanging the hell out of the song, he was doing just that. Not singing, sanging.

Dancing his butt off and sweating like a three-legged male dog, trying to get some girl dog booty. His eyes were closed tight and he almost had to feel his way around. I knew he could get a little crazy and out of control, but I'd never seen him like this before.

"All right! Sing it, preacher man, sing it!" Mitchell yelled, clapping his hands and patting his feet, trying to do what Zeke was doing. "You're the man! Don't make your move too soon now! Ha, ha, ha, ha!" Mitchell's laughter, along with the rest of our laughter and the music, was earsplitting. The noise in that little den could have raised the dead.

Ashton wasn't any better than Mitchell with all of his shouting and boosting Zeke to the limit.

"Bring it on home, preacher man! You better break it down for us! Chief's about to out do you!" Ashton spun around, and started doing the "primp." As old as the "primp" was from the 80's era, it still didn't go as far back as that 50's shit Zeke was doing.

Every inch of the den and kitchen floors was being worked overtime by our hustling feet. The only person even close to keeping up with Zeke's type of dancing was Curtis. They were two of a kind from virtually the same era.

I wasn't ready for the scary shit Zeke did next. Out

of the blue he yelled, "Whoa! Lucille! Lucille! Do it! Do it! Lucille!"

I kept staggering around, thinking I was dancing, and asking myself, *who the fuck is Lucille? And what does he want her to do?* For the longest time, I thought we had more company and they'd forgotten to tell me.

It wasn't 'til the song was getting ready to go off when I heard B.B. King singing, "Lucille! Lucille! Do it! Do it!" The same as Zeke was yelling. I was drunk as a fool for sure. With all the wine drinking on top of wine drinking, and uncontrollable laughing, there was only one conclusion to draw. Everybody else was drunk as hell too. And believe me, we had enough juice on hand for the job, plus extra. I was glad when that long ass song went off. I fell on the sofa, panting for air and worn out. Myilana, Ashton, and Curtis dropped down shortly after.

Dhelione and Mitchell danced their way to the next song. And Zeke refused to give up the floor, so Emberly paired with him. Her barely there movement said she had no intentions on dancing that time around, but she went ahead and did him a favor so he wouldn't be without a partner.

"Parrish! You better get up here and get your man! I'm fixing to sit my ass down," Emberly shouted to me over the music. "I hate for him to have to dance with the wind, but I'm tired, girl!"

Just as I opened my mouth to reply, my attention was drawn to another person, rushing out on the floor to dance. At first I thought I was seeing things as a side effect from the alcohol high. I took a doubletake, then closed my eyes and reopened them at least twice. That's when I realized my eyes weren't fooling me.

Renalia had leaped her way back in the den, and was on the floor dancing like a wild woman, gyrating, twisting, and jerking everything her momma gave her. She spun herself through the ones who were still on the floor dancing. Emberly swung around and moved out of the way just before Renalia spun into her.

"What the fuck are you doing!" Emberly frowned, shouting at her. "Have you lost your fucking mind, Renalia?"

Eric wasn't any help because he was doing it too dancing all over the place with no concern for anybody else, like they were the only ones on the floor. I guess the two of them had finished the bottle of wine they'd taken when they left, and were as high as the rest of us. No. Higher. Maybe they'd had more than one bottle. Renalia set her sights on Zeke and went for it. She abruptly started dancing all up on him touching him, rubbing him, feeling him, you name it. And to add insult to injury, he was grinning like a cheetah from ear to ear and doing all of the same kind of stuff right back to her. It wouldn't have been so bad if she hadn't been stark naked. That's right. Renalia was asshole bare, breasts flopping all over the place like she was on stage at the strip club. She looked to be getting the biggest thrill imaginable out of it.

With disgusted looks on their faces, Dhelione and Emberly hurriedly got out of the way, leaving Mitchell, Eric, and especially Zeke, three on one with Renalia. The three of them couldn't keep their lustful eyes off her for shit. The big ass smile on her face said that she had the men just where she wanted them. Three strong, and she was in control. She really started working her ass now. Rolling like she was on the river. The three men fenced her in and began groping her at random. They grasped almost every body part on her. She took turn after turn backing up in front of them and rolling her bare ass over their crotches seductively. Her ass was sure enough in the right spot, so the only thing preventing her from actually fucking them right in our faces was that they still had their pants on. The music was still going and they were still going with it.

Zeke really got nasty a few minutes later. He started trying to stuff her bouncing titties in his mouth. After two or three missed opportunities, he succeeded. He spun her around and sucked on her titties like he was the only one in the room. This going on, while Eric and Mitchell were clawing at her ass-cheeks and thighs. They squeezed, rubbed, swiped, and everything else short of throwing her down on the floor and ramming their dicks in her one at a time. She never lost her ear to ear grin. Even when Zeke began sliding down her breasts to her stomach to the front of her thighs, she smiled the entire time while helping navigate his head.

That negro actually fell to his knees, stuck his head between her legs, and started licking her pussy like a starving dog. The only thing she did was scream and open her legs for him to help himself. "Ooohhh yeah, baby! Taste that good stuff! It's good to you, isn't it! You haven't tasted anything that good in a long time, have you? Ha, ha, ha!"

Mitchell began howling like a wolf under a full moon. "Aww, yeah! Aww, aww, yeah! Save me some of them sweet goodies, man! Aww, yeah!"

Then Eric woofed, "Hell, yeess!"

These fools were definitely drunk, but their behavior couldn't be blamed entirely on alcohol. They were being who they really were on the inside, nasty dogs. And Renalia was a raving lunatic with no self-respect. The three of them eventually swooped her up and carried her off to the back with her screaming, "Come on, guys . . . do it to me! Let's fuck! That's what we're here for! I want all three of you! All three!"

I couldn't believe my eyes, nor could I say a damn word. Whatever high I once had was long gone, and my speech went with it. Emberly, Dhelione, and Myilana, were just as stunned. We sat there dazed, looking at the air as if air could be looked at.

Ashton and Curtis appeared astonished also. Nobody said anything for several minutes, then Curtis cleared his throat and mumbled rather uncertainly, "Do ya'll want us to get her out of there since she's drunk and don't—"

"That bitch is not drunk," Emberly cut him off angrily. "She know exactly what she's doing. I hope they fuck her 'til she can't walk anymore. Nasty ho." Emberly skipped over and turned the music off, then sat back down. "I swear, I don't even believe what I just saw. Renal—, I can't even say the bitch's name anymore. Damn!"

"They're just as much to blame as she is," Dhelione grumbled, looking flustered. "I don't believe that black, ball-headed ass Mitchell went back there. I really don't believe it."

"Well, believe it." I blew out a long, exhausting breath. "And so did that crooked dick, hypocrite of a preacher, Zeke. Did ya'll see what that son-of-a-bitch did right in front of us? Men are gonna be doggish no matter what."

Ashton cleared his throat, I felt, to correct me. But before he spoke, Emberly shot a mean frown at Curtis and said, "What are you waiting on? Aren't you gonna go join them? You know you want to, dammit."

Curtis snapped back at her, sounding offended. "I came here to see you, not her, or anybody else. How do you think you can sit here and tell me what I wanna do?"

"Yeah, Emberly," Dhelione complained. "He's not

the one being a dog. The bald-headed bastard, and the faked-out preacher are the ones."

Emberly had a quick change of heart. "Oh, hell, you're right. I'm tripping, ya'll." She slid her hand across Curtis's hand and told him, "My bad. I'm just freaked out by all of this weird shit."

He nodded at her. "It's cool."

"I don't mean to pry or anything, but has Renalia always been like this?" Ashton asked, glancing at each of us.

"Maybe we should be asking you that question," Myilana replied with attitude. "After all, you're the one who was fucki—"

"Come on, Myi." Dhelione stopped her from doing just what Emberly had done. "Now there you go. Why are you getting upset with him? What you're fixing to say isn't gonna help the situation one bit. You and him dealt with that issue and moved on, no need in bringing it up all over again. Besides, Ashton and Curtis seem to be the only two men in here with any kind of damn decency."

Myilana sighed. "You're right, I guess we're all a little agitated since we can't make any sense of the way she's been acting all weekend." Myilana softly smiled at Ashton. "Sorry."

"Don't be," he whispered.

Myilana was right about the incident taking a toll on all of us. Not only was it mind boggling, it was so distasteful. And as for Zeke, well, he wasn't my husband. I couldn't control who he fucked and who he didn't fuck, nor did I want to. Of course, I'd be lying if I said it wasn't a slap in the face to see him do what he did in front of me without taking a half second to consider my feelings. Even him doing that wasn't nearly as disappointing as knowing Renalia would openly have sex with men her best friends were already seeing just to get back at us. That thought kicked me in the teeth repeatedly. I felt it was safe to say Dhelione thought the same. If Renalia would do something like that in front of us, the ultimate reality check was she'd probably do much worse behind our backs.

No matter how deep I mulled it over in my head, I kept ending with the same conclusion, *It's over. It'll never be the same with her again. She's not our friend anymore.* I said it so many times, I didn't realize I'd said it aloud. "She's not our friend anymore. It's over."

"You damn right she's not our friend anymore," Emberly interrupted what I assumed were my thoughts, but instead was an oral statement.

"Huh?" I shook myself out of the daze. "What did you say, Emberly?"

"No, honey, you said it. I'm just agreeing with you," Emberly replied.

By now I was fully aware of my "aloud" thinking. I began slowly shaking my head in disgust. "I don't get it. Why would Renalia risk hurting our friendship like this?"

"Demonesha, dammit!" Dhelione barked. "Didn't I say she was possessed earlier? Her name's Demonesha 'cause she got demons in her."

Emberly shot Dhelione a questioning look and asked, "What the fuck is a Demonesha? Don't you mean, Emily Rose?"

"If Emily Rose had a damn demon, then yeah, her ass too," Dheilone snapped back, trying to be unconcerned, but it wasn't working.

"What do ya'll think Renalia's gonna say about all this when the show's over?" Myilana asked with sincerity. "Or better yet, what are we gonna say to her about it?"

"I'm not saying shit to the bitch, I'm beating her ass." Emberly leaped up out of her seat, heading toward the hallway. "Hell, this isn't the time for talk. We've been talking since yesterday. Hasn't helped, has it?"

All of us quickly rose to stop her. Curtis grabbed her first. The girls and I knew she wasn't playing worth shit. Emberly wasn't violent by nature, but when provoked, she'd start a fight in an empty room. At this point, she was the last person needing to deal with Renalia and anymore of her issues.

"Emberly, you can't just jump on her and fight her 'cause you don't like what she's doing," Dhelione said. "Damn, girl, this isn't high school."

"This isn't Platinum Plus's strip and fuck club either," Emberly replied.

Not only was I disappointed in Renalia, I no longer felt a desire to continue on as her friend. I'd never look at her, or feel the same way about her again. Not because of Zeke, but because I'd lost confidence in her. Most of all, I'd lost my respect for her. I wasn't sure if I could bear to look at her when she did re-emerge from that back room.

There were no grounds for me to be self-righteous with all the shit we'd done. That wasn't it. It was more a thing of loyalty. We'd been thick as thieves over the years, and even among thieves there is a certain code of honor that is never to be violated. Renalia violated our code, and unfortunately, the hands on the clock couldn't be turned back.

I finally came up with a way to prevent anymore trouble from breaking out. Things couldn't keep going on the way they'd been going. It was clear that Renalia had no desire to cooperate with us and we couldn't force her to. I went ahead and voiced my suggestion.

"Hey, ya'll . . . I think I've got a solution," I said hesitantly. "I'm not sure about it, but ya'll tell me what you think."

Emberly set her eyes on me. "You're gonna help me whup her ass? Not that I need any help. Her ass is the one who's gonna need help."

I shook my head. "No, not that. Maybe she needs to go."

My statement captured everybody's attention. Myilana started saying, "You mean—"

"Yeah, that's exactly what she means," Emberly answered for me. "And I agree with her. Let's give the whore, the door." She rhymed it like poetry.

"Whoever's in favor say, yay. Whoever's not say, nay." I waited for their responses.

"Yay." Emberly flung her hand up first.

"Yay." Dhelione went next. Then me.

The three of us parked our eyes on Myilana for her yay or nay. Considering everything Renalia had done to her it seemed her hand would've been the first one to fly up. Instead she was more reluctant than any of us. Easygoing Myilana, always putting other peoples' feelings ahead of her own. What could we say to her?

"Come on, Myilana. What's it gonna be?" I asked her.

She sighed wearily. "I guess, yay."

"All right, then! That wench can get ready to pack her shit." Emberly smirked.

Ashton and Curtis listened in silence.

Chapter Fourteen

Renalia

"Yeah, come on, guys . . . give it to me! Let's get this party going!" I squealed, as Zeke and Mitchell hastily lay me down on the bed so we could get the real fucking started.

Eric and I had already fucked less than an hour before. When the four of us made it to the back bedroom, he told the guys he was going to stand aside with his wine and watch while I gave them some of the same sweet treats I'd given him earlier. Then he let out a grand laugh and said, "Just save me some! Don't get it all! I want some more of that good stuff when ya'll get through!"

I couldn't help but blush, I was getting just what I wanted.

Zeke was so busy hogging my pussy, I could barely make my way to Mitchell's dick for some good ol' fashion sucking pleasure. Mitchell finally got his pants and underwear down and dropped them to his ankles. I took his big, black, shiny cock in my mouth and I worked it overtime for him. At the same time I was doing this to Mitchell, Zeke was working on my throbbing pussy with his long tongue. It was easier than I thought to fuck two men at one time, considering I had never done it before, nor did I ever think I would.

The wine I'd gulped down so fast instead of gradually drinking had put me on cloud nine. My emotions were racing on overload, and my heart was yanking me in ten different directions. How could I not have some mixed feelings about the whole thing? But I somehow managed to cram all of the different stuff I felt into one big melting pot, and what I got in return was one of the most intense horny feelings I've ever had in my life.

Or maybe it was just the revenge factor keeping me soaring on an incredible high I'd never experienced before. After all, revenge is known to make a person do some messed up shit in hopes of finding satisfaction. But in the end the person's usually left with even more regret than when they started. At that moment, I didn't give a damn which one it was. I just wanted to seize the moment and satisfy my desires. I tried not to think too hard about how my four best friends had turned on me like poisonous tarantulas, making it seem like I was the villain because I was outspoken. It was no secret to them that I was the one with a little more complexity, and it had never been a problem before now.

If they had taken the time to search the situation more carefully they would've realized there's a big difference between outspoken and unreasonable. Maybe they already knew and didn't want to be fair to me. *To hell with them*, I told myself quietly. I decided right then and there to fuck every man in the cottage who had two legs, two arms, and a big delicious dick. Not only that, I was going to do it before the night was over.

That meant I needed to persuade Curtis and Ashton, even though they didn't join in on the first go around. What could those bitchy, so-called friends of mine do about it? Not jack shit because they didn't have papers on any man in there. They fucked married men just like I did, only I wasn't limiting myself to just one per night anymore. I wanted as many as my pussy would take without closing down on me.

Too bad Dhelione couldn't suck Mitchell's dick as well as I could. If she had maybe he wouldn't have been back there with me. *Oh yeaahhh, this smooth, chocolate dick is sooo good,* I told myself silently as I sucked and licked her man's stuff nonstop. He had the blackest, shiniest dick I'd ever seen. Mitchell stood steadfast at the end of the bed, feeding me his dick like a sweet lollipop.

If Eric wasn't a watcher before that moment, he sure as hell was now, and a very enthusiastic one too. He looked aroused and happy as a camper in Connecticut, watching me blow Mitchell like giving a blow-job was going out of style. Zeke changed positions, and was now kneeling in the bed thrusting his big dick in and out of me from behind doggy-style. His dick was huge just like I like them. Parrish had bragged about the size of his cock many times in the past and now I knew for myself. She was right on target.

If Zeke wasn't careful he could cripple somebody with his heavy hardware. He was damn near poking my upper intestines. I would've been lying to myself if I'd said I didn't feel a slight aching twinge when he first entered me. It was a bittersweet twinge, the kind I could definitely get used to. For me to walk away from something that big and good would've been the craziest thing I'd ever done. I didn't move from that spot. The way he gripped around the insides of my thighs and thumbed my clit while pumping made me crazy. Zeke knew how to get his thrills, while at the same time making sure a sister got hers. He reminded me of an untamed wild man, handling my pussy with all kinds of grunts, groans, and out of control body trembling.

He hadn't said a *real* word since he'd first started eating my goodies in the den. To top that, he suddenly yanked his dick out of me and started cramming it in my asshole. I wasn't use to that kind of shit, but it wasn't so bad. I let him do his thing. He must have really liked giving it in the ass because only moments later he was growling about how good it was and how he was getting ready to cum.

"Oohh, yeah! Oohh, yeah! I'm getting ready!" he mumbled.

Right after Zeke filled my ass with cum, Mitchell spurted his thick juice all over the place too. Then Zeke fell across the bed, huffing like he had just finished running a marathon. Seconds later, Mitchell fell on top of me, trying to stick his dick in my pussy to fuck. I was already lying on my back, I just opened wide and let him in. We kissed and licked all over each other's mouths. After he was in, he worked his shiny black ass just as relentless as Zeke had done. I was surprised that I was able to take him thrusting in me so vigorously after taking all the fierce ramming of horse dick Zeke.

Mitchell's dick wasn't mini-meat size, but compared to Zeke's it was child's play. I sailed through Mitchell's humping effortless, and still managed to have me another intense orgasm along with him. The second

Mitchell rolled off me here came Eric. I stopped him in his tracks, taking a few minutes to catch my breath. Six or seven minutes later, Eric was on top of me humping my brains out. I squeezed and rubbed his fervent ass-cheeks as he rolled. Eric was a gentle lover. He liked to do it slow and easy for the sake of savoring every little drop. He and I took our time arriving at the end. This time Zeke and Mitchell were the watchers. Neither of the men had taken their pants all the way off, only dropping them to their feet. That proved they were there to fuck me only, and no other kind of funny shit was going to take place.

When Eric and I finished, I lay across the bed with a broad smile on my face, listening to the guys tell me how beautiful, and how fine, and how marvelous, and how delicious I was. What a big turn around in the way things had been going for me all weekend. I'd gone from one stupid man telling me he didn't want me, to three very smart men telling me they wanted everything I had to offer. The ultimate fantasy for any real woman had come true for me, which was to have the undivided attention of at least three men at one time while being intimate. What more could a girl want?

I told the guys I wanted to do everything we'd done back over as soon as I ran into the bathroom and took a five minute shower to refresh myself. They were as excited about a second round as they'd been about the first one. Neither of them moved a muscle to leave. I jumped in the shower in a split second to clean kitty-kat up. As the warm, exhilarating water ran down my body, I felt the semen from my three guys trickling down the inside of my thighs.

A tingly feeling cascaded over me causing me to smile on the inside. *Sweet revenge. How good it is,* I thought while washing myself. Myilana thought she had it going on the way she'd managed to confuse Ashton and trick him into saying all the bullshit she wanted to hear. Little did she know, I was about to get my man back where he belonged—with me. After I finished weaving my web, he wasn't going to resist me. And as for Curtis, he would be my big healthy bonus. Those wonderful thoughts jingling throughout my mind were making me extra horny all over again.

I was so caught up with getting back to screwing my guys again, I almost forgot to take my medicine. It had already been two hours past the time since my last dose. I couldn't afford to go any longer because I was already having to wish away the slight fatigue that was beginning to ease up on me. The minute I swallowed those two pills I was back in the room grinding on the dicks once more. Sponging my pussy with hot, sudsy water while I showered proved to be just what I needed to get rid of the teeny bit of tenderness I'd felt earlier.

One after the other they fucked me and came again. The looks on their faces were pleasure-filled after we were done. I was happy with the job I'd performed in satisfying them. And I was extra happy about the way they'd satisfied me and helped to give me a brand new outlook on things. Before we went back to the den I slipped into a short nightshirt, dabbed on some perfume, and prepared myself to entice my next two fellas.

Chapter Fifteen

Parrish

The four of them had the nerve to come barging back into the den, one after the other, laughing and talking as if nothing had happened. Renalia was really pushing the envelope with what she was wearing in the presence of everybody. She wore this really-too-short nightshirt. I guess we couldn't complain too much. At least she wasn't butt-naked anymore. She and Eric went into the kitchen, bombarding the food. Mitchell followed them. The nerve of them, playing this thing so casual.

On a second notion, I began to think about the whole thing and told myself maybe they were the ones who knew the true meaning of being fully liberated, and the girls and I only thought we knew with our small time dealings. My final conclusion was, if being fully liberated meant doing what Renalia had done with three men at one time, then I would never be all the way liberated.

Zeke didn't follow the others into the kitchen, instead he dropped his laid back ass down on the sofa near me and said, "Hey, baby girl. Have ya'll had as much fun as we've been having?"

I slid farther over, making sure his nasty ass didn't touch me. "Can't say we did," I replied nonchalantly without looking at him. But from the corner of my eyes I saw his reaction to my brush off. The depraved smile on his face shrunk to a bothered look.

"Something wrong, baby?" he asked.

"Not with me. I'm picture perfect," I told him without delay.

His wrinkly forehead deepened as he stared at the side of my face. "You sure? I mean, you seem a little stressed."

"I told you I'm fine. Please don't keep asking me." I still never looked his way.

"All right. If you say so." He sighed. " 'Cause I know you don't call yourself upset about that little quick fun we had back there. Like the lady said, we're here to have fun, right? We didn't do anything she didn't want us—"

"Zeke stop, okay." I held my hand up, stopping him before he went any further. "You're not my husband, you don't have to justify anything to me. I agree with you, we're here to have fun. She wanted it, ya'll gave it to her. End of story." By now I forced myself to look at him.

I refused to give him the satisfaction of thinking he'd gotten under my skin even a smidgen for doing what he'd done. I wasn't a jealous fool, acting out about somebody else's husband like Renalia had been doing over Ashton. Zeke wasn't worth that much to me. Hell, my own husband wasn't worth that much to me. I'd noticed the way Mitchell was carefully peeking at Dhelione from the kitchen. His wariness said he wasn't ready to exchange words with her yet. At least not like Zeke was doing with me.

"All right, baby girl." Zeke shook his head like a donkey. "If you say so." His faked out response made me think he didn't really believe what I'd told him, which didn't matter to me as long as he went along with it anyway and left me alone.

Renalia was stretching her neck to the extreme, trying to hear any negativity she could use to start an argument with the girls and me. It was no surprise when she interfered Zeke's and my conversation. "What's up, Zeke? Is there a problem?" She asked sarcastically.

"I guess not," Zeke replied.

"Oh, okay." The carefree smirk on Renalia's face meant she wanted some chaotic shit going again.

She wanted to see the surfacing of whatever hostility she believed we were hiding. That way she could throw in our faces the same thing we'd told her about not letting sex with a man damage our friendship. She would never have admitted that her act was totally the opposite of what we'd talked about.

I didn't give Zeke any satisfaction when he'd questioned me, and I wasn't going to give her any. Emberly and Dhelione looked like they were about to explode. I knew I needed to address Renalia before they did.

"Renalia." I stood up. "Can the girls and I have a word with you in private, please?"

She stopped nibbling from the hors d'oeuvres on her saucer and looked at me.

"Have a word with me in private?" She puckered her brows as if confused. "When did we suddenly become so professionally correct? I mean, you asked me that question like we're in a business meeting or something. Are you uptight about anything?" That same funky ass smirk of hers was working overtime to get a rise out of me. I wasn't having it.

I inhaled smoothly to keep from becoming any more stressed than I already was. "Nothing to be up-tight about, hun. So what's up? Can we holla at you or not?"

She burst into a loud scornful laugh. "Now you sound like a ghetto girl from around the way. There's got—"

"Shut the fuck up, bitch!" Emberly jumped out of her seat, heading straight for Renalia. Curtis, Dhe-lione, and Myilana grabbed her and held on to her.

"Bring it on!" Renalia shrieked. "Let her go, don't hold her! Let her go!"

"Shut your damn mouth, Renalia!" I demanded. "You know as well as I do, if they let her go you'll have a well whupped ass. Something you've been asking for all weekend. Did I say that non-professional enough for you?" Now I was scorning her.

"Nobody's got to tell her shit in private," Emberly snarled, burning her eyes into Renalia's. "Bitch, you're gone! Get your shit and get out." Emberly scuffled to get by Curtis, Dhelione, and Myilana, but they had boxed her in.

"Leave? I'm not going anywhere!" Renalia refused. "I have as much right to be here as anybody else. You can't kick me out 'cause of a disagreement, or 'cause I did something you don't like. I know what this is about. It's about me fucking ya'll's men, and them lik-ing it! Get over it!"

"Renalia, nobody gives a shit about who you fucked," Dhelione jumped in. "Hell, these men aren't our husbands. You can fuck them again if you want, you just won't do it up in here."

Renalia twisted her poison lips and transferred her twice as poison look to Dhelione, then said, "Oh, you don't give a shit about me fucking these men 'cause they're not your husbands, huh? Well, lah-tee-dah, guess what? I fucked your husbands, too." Before she got the last word out, Dhelione had already shot past everybody and ran up on her. Dhelione whacked her in the face. They entangled in a cat-fight, licks flying all over, and Dhelione getting the best of her.

Dhelione slung her around, fisting her like the light-weight she was. If it hadn't been for Eric and Mitchell taking hold of Dhelione and restraining her, there wouldn't have been much of Renalia left. She was getting ragged up pretty bad. Shame on the rest of us. We didn't move a muscle or lift a finger to help her. Extra shame on me because I was wearing a big smile on the inside and rooting for Dhelione the whole time.

Beat her ass good. That's it, show her who's boss, I bragged to myself 'til Renalia let out this excruciating cry like a wounded animal. Mitchell had tugged Dhelione back to the sofa against her will and was holding her there. Eric was trying to calm Renalia down, but the deafening scream coming through her lungs was unbearable.

"Get away from meeeeeeee! Don't touch meeeeeeee!" Her tears were streaming forcefully to match her vigorous cries. "I hate you! I hate all of you! You can't judge me! Who are any of you to judge meeeeeeee!" I'd never seen anybody crying so hard and screaming so loud at the same time.

She reminded me of a little girl who felt she'd been wronged and was throwing a severe tantrum. Behind the tears, the red eyes, the messed up hair, and the torn nightie, her ferocious face looked completely vulnerable. If I hadn't known better I would've sworn she was acting out over something more painful than this one incident with us. There seemed to be a lot of pain seeping through her eyes despite how hard she was trying to hide it behind the anger.

Nobody said anything. We just stared at her as she outpoured like a neverending waterfall. She must have felt all alone. My anger was beginning to transform into pity. I just had to say something, "Renalia, please calm down and—"

"No!" she cut me off instantly. "Ya'll want me to leave? You don't have to tell me again, I'll leave. I thought ya'll were my friends, but you know what? I don't need friends like any of you. I left his ass, and I can leave ya'll's asses too!" She stormed out of the kitchen, heading to the back. The girls and I looked at each other in bafflement about her last statement.

"What in the hell is she talking about?" Emberly frowned. "She left him, she can leave us?"

Myilana shook her head. "I don't know."

"Me neither." I shrugged my shoulders.

We looked at Dhelione. She slightly rolled her eyes. "Hell, don't be looking at me. I don't know what she's talking about."

As the four of us stood there, trying to figure out what Renalia was talking about, Curtis gestured for Zeke, Mitchell, and Ashton to follow him into the kitchen where Eric still remained. The girls and I continued speculating.

"Do ya'll think she's talking about her husband?" Myilana asked, looking concerned. "I mean, leaving him? That's the only sense I can make of it."

"She hasn't said anything to me about leaving her husband," Emberly replied. "Has she said anything to either one of ya'll?"

"No. Let's go try to talk to her. That's the only way

we're gonna find out what's going on." I gestured for the girls to follow me.

Before we made two steps, Renalia was already coming from the back wearing a thick green robe tied in the front. She abruptly stopped at the front door as if she was going to make a speech to everybody. She not only captured our attention but the men's too. The detached look on her face was hardly readable, and her eyes were like black pit holes, leading to an empty vault. One of my best friends had turned into a human frame with skin and no soul. I asked myself silently, *what's wrong with her? How'd she get so bad, so quick?* Her entire appearance had changed.

The others gazed at her with as much disbelief as I. She didn't even look like the same lowdown Renalia that had willfully sexed up our men less than an hour ago. At least then she seemed more alive. She looked all but dead now.

"Renalia, please. Let's go in the back and talk," I begged calmly. "If something's wrong with you, we wanna know."

Her red, watery eyes pierced through me as she slowly answered. "If . . . if something's wrong with me? Parrish, you know what's wrong with me. You're one of the so-called friends who helped make something wrong with me. Or did you forget your part in all this?"

I let out a soft breath. "Listen, Renalia, I'm not talking about the stuff that has happened here this weekend."

"Really? Then . . . then what are you . . . you talking about?" Renalia's hesitation was so robotic, it gave me a terrible eerie feeling.

"Come on, Renalia. There's gotta be something else

wrong with you." I paused. "What about the statement you made a few minutes ago? Something about leaving him . . . and leaving us too? What did you mean?"

"I don't know what you're talking about," she denied it.

"Please, Renalia." I began to slowly walk toward her. "Let's just—"

"Let's not." She nervously stuck her hand in one of her pockets, and when she pulled it out it was wrapped around a black handgun, pointing right at me. "Don't come any closer."

I gasped in shock. I was too scared to take my eyes off Renalia, but I heard everybody else gasp also. Now my words were coming out like a robot. "Renalia . . . what . . . are . . . you doing with a gun?"

"I'm pointing it at you, Parrish," she said sarcastically. "That's what I'm doing with it."

Tears formed in my eyes, I was so afraid. I didn't know what else to say, nor did I understand what was truly going on with her at that moment.

Dhelione broke her silence, sounding nervous and unsure too. "Renalia . . . please . . . put that gun down before you hurt somebody."

"Yeah, Renalia . . . you don't wanna hurt anybody." Emberly trembled. She talked slower than I'd ever heard her talk before. "Where'd you get that gun from anyway? Is it loaded?"

"She got it out of my jacket pocket," Curtis answered Emberly.

Emberly gave him a "tell me you're kidding" look. "Your jacket pocket? Where was your jacket? And why was a gun in it, Curtis?" Emberly forced herself to talk calmly.

"My jacket was in the bedroom where we were earlier. And a gun was in it because I'm a police officer, Emberly," Curtis's defensive reply was filled with tension.

"That means the gun is loaded. Why the hell would you leave a loaded gun lying around, Mr. Police Officer?" Emberly smart-mouthed him back. Their irritation was no doubt caused by the strenuous situation we were all in.

It was enough knowing that Renalia had suddenly started acting unstable, now she was holding a gun on a house full of people. We were in a very hostile environment, not knowing what she was going to do next. It was natural to want to blame somebody.

Curtis exhaled deeply, and took his time replying to Emberly, "I didn't leave it lying around. It was in my pocket . . . in the room . . . out of everybody's way. She had to go looking through my things to find it. And how the hell was I supposed to know you had crazy folks in here?"

"Crazy?" Renalia raised her voice. "Who the hell are you calling crazy!"

"Nobody, Renalia. Nobody's crazy." I thrust my hands in front of me to calm her so she wouldn't do anything drastic. "He didn't mean that."

"No he didn't," Emberly backed me up. "Look, Renalia, this is nonesense. Put the gun down before—"

"Before what?" Renalia took over. "Before I hurt somebody? Yeah, you've already said that, and you wanna know what I think? Huh? Do you? Answer me!"

Instead of answering Emberly jerked in-fear at the sound of Renalia's demand. I replied in her place, hoping to smooth over the anger. "Okay, what do you think, Renalia?"

"I think . . . I don't give a shit what any of you think,

or if somebody does get hurt. Why would I? None of you gave a shit about hurting me."

"That's not true, Renalia," I disagreed with her. "We didn't deliberately try to hurt you. It's just that—"

"It's just that what?" Renalia refused to cooperate. "Spare me your lying bullshit. Ya'll were throwing me out like Mississippi trash. And that's not the worst part, the worst part is none of you was ever gonna look back again. All because things got out of your perfect little order this *one* time. Of all the years we've been friends, this *one* time things didn't go the way they were supposed to," she paused, looking hurt. Tears began dripping down her cheeks again. "What happened to being together through the good times *and* the bad times? I mean, aren't *real* friends supposed to be there for the good and the bad too? I may not have a lot in my life, but I thought I'd always have my friends around. That's the one thing . . . the one thing that's kept me going through all of the shit I've dealt with this year."

"Dealt with? This year? What—"

"Shut up, Parrish!" she shouted. "You don't know anything, and you don't wanna know anything. If you did you wouldn't have been so quick to judge me. None of you would've."

As she talked, Curtis was slowly easing up on her. He had been taking step by step, trying to get closer to her. We knew he was going to take the gun from her if he could get close enough, so we made sure not to look in his direction and give him away. Just when he got ready to make his move, she quickly turned and fired at him. He let out a loud agonizing roar and fell backwards on the floor. The girls hollered. The men gasped. I was too devastated to say anything right then. I didn't know where the bullet hit him, but his chest area was splattered with blood and he wasn't moving. Maybe he'd just fainted from being shot. I hoped. But he lay there motionless. The thought of him being under a fainting spell seemed out of the question.

My delayed scream now came. "Oh my God!" I thrust my hands to my mouth, muffling my scream. But Emberly's horrific cry couldn't be covered up. She dived on the floor near Curtis with tears gushing from her eyes.

"Nooo! What have you done?! You shot him!" Emberly vigorously rubbed and pulled at Curtis for him to make some kind of movement. "Curtis! Curtis, please don't die! Open your eyes!"

Ashton ran over and kneeled down beside Emberly. He stuck his hand under Curtis's neck to take his pulse. It only took me a moment to read the dreadful news on Ashton's face, even though, he hadn't said one word yet.

Emberly must have read the same news on his face that I'd read, because seconds after they locked eyes with each other she began shaking her head and crying much harder. "No! No! No! Tell me he's okay! Tell me he's okay!"

Aside from her weeping and wailing, the rest of us were stone quiet, waiting on edge for Ashton to tell us something. He slowly shook his head, staring at Emberly and semi-whispered, "I'm sorry, he's dead."

"No! No! He can't be," Emberly cried. "He can't be dead!"

Ashton pulled Emberly away from the body and lead her over to where Myilana was standing and he remained near them. Myilana wrapped her arms around Emberly to comfort her.

Chapter Sixteen

We were all in awe. My heart skipped a beat. The chief of police of our little town lay dead as a doornail right in front of us. And his killer was standing in her same spot holding the gun on us that she'd shot him with. Things couldn't get any worse. Or could they? I glanced at the others. They were horror struck. I knew nobody else was about to make a move on Renalia after what had happened to Curtis. I needed to hold it together long enough to get the gun away from her before somebody else got shot.

"Renalia, this is insane. You just killed the chief of police. How are we gonna explain this? What are we gonna do? We're in a lot of trouble. These men are not even supposed to be here, tell me you understand that? What about our families?"

Renalia looked just as distraught as the rest of us, and my many questions only stressed her all the more. She transformed from one painful expression to the other, and the tears still came. To top it off, she was in denial.

"He's not dead. What do you take me for . . . some kind of an idiot?" she questioned.

"Not dead?" I couldn't believe what I was hearing. "Renalia, the man's body is as stiff as a board. He couldn't get any deader if you shot him ten more times."

"I shot him in the shoulder . . . that's how I know he's not dead," she exclaimed. "He's a cop. Cops do shit like that to trick people so they can get the ups on them."

"Shit like what? Being dead?" I asked her.

"No, playing Possum . . . pretending to be dead." She searched his lifeless body with her eyes, then took careful steps toward it. After kicking it two or three times near the wounded area and seeing it wasn't going to move, her face went blank. She knew he was dead.

She began trembling, and slowly eased away from the body 'til she was back in her spot at the door. The gun shook in her hands. While she was in a vulnerable state I figured it was a good idea to keep trying to talk the gun away from her.

"See, he's dead," I carried an easy tone. "Now put the gun down before somebody else gets hurt. We're already in enough trouble as it is."

She rested her regretful eyes on me and said, "You're not in any trouble. None of you are. I'm the one who pulled the trigger. I'm the one who's in trouble."

"We're all in trouble one way or the other 'cause we're not supposed to be here," I told her. "It doesn't matter what the police say, Renalia. We're all going to suffer from this. A man is dead. A very important man. We need to go ahead and call somebody before we make things worse."

Her regret turned to anger in seconds. "No," she snapped. "Nobody's calling anybody."

"Renalia, please. Not calling the authorities right now is going to make things worse," I pleaded.

"Really? Is that what you think?" She freaked out. "Well, I've got news for you. Things are already worse for me! Have been for a long time! And this shitty situation isn't gonna be any different!"

"Renalia, what are you talking about? Stop talking in riddles and say what you've got to say," I urged her.

"Okay! You wanna know what I've got to say? You wanna know? I'll tell you!" She crammed her hand in one of her pockets, then chucked a bottle of prescription pills at me. "Take a dose of those four times a day for the next seven months, then tell me things aren't as bad as they can get!"

I picked the bottle up off the floor and read the label. "Em-tri-va? Em-tri-va? What is this? I don't know if I'm pronouncing it right. What's it for, Renalia?"

She didn't answer me right away, she seemed to want to disappear in thin air.

Dhelione moved closer to me and reached for the medicine bottle. As she read the label, I asked her if I'd pronounced the name of the medication correctly. She shook her head in puzzlement and replied, "I'm not sure. Em-tri-va. It sounds right. But what is it for? What is it for, Renalia?"

Renalia still wasn't talking, just stood there pointing the gun. By now Eric had made his way over to us and gently took the bottle out of Dhelione's hand to read it.

"Do you know what it's for?" Dhelione asked him.

A look of sickness came over Eric as he answered her reluctantly, "It's Emtriva. An anti . . . anti-HIV medication."

"What?" I just knew I'd heard him wrong. "That can't be right. How do you know that? I didn't see that. Does it say that somewhere on the label?"

"No," he replied. "It doesn't say it on the label."

Dhelione frowned at him. "Then how the hell do you know that for sure?"

"I know for sure 'cause I have a relative . . . a first cousin who takes it too. He's HIV positive."

Dhelione thrust her hand to her mouth and looked at Renalia. "Oh God."

I looked at her too. "No, No, that's not right. "

The tears continued falling from Renalia's eyes. She took her time searching each of our distressed faces. After a few minutes, she mustered up seven heartrending words. "Welcome to the world of Aids, Gentlemen."

The only man in the room who hadn't slept with Renalia was Curtis, and he was dead. Eric, Ashton, Zeke, and Mitchell were beside themselves. Zeke didn't handle the news well, at all. He instantly flew into an anxiety attack, panting, wheezing, and grasping hold of his chest. When he fell to his knees in front of the garbage can vomiting everywhere, I could only imagine what he was feeling. He'd just performed oral sex on Renalia, among other things, not long ago. My sympathy was with him, but I kept in mind he'd brought it on himself.

The moment he lifted his head from over the garbage can, he let Renalia have it. "You little nasty whore, I'm gonna kill you for this. What have you done to me? Oh, God, what have you done to me? You've ruined me. I swear, if I've got anything, you're a dead woman, you, bitch!"

Renalia pitched Zeke a vicious glare. "Shut the fuck up, preacher man! You're gonna do nothing! Nobody forced you to fuck me. Nobody ever forces doggish ass men like you to stick your dicks where they don't belong. In this case your tongue too. Greedy men like you always want as much pussy as they can get. Too bad you got a little too much this time. You're getting exactly what you deserve. Hell, I don't feel sorry for your black ass. And as for killing me, well, don't you know? I'm already dead ... and so are you." She paused, then set her eyes on Mitchell, then Eric. "So are all of you."

Eric peered back at her angrily. He looked like he wanted to rip her spine out. "How could you not tell us?" he asked her through tightened teeth. "Huh? How could you? I mean, that's like malicious intent or something."

"It's not *liiike* malicious intent, it *isss* malicious intent," Renalia bragged with smugness. "Just accept your fate and live with it. That is, until you die in about a year or so."

"A year or so?" I spoke ahead of Eric. "Renalia, lots of people live with AIDS for years at a time. Just 'cause you have it doesn't mean you're gonna die in a few months."

"That's exactly what it means for me," she replied. "My doctor gave me eighteen months, tops. Evidently, my blood cells aren't up for a fight like other people."

I was heartbroken with grief for her. "Renalia, why didn't you tell us? You've been going through all of this alone? We're your—"

"My friends?" She gave me a look of contempt. "Is that what you were gonna say? What a joke. Considering the way *my friends* acted over my other little problem with Ashton, I know for a fact I made the right choice not telling ya'll about this one. Off hand, I'd say you wouldn't have understood too well, just like that sorry ass husband of mine. He's the one who gave it to me. He was diagnosed first. And now, after all this time goes by, he up and tells me he's moving back to Detroit with his family. Say's he can deal with things a lot better without the pressure of me blaming him all the time. Ain't that shit a trip? I mean, who the hell should I blame if not him?"

"Oh, Renalia, I'm so sorry." I couldn't have been more sincere, but she mocked my every word to her.

"Sure you are. I can see you now, and them too, prancing around being careful not to touch anything I touch. Turning your noses up at me behind my back 'cause I'm no longer clean and classy like ya'll. Pretending to care, but wishing I'd go somewhere and ball up in a corner and die before I infect you with my contagious germs. Oh, yeah, ya'll would've been real supportive."

"Renalia, none of that negative stuff you're saying is true." Dhelione tried convincing her now. "Being in a relationship triangle comes nowhere close to having . . . having AIDS. I'd like to believe we would've been much more sensitive about something like this."

"So would I," Renalia replied. "But the fact is, I don't. That's why I took control of the situation and fixed everything so the four of us will be together for eternity. See, I've been a better friend to ya'll than ya'll have been to me. We may not all go at the exact same time, but I'm sure our time won't be too far apart." This crazed look came upon her.

"What are you talking about?" I asked her.

"You didn't think I was kidding around when I said I'd been fucking your husbands, did you? Yeah, I started fucking them about three months after I found out I was sick. You see, I couldn't bear the thought of dying and leaving my best friends behind. I knew if I gave it to your husbands, they'd give it to ya'll, then our friendship would be inseparable. Good thing they went ahead and acted like the dogs we've always known them to be. Hell, I didn't have any problem getting each one of them to fuck me over and over and over again."

Renalia had gone off the deep end, and from everything she'd said she was trying to take us with her. I had so many mixed feelings I couldn't even think straight. Like Zeke, I felt like vomiting, or worse, dying. And to think, I thought things couldn't get any worse than Renalia shooting Curtis. At least her unexplained behavior for that weekend was now accounted for.

Her crazed look intensified. "Don't look so surprised, ya'll," she said. "We've been talking about how whorish our husbands are for years . . . you guys had to know your men weren't gonna turn down a chance to screw one of their wives' best friends. And guess what? I had each one of them in their own perverted little way thanks to all the details ya'll shared over the years."

The one question I couldn't get out of my mind, I slowly opened my mouth to try and ask it. "Why did you do all of this, Renalia? Why?"

Dhelione answered before Renalia. "Why, isn't the question. How? That's the question. How could you?" A few tears trickled down Dhelione's cheeks.

Renalia taunted us. "Aww, don't be so sad, guys. If it makes you feel any better you can look at the bright side of things. Myilana's gonna be the first of ya'll to die because she's had a double dose from both her men." She turned to Myilana and asked real cool. "Still want your precious Ashton, Myi?"

Other than Renalia's stone face, there was nothing but sorrow in the room. If everybody else's hearts were hurting half as bad as mine, they were in a terrible shape.

Why? Why? Why? I went into a trance repeating the same question in my head. Just as I came out of my deep-daze seconds later and refocused on our heart-breaking circumstances, I noticed a look in Eric's eyes. A look that said he was about to try something against Renalia. As bad as I wanted somebody to succeed in getting that gun away from her, a good *off-guard* moment wasn't to our advantage right now. My words of protest didn't ring-out fast enough, he charged straight for her. Bang! Bang! The sound of the two gunshots jolted me severely, then I watched him fall to the floor.

"Nooo, Eric!"

"Oh my God!"

"Renalia, no!"

"Oh, shit! Oh, shit! Oh, shit!" Zeke was squealing like a scared little kid in harmony with everybody else.

I began trembling almost uncontrollably. Renalia had shot somebody else, and by the looks of his still-ness he was dead too.

"You crazy, psycho bitch!" Zeke exclaimed. "There's no doubt in my mind the bitch is psychotic, ya'll!"

"Stop calling me psycho before I shoot you too, nigga!" Renalia yelled back at him. "It's his fault! The dumb son-of-a-bitch tried to attack me! I had to shoot him! How fucking retarded could he be, thinking I wouldn't shoot him if he ran up on me like that! What? He didn't see what happened to the chief? For all of you who don't know, this fucking gun has fifteen bul-lets in it. Fifteen! So stay the hell away from me!" She paused in thought, frantically rubbing through her hair with one hand. "I know, I know what to do! I'm gonna have to tie everybody up."

"What?" Emberly gasped.

"Tie us up? Please, Renalia, don't," I pleaded.

"She ignored me and shouted, "Shut up Parrish! Just shut up! I can't think with all your damn begging! Get down there and see if Eric's breathing or not." She shoved the gun outward, aiming directly at me.

"No," I mumbled after checking his pulse. "You shot him twice at point blank, Renalia. How could he be alive? This has gotten way, way out of hand."

"You're right, it has." She nodded. "And the only way to make sure nobody else gets hurt is to tie ya'll up like I said. If I don't, you'll keep trying foolish shit. And I don't need that right now. What I need to do is think. Think about what I'm gonna do. Think about what my options are."

"Our only option is to—"

"Did I say anything about *our* options, Parrish?" she shut me up quick. "No I didn't. I said *my* options."

Nothing I said did any good. And with two dead bodies on our hands, nobody else was brave enough to try and get close to her to get the gun away. She ordered me to go into the kitchen and get the two rolls of duct tape we'd seen under the sink earlier that day when we were cleaning up. I had no choice but to tape everybody's wrists and ankles together as tight as they could bear. Then she insisted I sat on the sofa and tape my own ankles together, leaving my wrists for her to do. She quickly did it with no problem. Thank goodness she didn't tape our mouths shut. Everything was happening much too fast. We'd gone from what was supposed to be an annual weekend of fun, to a weekend of pure tragedy. I didn't know how much more I was going to be able to endure.

There we were tied up and helpless at the hands of a damn maniac. Each one of us worked and twisted our wrists and ankles, trying as hard as we could to get free. It was hopeless. The inelastic duct tape wouldn't give. Without a knife or something sharp our efforts were useless.

After about an hour of Renalia's supposed "pondering" in the kitchen by herself, she slid out of her chair and strolled back into the den with that same crazed look in her eyes as before. I couldn't read her mind, but I just knew I wasn't going to like what was about to come through her lips.

"I know what I have to—"

"Excuse me, Renalia," Emberly cut her short. "I need to use the bathroom."

Renalia sighed. "Hold it 'til I'm done talking."

"I can't. Come on, Renalia, I've really gotta go. That wine's working on me. I'm surprised you don't have to go yourself."

Renalia cut her legs loose, then her hands. Emberly wasted no time attacking Renalia the second she was free.

"Oh my God! Please stop!" Dhelione screamed to the top of her voice. "Don't do it! Stop!"

Like Dhelione, Myilana was screaming for them to stop. I was too frightened to get a sound out as I watched them roll around on the floor, wrestling for the gun. Once Emberly was free from the duct tape, she quickly grabbed Renalia's hand while they were near each other. She took the only opportunity she had, or probably would ever have, to get that close to Renalia. It was a brave thing for Emberly to do, but I feared for her life. As the two of them scuffled and scrapped for control, I held my breath. Both of them had their hands on the gun, and both of them were fighting violently. I wished so badly that one of us had been in a position to help Emberly, but we couldn't.

"Oouuchh, you bit me! Stupid bitch!" Renalia cried out.

Their struggling intensified. Now the gun was out of sight and in between them. Emberly had managed to come out on top of Renalia. She was getting the best of her, which was no surprise considering all of the feistiness we knew she had. The gun went off in the middle of their tussling, and they both stopped moving. They were as still as the dead bodies not far from them. Either one of them could have taken the bullet.

"Emberly! Emberly!" Myilana cried out. "Say something!"

There was no answer right away. Then Emberly began slowly picking herself up off Renalia.

"Emberly, are you okay?" I was able to breathe again.

"Yeah," she mumbled as she kicked Renalia twice, checking for movement. There was none. "The gun's on the floor with blood on it. Blood's all over it. Oohh, I killed her," Emberly cried. "I didn't wanna kill her, I just wanted to get the gun away from her. Now she's dead."

"Oh my God, Emberly, I thought . . . I thought she'd shot you," I weeped.

"No, I managed to turn the gun on her in case it went off. I don't know how, but I held it like that since I couldn't pry it out of her hand. She scared me shitless." Emberly was shivering as she kicked the gun away from Renalia's body.

"Cut us loose!" Zeke ordered Emberly. "Are you sure that crazy bitch is dead?"

"She's not moving and blood's everywhere. Yeah." Emberly grabbed the knife off the table and began cutting Dhelione's hands loose.

Zeke wasn't convinced about Renalia. "Why the hell didn't you check her pulse?" Zeke asked Emberly. "If she was crazy enough to think they were faking after getting shot, how do you know she's not faking?"

Dhelione's hands were loose. Emberly began working on her feet.

"Watch out, Emberly!"

"Turn around!"

"Oohh!" By the time our cries warned Emberly, Renalia had gotten up and grabbed a wine bottle and shattered it over her head, knocking her out. Then Renalia staggered around, holding her bloody side with one hand, searching around on the floor for the gun. That gave Dhelione very little time to finish getting the tape off her ankles.

"Hurry Dhelione!"

"Hurry up!"

"Please hurry!"

Just as Dhelione stripped the tape away and jumped up to tackle Renalia, Emberly began moving. We hollered and hollered for Emberly to get up and help Dhelione. With Renalia injured and no gun in her hand, there was no reason the two of them couldn't stop her once and for all. Emberly responded to our hollering and got up as quickly as she could. Despite being a little off balance and out of it from the head lick, she was on her feet. But she didn't catch up to Dhelione in time for both of them to overpower Renalia before she got hold of the gun again.

The first bullet struck Dhelione, and I watched her fall to the floor like she was falling in slow motion. If that wasn't bad enough, Emberly was now in the middle of making her move, so Renalia didn't waste any time pulling the trigger a second time and struck her down. Within a few minutes, two of my best friends in the world were gunned down right under my nose by another best friend, and I couldn't do one damn thing about it. I'd never felt so helpless in my entire life.

Renalia moaned in agony. She looked like she was in severe pain from her bleeding side where she'd taken the bullet. She put pressure on it with her hand and wasted no time limping over to make sure Dhelione and Emberly were really dead and not faking like she'd done. By now I was numb. I didn't have anymore tears in my glands to shed. I no longer believed the rest of us were going to make it out of there alive. I kept asking myself silently, *how did this happen? Oh, God, How?*

Chapter Seventeen

Four dead. The bodies were piling up by the minute, and Renalia no longer wanted to talk to anybody about anything. The others were continually trying to get through to her and find out what she was thinking since the last incident happened, but she refused to say anything to them. I didn't have to ask her what she was thinking, because I already knew by the uninhibited look on her face. She had nothing more to lose. And that wasn't the worst of it. The worst of it was killing had become easier for her now. I always heard if a person manages to kill once, it's much easier to kill again after that. All the reasoning and pleading in the world wasn't going to budge her one bit.

Pretending I didn't see how hard Zeke was working to flip his cellphone open and press the speed-dial key for 911 wasn't hard to do, because I didn't think it was going to work anyway. It was one of many attempts that would probably leave him with a bullet in his body just like the ones before. When he first whispered his plan to us, I didn't have much confidence in him getting the call through, but a big part of me still hoped he'd pull it off.

God, help us all, I said in my head. *If she catches him . . .*

"Hey, Renalia, why did you shoot both of them? They were your friends!" Zeke suddenly began shouting all of these different questions at Renalia. "Hey, do you hear me? Why did you invite us way out here in the middle of nowhere on LeSewer Road in this cottage just to shoot all of us? I don't wanna die! Don't kill me! You've already killed the chief of police! The chief of police is dead, and you killed him! This cottage isn't hid that well out here on LeSewer Road, somebody's gonna find us after a while! Just go ahead and let us—"

"Shut up!" Renalia finally broke her silence. Oozing toward Zeke, she stopped in front of him with this enraged scowl. "Why the fuck are you running your mouth like that? Hollering at me about shit that's over and done with! We know where we are, and we know what's happened here! What's gotten into you?"

Zeke didn't answer. There was a moment of quietness while Renalia waited on him to reply to her.

"Answer me!" she demanded. "Why are you yelling about this shit? Say something you crooked dick piece of shit!"

Zeke cautiously rotated his eyes down at the gun in her hand, then raised his voice again. "'Cause you're not gonna get away with this! You might as well untie us and let us go before things get any worse for you! You've already done enough! My God, you killed the chief of police! The police are probably on their way right now!"

I wished Zeke would stop shouting at her and provoking her even more than she already was. If he didn't, I was afraid she would speed up his killing. I was too deadened to tell him to hush.

As she stood scowling at him, her eyes went crazed all back over again. "And just why would the police be coming out here? Huh? They don't know what's going on out here."

"Yes they do," he told her. "They know 'cause I got them on speaker phone. The line's been open all this time, and they heard everything we said. Now let us loose, they're on the way."

Her eyes really bugged out with rage after hearing him say that. "Maybe they are on the way," she mumbled. "Too bad they won't get here in time to save you."

Bang! She shot him point blank in the head without blinking so much as an eye.

"Oooohhhhh!! Nooo!!" Myilana screeched out distressfully. Tears flooded her face.

I closed my eyes as tight as they'd fasten, momentarily. I had to at least try for some mental relief, if only for one moment. Zeke's body fell over like an oversized domino, and his eyes were still wide open. His cellphone lay on the sofa behind him. If I saw it from where I was sitting, Renalia couldn't help but see it.

She picked the phone up, held it to her ear and spoke loudly. "Somebody there? Hello. Who's there? Hello!"

I guess there was no response. She angrily threw the phone across the room against the wall; it sounded like it had broken into a hundred pieces. Then she walked back to the oversized chair and dropped down in it while staring out into space. Her reaction was proof that she no longer had any hesitation about taking a human life. She'd sucked the last drop of wind out of five people, and I didn't believe she would think twice about doing it to us. She still held on to the gun like it had mutated into a part of her hand, so nobody dared say anything to disturb her from the daze.

Myilana's sobbing was the only noise in the room for a short time, then out of the blue, Renalia mumbled pitifully, "I'm sorry. I'm so sorry. I'm so . . . so sorry for what I've done. I know it doesn't mean much now, Parrish and Myi, but for what it's worth, I couldn't have loved you any more if you were my own flesh and blood." She apologized to us, but never looked our way, just continued gazing out into nothing.

We listened attentively as she stuttered on. "I don't expect ya'll to forgive me . . . 'cause I can't even forgive myself. It wasn't supposed to happen like this. I didn't plan it this way. Dhelione and Emberly weren't supposed to die before their time, none of us were. The five of us were supposed to die one at a time as the disease took over our bodies. That was the plan. But now . . . but now, it's all messed up. And there's no turning back. We've got to see it through to the end."

Renalia's mind had become twisted enough to believe the shit she was saying to us. She actually made sense out of fucking our husbands so that we would catch the disease and die along with her. Now she had the nerve to be apologizing because we weren't dying the way she'd planned it. I wondered if she had ever considered the fact that whether she shot us with a gun or injected us with the AIDS virus, she would still be our murderer.

I didn't need to ask her what she meant about "seeing it through to the end", I already knew. But Ashton did ask her carefully. "What do you mean, Renalia? You said we've got to see it through to the end. What does that mean?"

She still didn't look directly at any of us when she

answered him, "Zeke said the police were coming. If that's true we can't be here when they get here. They'll separate us. And I'll spend my last months locked up in some dark prison cell. I can't die in prison. I won't."

"I understand what you're saying, Renalia, but there's nowhere to go," Ashton replied gently. "Where in heaven's name can we go to get away from all that's happened? There's nowhere to go. Nowhere."

"Yes there is," she whispered, then slowly turned her eyes down at our friends' dead bodies on the floor. "We can go where they are."

Ashton furrowed his brows. "What? Renalia, they're dead."

"Yeah." She barely nodded.

Ashton, Myilana, and Mitchell were taken aback at what Renalia said. They looked sicker than ever now. I, on the other hand, didn't react in the least, because I had braced myself for her "so-called" plan. I'd already forced my heart to accept the possibility of us not getting out of there alive. There was no need in making a fuss over the inevitable. My same realization didn't go for Myilana, she was torn apart. I hated that I didn't have any comforting words or best friend support for her. But even if I'd have known what to say, it wasn't going to come out because my wounded emotions had been shut down for a while now.

Renalia slid out of the chair, strolled over in front of Mitchell and raised the gun on him. He sounded like a little boy begging her not to shoot him. "No, please don't. Please don't." Tears poured from his eyes. "I've got a wife and kids at home. Please, don't take me from my wife and kids? They need me."

Renalia didn't flinch an inch in remorse when she answered him, "Did your wife and kids need you when you got a phone call from another woman and broke your damn neck trying to get over here to fuck that other woman? Then after fucking her, you fucked me? On the real, I'd say your family's better off without you."

Moments after she shot Mitchell, there was a knock at the door. A man's voice called to us. "Hello! This is the police! We got a call about this address! Open the door! We need to check things out!"

Hearing that police officer at the door gave me something I hadn't had in hours . . . hope. Renalia couldn't stop Ashton, Myilana, and I from joining forces, screaming like mad folks to the police, so she did the only thing she was able to do. She started shooting us, one after the other. I watched Ashton fall back on the sofa after taking a bullet in the chest area. Then Myilana took one in the head and fell to the floor.

Please, God. Let the police hear the shots and bust in, I said a silent prayer because it was my turn now. The tiny amount of hope I'd regained when I first heard the officers at the door disappeared as fast as it came when Renalia started shooting the last three of us. She turned the gun on me at the same time the police broke the door open and stormed in.

"Drop it! Police!"

"Put the gun down!"

"Put it down, Lady, put it down!" The three officers yelled at Renalia repeatedly while holding their guns on her. She never turned around to look at them, just stood there with that same crazed stare.

One of the police officers repeated the demand to her very slow but firmly, one last time. "Lady! Put-the-gun-down-on-the-floor! And raise your hands in the air, now!"

She didn't seem the least bit concerned with their warnings. She fired the gun anyway. The bullet pierced my delicate body, knocking me to the floor. As I fell, I heard multiple shots from what I believed were the policemen's guns shooting at Renalia. She hit the floor right after I did. The pain from the bullet that struck me was unbearable. I lay on my back in misery. And Renalia lay with her jaw against the floor, facing me. Things were a little fuzzy, but her body seemed to be slightly twitching. Her distant, dead eyes were the last thing I saw before everything went black.

Chapter Eighteen

Myilana

I was in a coma for six weeks. When I finally woke up my sister told me nobody thought I would survive. The doctors explained to me that if the bullet had lodged only three centimeters lower in my head, there wouldn't have been any way for them to remove it, and I would have in fact died. I burst into tears and thanked God immediately. As time went on, I found out Parrish and Ashton had miraculously survived and were doing well. That was great news to hear. I cried happy tears for them.

Under the critical circumstances, I didn't expect Ashton to come see me at the hospital even in a big city like Memphis. But that didn't stop me from wanting him to. Day after day went by and left me wondering why Parrish hadn't come to visit me yet. It bothered me that I hadn't seen her or gotten so much as a phone call from her. Everybody else I knew, who wasn't angry with me about what I'd been involved in, had come for a visit after they heard I was awake. Why hadn't she?

I lay in my bed every morning for weeks, listening to one family member after the other tell me how blessed I was to be alive after such a tragic ordeal. And of course, they never let me forget how I'd brought that tragic ordeal on myself. Thank goodness I had a private room with all their mouthing going on. Still, it didn't take long for the news to spread in our small town and other nearby towns. Somebody even brought me a copy of the local newspaper report on the story. The headlines read: *Secret Sex Party Ends In Shooting Massacre—Seven Of Our Own Dead.*

I didn't have to read any further, just seeing the headline segment disgusted me. Not to mention, it made that awful weekend come rushing back to my memory. Now on top of all the health issues I was dealing with, I had to start grieving about my dead friends so quickly before my own recovery. I wondered who could've come up with such a brutal headline. Evidently, the editors of our little hometown paper had learned some ruthless media tricks from the tabloids. As bad as the scandal was, I didn't have the strength to worry about my appearance or what people were saying about me.

I felt grateful to be alive, but my surviving came with a high price. Unlike my seven friends who died that horrible night, I didn't have the excuse of death to keep me from being persecuted and strung up on a pole to burn by our judgmental citizens. I had to face the music of answering hundreds of questions over and over again for the police. From what my questioning officers told me, Parrish and Ashton had already made their statements during my coma. I kept asking myself, *why do the police keep asking me so many of the same kinds of questions?*

After thinking about it a while, I realized there were many reasons for their intense questioning, but one of the main reasons was because their chief had been involved and was found dead with the others. Not to mention, Zeke, a well-known, important preacher from one of the largest churches in the area was there too. The police interrogation was pretty bad, but I survived it. Then I finally made it home from the hospital only to find I was out of the pot and right back in the kettle, answering hundreds of additional questions from my husband, Reginald. The tall, brown, halfway handsome, pain-in-the-ass, almost drove me insane.

One of Reginald's continuous questions was why, why, why. The truth wasn't pretty, but I went ahead and told him what he wanted to know about that night. I didn't go into detail about what our club stood for, or how we had done our thing with other guys throughout the year, but I was honest with him about why the five men were at the cottage with the five of us on that particular day. Besides, it was too plain to ignore. I couldn't have hidden it if I'd wanted to.

Even with me explaining my reasons for doing what I'd done, and reminding him of his many years of cheating, he was still outraged. He flew into a fit, cussing like a sailor every single day, and threatening all kinds of legal battles to divorce me and take our ten-year-old son, ReShad, away. Reginald not only became verbally abusive, but there were times when he actually almost hit me. Of all our years together, he'd done plenty of explicit dirt, but he'd never laid a finger on me through violence. I knew then it wasn't going to work.

Only one thing forced him to calm down and realize he wasn't so perfect either. And that was when I told him about Renalia being HIV positive, and confessing that she'd been sleeping with him and my other friends' husbands so she could pass the disease on to us. I thought I was going to have to resuscitate him afterward. He was devastated about it. But at least he had to let up on me for a while, because now he had his own nasty demons to deal with. Their names? H, I, and V.

He never admitted to me openly that he'd slept with Renalia, but he didn't waste any time contacting his doctor to get checked out. The process he went through of testing and waiting for the virus results kept him preoccupied for a while; long enough for me to have the opportunity to figure out what I was going to do about our miserable situation. After a little over two months of being back home with him, I began making preparations to leave permanently.

I needed some peace; some time alone with my son to focus on him and a full recovery. Physically, I was doing well because I was able to get around and do lots of basic stuff; things were almost back to normal in that area. But mentally, there wasn't any peace for me as long as Reginald was in my presence. Luckily, he didn't fight me about my decision to leave as long as I agreed to let Shad finish the school year out at home with him so the bus schedule, among other things, wouldn't be disturbed. Shad, of course, would be with me on weekends. Then at the end of the school year, we would agree on a fair custody plan. I had no problem with that because it was the right thing to do for Shad. Plus, It would've been a lot of pressure on me getting him to and from school everyday in my condition.

I believed Reginald's cooperation had a lot to do with the fact that he still hadn't tested positive at that point, and the periodic tests were driving him crazy.

They were driving me crazy too. The thing worse than knowing was not knowing, and having to keep going back and waiting all over again for a yes or no, positive or negative. Eventually, Reginald indirectly blamed me for "my crazy friend's seduction" as he put it. But he still didn't own up to his part in all of it. That told me every time he looked at me, he was reminded of Renalia and his own choice to sleep with her. He may not have been there that night, but he was still guilty as sin.

It took me a week of phone calls to have the electricity and other utilities turned on in the apartment I'd chosen to lease, which was as far as I could get from our house. The complex was on the opposite side of town in a nicely secluded area without a lot of traffic. My two brothers made sure all the furniture I purchased was brought in and set up with no problems, and my mother and sister took care of the rest. They really fixed the place up for me. The three of us pretty much had the same taste in everything, so I knew they would do things perfectly.

They wouldn't let me do any labor. When they finished, all I had to do was bring my clothes and move in. It was beautiful—a little smaller than what I was used to, but very cozy. I'd always had a supportive family, and I'd always been supportive of them in their "not so great" times too. No matter what the situation, we were tight despite our different views on certain issues.

A week in my new place and I'd already fallen into a nice, tidy routine, which hardly ever included going on the outside, or having anyone over to visit. I even made up constant excuses about getting plenty of rest to avoid visits from my family. As long as they could reach me on the phone and hear my voice they went along with me, but I knew I wasn't fooling them, especially my mother. She finally went ahead and told me she understood me wanting to be alone for a while and wouldn't push, but she made me promise if I became too depressed and needed to talk to let her know. I appreciated her for respecting how I felt.

Since the first day I came out of the coma and was home a week or so later, I hadn't had much time by myself. Somebody was always with me. Whether it was a visitor, a family member, or Reginald, somebody was always there. I wasn't left with time to go into deep thought about all the stuff that happened on that dreadful night, or the things that happened afterward. Now that I was alone in my own space I could take some time to really think. It wasn't long after that reality hit me and it hit me hard.

I grieved for my dead friends and I grieved for their families. I grieved that I'd almost died and I grieved from the guilt that I didn't die like my friends did. I grieved about the possibility of still dying if I eventually tested positive. I grieved about how one bad incident had turn everything in my life upside down and there was no way for me to go back and fix any of it. I mostly grieved that in the end, the one that would hurt the most was Shad, if he had to grow up without a mother because of my bad choices.

My grieving list was a mile long, and on top of it all I still hadn't seen or talked to Parrish yet. I had been trying to contact her since I left the hospital. I'd left several messages on her home phone and cellphone for her to call me, but she hadn't. Not hearing anything back lead me to believe that maybe she wasn't getting my messages. That continuously worried me. I'd become a recluse, so if I didn't get her by phone there was no other way for me to reach her.

Then there was my job. What was I going to do about it? I was collecting leave of absence benefits that were due me. After careful consideration of all the consequences, I came to a decision not to go back to work when my benefits ran out. I would mail the company my letter of resignation. I just couldn't deal with the pressure of the job and the people. Financially, it wasn't a big issue, because I knew I would be okay. I had a very nice lump of savings that only me and my mother knew about. With my medical insurance and emergency nest egg, I could afford to be off work a while.

Bernadine's husband in the movie *Waiting To Exhale* taught me, and probably millions of other women, how not to trust a cheating husband with all the finances, just in case he decided to up and fly the coop one day. A girl could still survive with dignity. Glad I took that movie seriously.

Chapter Nineteen

I spent most of my time on the sofa with the remote control and a box of Kleenex, thumbing through the channels and crying 'til my eyes swelled. Except on the weekend when Shad was with me. No way I was going to upset my baby boy with hopeless tears.

When I took into consideration everything I'd gone through, I knew in my heart I was in denial about one particular thing, or should I say one particular person. That person was Ashton. Being alone forced me to admit to myself that I really wanted to see him. I had wanted to see him from the beginning, but I kept reminding myself it was impossible. So I blocked out my feelings, and kept on blocking them out because I didn't want to deal with them. I pretty much accepted the reality concerning most of my issues, even though it hurt like hell. But I had no idea how to approach the Ashton dilemma.

After all, this man and I had openly admitted our love for each other just a short time before the disaster happened. Given that both of us survived, what would come of that supposed love? Did it still mean anything? I hadn't seen or heard from him, but my feelings were as strong as they were the night we confessed. I couldn't forget how he constantly whispered he loved me during the ordeal.

As I sat on my sofa, clinging to a wad of Kleenex tissues, my mind rambled. *I wish I knew if he tested positive? If I could just* ... The doorbell interrupted my thoughts and tears. I grabbed the remote and powered off the TV.

"Who on earth could that be?" I mumbled as I got up and walked to the door.

I certainly wasn't expecting anyone, least of all on a Tuesday night. When I peeped through the eyehole on the door, I couldn't believe who I saw. I thought my eyes were fooling me. I jerked my head away from the door and began fluttering my lids like something was in my eyes. The bell rang again. I peeped through the hole a second time. Nothing changed. I saw who I saw. When I jerked away from the door this time, my heart rate increased and the tears really came. I folded my arms, hugging myself as if I had suddenly gotten cold. *Oh my God. What am I gonna do?* I thought.

I was so surprised, I didn't know what to do. I just stood there 'til the doorbell rang again. There was no avoiding opening it, so I sucked it in, held my breath, and unlocked the door. There stood my beautiful lover. We shared instant eye to eye. There was so much love in his eyes, I could practically feel it penetrating through my body. It was a real defining moment for me. At that moment, my heart told me without a shadow of a doubt, I loved him deeply.

He walked in without me telling him to, and slowly

closed the door behind him, never taking his eyes off of mine. His glowing face was like a bright lamp in my dimly lit living room.

"Hi," he said softly.

"Hi." I, like him, couldn't take my eyes away.

He stood close in front of me, and gently wiped down my jaw with the back of his hand, drying my tears.

"I stayed away as long as I could," he whispered. "I couldn't wait any longer. I had to see you. I love you so much." He eased his lips to mine and kissed me very softly.

Not only was his mouth talking, but his presence spoke just as loud. We embraced and squeezed each other tightly. I felt better at this moment than I'd felt in a long time.

"Where've you been? Have you been okay?" I asked him.

"Yeah, I've been okay. Just wanting to see you real bad. Real, real bad." He released his hug and looked at me. "I knew I couldn't get in touch with you 'cause things have been so crazy. But a day doesn't go by without me thinking of you. I finally got tired of waiting and gave you a call."

"On my cell?"

"Yeah, but it wasn't on. The message said out of service."

"I know. It somehow got lost when my family picked my things up at the cottage so I had it disconnected. How'd you find me?"

"You're not gonna believe this, but I was desperate. I had my sister call your home number from a pay phone."

"And she agreed to do that?"

"Believe me, she didn't want to at first," he chuckled. "But she loves her big brother. I told her how much you mean to me. Once I got her to understand my feelings for you, she did it willingly. "

"Really?" My heart was touched.

"Really."

"What happened when she called?"

"A man . . . probably your husband . . . told her you didn't live there anymore. Said you had an apartment on this side of town. It was easy after that."

I didn't respond right away, just slowly nodded at him. He continued, "You look so beautiful with your new hair cut. I knew you would. How are you adjusting to it being short like that?"

"Considering the reason it was cut, or should I say shaved, I couldn't be happier. I don't think it's something I would've done by choice, but over the months its grown on me. I like it. Takes about five years off."

"You said shaved. It was shaved?"

"To the scalp. Only way for them to do the surgery."

"I can't tell. How did it grow so fast?"

"My hair has always grown pretty fast. Besides, it's been over four months."

"Yeah, but that's still a lotta hair for only four months." He laughed quietly. I laughed with him, then his faced turned serious. "So you left him, huh?"

"Yeah. I couldn't stay. Everything came crashing down after I left the hospital and went home. What am I saying? It wasn't a home. It hadn't been a home in years. Our separation was a long time coming. Even if it hadn't happened like this, I think I would've eventually gotten tired of all the games. I mean, that's why me and the girls started the so-called club in the first place, remember? Trying to get back at our husbands.

In the end nobody won, right?" My heart was now aching from recalling the sorrow. "What about you? Are things okay with you and your wife?"

"Nahh. About as bad as you just described. Maybe worse. But I guess most of it was my fault from years and years ago. This thing here just put the icing on the cake. From what she says, I did to her what you say he did to you. Ain't that something? I waited too late before I realized any of it. My change don't mean much now. Not to her, anyway. Weird thing is, I went into my marriage cheating on her, and kept it up pretty much the whole time. But as much as I love you I can't see myself doing that kind of shit. Anyway, while I was recovering from the gunshot, we moved into the husband and wife routine for a minute, but it wasn't working." He paused and exhaled like he was weary. "You know what?"

"What?"

"I don't think a person can go back to being the same after going through what we went through, and living to tell about it." He paused again. "When I told my wife about the HIV . . . that's when she really snapped. I didn't have anymore peace after that. The police even had to come out to my house a few times 'cause she wouldn't let up with the fighting. The last time they came, I left. I moved into my other house."

"That pretty two-story house right outside of town?"

"Yep, that's the one. The only one."

I teased him. "You sure that's the only one? I mean, my-my, you must be a man of prestige and privilege. In these parts, we don't have a lot of people who are able to leave one big beautiful house to their wife, and move into another one almost just like it. Why you must be a wealthy kind of guy since you got it like that, aren't ya?"

He smiled back at me, but still in a serious way. "Only if I can have you. Without you my wealth is nothing. Are you sure it's over with you and your husband?"

My forehead slightly wrinkled, indicating my seriousness. "Of course I am. The only thing me and him got left to talk about is Shad."

"Good." He exhaled a sigh of relief. "I don't know about you, but my divorce is already in progress. As soon as it's over we can—"

"Don't." I feared what he was going to say. I couldn't bear to hear it, because I knew we couldn't have it. The timing was all wrong.

"Don't what? Don't ask the woman I love to marry me? Too late, I already did." He leaned into me and kissed me on the lips sensually. I pulled away. My heart was saying yes, but my good sense was saying this was impossible.

"Ashton . . . this is too much . . . too soon." I hesitated. "I mean, I don't even know if, if—"

"If what, baby? You just told me it's over with your husband, didn't you?"

"That's not all I'm talking about. There's so much more to consider. For one thing, what about the tests? What about yours? Mine tested—"

"Stop," he said. "My first test was negative, Myilana. And I've had several more since that one. All negative. Now, the doctor explained to me that the virus can show up anytime within a year of being exposed to it, so I have to keep testing 'til who knows. But I don't care whether you're positive or not. The only thing that matters to me is that we're together. We can beat this thing. I hope you feel the same way." His sincerity moved me to more tears.

"I wish it was that simple."

"It is that simple. Why wouldn't it be? It's not like people don't know why all of us were in that cottage together. They just don't know who was with who. And even if they do, who cares? We're grown, we make our own decisions."

"Ashton, there are other people in our lives that we have to think about. It's not just us, you know. We have children to consider. This small town isn't ready for change like this from people like us."

"Like us?" He frowned.

"Yeah, like us. Dignified. Isn't that the right word for Coldwater citizens of our status? Supposedly? I mean, I know it's bullshit, but it's true."

He chuckled at my sarcasm. "You're right. Some of the most hypocritical people in the world live right here in this little town, but they still judge other folks like they haven't sinned a day in their lives. They think as long as it's done in the dark it's all right. But by no means can it be brought to the light, even if deep down a person wanna try to make their wrong, right. Damn, what do they think about that?"

"It's a mouthful, but it just about sums things up." I nodded. "Look, Ashton, it's so wonderful that you haven't tested positive, and don't care whether I have or not. I guess that helps me know how much you really care, but it's not the real issue."

"Nothing's the real issue, baby. We don't have to have issues unless we create them. We can't let other people live our lives for us. We've made our own mistakes and paid for them . . . now we can make our own choices. And I choose us."

I slumped my head over and walked away from him to sit down on the sofa. He followed and sat beside me.

"Just to let you know . . . I've had several tests and I'm not positive either."

He opened a big smile. "You're not?"

"No."

"Oh, baby. That's wonderful. See, that's a sign. We can be together if we really want to. Nothing's stopping us."

"Ashton, I don't—"

He took me in his arms and began kissing me passionately. His warm tongue felt so good touching against mine. He caressed my backside gently. I gradually leaned all the way back on the sofa with him leaning on top of me as we continued kissing. My adrenalin was amazing. Ashton's body felt so good on top of me. He made me feel things I hadn't felt in a long time, in months. I was beginning to feel alive, like a woman again.

His presence excited every muscle in my body. During our kiss, he lifted his head from time to time and gazed at me, showing me all the intense emotions that were in his soul. He ended our tongue-locking kiss, and began planting smooth, random kisses all over my face 'til he reached my forehead, then he planted his famous endearing kiss in the same spot so perfectly.

After that, all of my logic vanished. My body, mind, and heart turned to silly-putty. I was his for whatever he wanted. I began pulling at his shirt to take it off; and he helped. I then unfastened and opened his pants as he held himself over me, never taking his eyes away from mine. He took the liberty of taking his pants off, along with his shoes.

He easily pulled my baby blue nightshirt over my head, leaving nothing but my panties intact. In the blink of an eye, he took those off of me too. Our naked bodies entwined felt so fervent and moist. His dick was extra strong and hard. I wanted him in me so badly. I slowly parted my legs, letting him know I was ready for him to come inside, but he stopped all activity and didn't budge anymore. He stayed there on top of me, staring as if he was trying to see inside my mind.

I wondered what he was thinking as he stared at me so insistently. Then, as if he'd heard my thoughts, he asked me, "Wanna know what I'm thinking?"

I gently nodded. "Yeah."

His answer was so seductive and soothing. "I'm thinking how beautiful you are. And how much I love you. And how bad I want you."

He had caressed and kissed me so good, my body was severely overheated. If he wanted me so badly, didn't he see I was lying there fully ready for his taking?

"I'm here. I'm yours. You can have me," I whispered while stroking his back.

"No, baby. I don't mean just for now. Touching you and kissing you made me get carried away. Now here we are naked. The truth is, I didn't come over here to get you into bed. I mean, that's a good idea . . . but it's not why I came. I came to tell you how much I love you and how much I need to be with you from now on."

"Ashton, all I have to give is right now. I just can't make any long-term plans like that. Don't get me wrong, I wanted to see you just as bad as you say you wanted to see me, but no matter how much my heart says yes, I've got to think as realistically as I can. Please try to understand?"

"As bad as I don't want to accept you telling me no, I do understand."

"Baby, it's not a no."

"What is it then?"

I kissed him gently on the forehead and said, "It's a, wait-a-while-and-let's-see-what-happens."

His gentle okay led us into a tight hug, then he motioned to get up. I pulled him back close to me.

"What are you doing?" I asked. "I didn't mean wait a while to make love, I meant wait a while to see where our relationship goes."

"I know, baby. I know what you meant. And I know you're right about it, 'cause this is a mistake. I apologize for doing this to you."

I was confused. "What are you talking about?"

"Putting you at risk like this. That wasn't my intention, but I still ended up laying here on top of you getting ready to expose you—"

"I thought you said you hadn't tested positive?"

"I haven't."

"Then how are you putting me at risk? If both of us are still negative, how can you be putting me at risk, Ashton?"

"Because."

"Because of what?"

"Think about it. What if you haven't contracted any of the virus in any form? You haven't tested positive yet, so there's a real big chance you won't."

"I know that. The same goes for you too."

"Maybe. But what if . . . what if it's in my cells and just hasn't shown up? Here I am getting ready to have unprotected sex with you, exposing you to it all over again. That's real responsible, ain't it?"

"Ashton, please. I can say the same thing for myself. I mean, what if you don't have it in any form either? And it just hasn't shown up in *me* yet? I was getting ready to do the same thing to you with no protection."

I exhaled. "Look, we can only go by the test results. There's no way for us to know what the outcome of any of this is gonna be."

"You're right, but the least I can do is try not to hurt you any more than I already have."

"How have you hurt me?"

"Being with her at the same time I was being with you. I mean, she wasn't real to me like you were. I was just doing it 'cause I could. I knew I loved you back then, but I didn't wanna have to deal with it. If I hadn't been with her maybe none of—"

"Been with who, your wife?" I said teasingly, trying to lighten things up since he was so frustrated with blaming himself.

"No. Renal—"

"I know who you meant, I was just joking. Baby, all that's in the past. It's over and done with, let's leave it there. Besides, even if you hadn't been with her, she was still determined to get me. Did you forget she slept with my husband on purpose just to pass the virus along? She betrayed all of us like that?"

"Yeah, I'll bet that was a hard pill for you to swallow, wasn't it?"

"It was. But I did, and I'm dealing with it. That's all I can do . . . that's all you can do."

Ashton was a man in every way, but at this moment he seemed so delicate, so vulnerable. He lay his head on top of my breasts. "I have to keep reminding myself, I'm not a normal man anymore. I'm possibly diseas—"

"Be careful. Whatever you say you are, remember I'm that too, because I was doing the same thing you were doing." I sighed. "Listen, baby. We don't even have the virus yet, and you're already giving up. Don't label us. We haven't done anything a few billion other people on the planet haven't done. Even if we do get sick, the worse thing folks can say is, they're sick. We're not celebrities like Magic Johnson, but if he can survive and go on with his life for all these years, we can too. Right?"

"Right."

"But I do agree with you on one thing." I admitted.

"What's that?"

"We've got to start being more careful and practicing safety. We can't do what we used to do. That's how we ended up here in the first place. Stop beating yourself up, okay?"

"Okay."

"One last question." I lifted his head from my chest. He parked those beautiful browns in mine again.

"What?"

"We're not gonna make love, are we?"

"You got any protection?"

"No. You?"

"No."

We kissed. As bad as I wanted to, Ashton and I didn't make love that night. We put our clothes back on and fell asleep wrapped in each other's arms in my bedroom later on.

Chapter Twenty

It was hard to believe almost a year had gone by since that atrocious night in October of '99, but it had. And now it was September 17, 2000. Thirty days to the anniversary. I wasn't sure how I would feel when the day finally arrived, but I expected to be very emotional. So much had happened since then. Ashton's divorce from his wife was finalized in the early summer of 2000. And because I went ahead and filed for mine a few weeks after he started visiting me at my apartment, I was a free woman too, but not for long. Ashton and I were married in a private ceremony shortly after both of us were able to bury our divorce papers in an iron chest, forever.

Before I moved in with him, he and I, along with Shad, had so much fun redecorating his two-story house on the outskirts of town. Five bedrooms, three full baths, a living-room, den, and a huge kitchen was what we had to work with. Ashton spent a lot of time spoiling me and Shad. It made me happy the way Shad grew to love him during the time we were seeing each other before the marriage. As a matter of fact, the marriage couldn't have come so soon if Shad had any unsettling emotions about it. Thank goodness that wasn't the case. Shad loved Ashton, and Ashton loved Shad. They were great with each other.

Reginald and I shared custody so when Shad wasn't with him, he spent more time hanging out with Ashton than he did with me. After it went on for so long, I started teasing them about my jealousy because they were leaving me out. They always tried to fix it up with some kind of bribe that resulted in the three of us laughing all over the place.

Surprisingly, Reginald didn't make a big stink of the new man in his son's life. That probably had a lot to do with the new, younger tenderoni he had living with him. His nose was wide open. And though she was a bit young in my opinion—twenty-five—I liked her because she seemed genuine. But more importantly, Shad liked her. One of her best qualities was how she had somehow managed to turn Reginald into something more than a heartless bastard.

Unfortunately, I didn't get much of an opportunity to form the same sort of bond with Ashton's children because his ex-wife rarely let them come over, if ever. She was still bent out of shape about the way things had gone down with her and Ashton. She'd walked away with a very nice pile of their finances after the divorce, so much that she didn't have to work if she didn't want to. And even though she had boyfriend after boyfriend, she still refused to kill the bitterness between her and Ashton.

I told him it wasn't inconceivable that one was still in love with him. He told me, "She's about as much in love with me as you are with Reginald." That statement sure as hell kicked my theory out the door because I knew I wasn't in love with Reginald even a little.

Life with Ashton agreed with me, I was happy again. In spite of all the bad things that had happened, I was able to smile and really feel it, not just paste one on for others. Ashton and I always talked about how grateful we were to have a second chance at life, this time with each other. I wasn't a recluse anymore. I started getting out in society again. Of course, not without some stares here and there, but it wasn't anything I couldn't get used to.

A few things about my new life came easier than I thought it would, like being an *almost* housewife. If somebody had told me five years prior that I would be an *almost* housewife at thirty-four, I would've told them they were crazy. When I resigned from the mortgage company it was for that time and that place. I knew if I wanted to, I could always find a good job in my line of work somewhere other than my hometown.

Now that I was married to Ashton, he told me working for somebody else was out of the question. I agreed. My accounting talents and business knowledge joined forces with his expertise in running the three day spas, and managing his properties. Ashton was pretty well off financially. I didn't find out how well off 'til after I married him and took over the books for the businesses. Working the books and doing payroll from my own spacious office at *home* was where I came up with the expression, "almost housewife."

I didn't spend much time at the spas, but one of the first things Ashton wanted me to do at the Coldwater location was be there with him when he dismantled his little love room. He told me he really needed me to see him do that. We turned it into an extra employee break room. How about that?

Our HIV testing had been ongoing for nearly a year, and we were both still clear. To us, that was a sign of good grace. We vowed that we would always be thankful for what we had overcome, and we would never take it for granted, or take each other for granted either. We also made that same vow to God. I once told Reginald he should do the same because he'd been blessed enough to still be in the clear too.

As great as things were, I sometimes found myself very sad when I thought about Parrish. Her old phone numbers had been disconnected months ago. If she had new ones they weren't listed. All of my attempts to contact her had been unsuccessful. Almost a year had slipped by and not so much as a letter in the mail came from her. It was like she had dropped off the face of the earth, which was hard to do in our little town. Then I heard her husband had up and sold the house and moved the family to Memphis during the early spring. That told me why there wasn't much talk around town about how or what she was doing. Being all the way up in Memphis, and deliberately staying hid, nobody would know anything to talk about.

I longed to see her so badly, I hired a private investigator to find out if she was really in Memphis, and if so, where. When he brought me the information, I found myself standing at her front door one day. To be exact, it was shortly after Ashton and I got married. Talk about a bad idea. It was that day when I learned the truth about why she hadn't returned any of my calls or answered any of my messages. Parrish had been avoiding me and everybody else in town because she'd found out she was HIV positive while she was in the hospital. She had no desire to see anybody, ever again. Including me.

I'll never forget the conversation I had with her husband when I asked him if I could talk to her for a few minutes, just to let her know I was there. He peered with his black beady eyes into mine and said, "You get the hell away from here, dammit. The last thing Parrish needs is to see one of her *whores in crime* from back in the day."

Parrish had always told us about his cold, ruthless eyes when he became angered, but he never seemed to anger in our presence. As I looked at him at that moment, I realized she hadn't exaggerated. Still, I wasn't going to be intimidated so easily.

"Look Larry, I didn't come here to see you. Why don't you let her tell me if she doesn't want to see me?"

He thrust his hand in front of him, pointing his finger at me angrily. "Hey! Can't you take a fucking hint?"

"I guess not. So please lose the hints, and stick to the facts."

"Out of all them phone calls you made to her, and all them damn messages you left, how many did she return? Huh, how many? She knew you had been in a damn coma, but she still didn't want to see you. Know why?"

He was really pissing me off now. "No, but I'm sure you're gonna tell me."

"Damn right I'm gonna tell you. You and the rest of them dead bitches are the reason she got this shit. When the doctor told her she tested positive she said she was glad the others died, and she wished you'd died too. She said she never wanted to see your conniving ass face again."

Tears began trickling down my cheeks. "I don't believe you."

"I don't give a fuck what you believe! My wife is sick everyday of her life. Some days she can't even get out of the bed. That gunshot almost killed her, but it didn't.

Instead, I'll tell you what it did do. It caused so much damage to her system that her system couldn't make up the antibodies it needed to help fight the damn virus. That's why she got so sick so fast. She's dying with AIDS . . . let her go in peace. Stay away from her. She didn't wanna stay in that little ass town down there 'cause she knew how folks would act if they found out. As much as it hurt her, she left the only home she's ever known." He paused, burying his chin in his chest for a second, then lifted his eyes back up at me. "Don't you ever come back here again, got it?"

The slammed door in my face was a harsh cue to leave. When I made it back home and told Ashton what happened, he comforted me. He also chastised me for going up there alone.

"Baby, why on earth did you go all the way up there by yourself? You were supposed to tell me when the investigator found out where she was. I should've went with you."

"I know," I replied. "I couldn't help it. When he told me where she was, all I could think about was seeing her. I jumped in the car on impulse and left."

"Yeah, you did. Left me a note?" His soft frown and questioning eyes came at me from across the room. "How could you leave me only a note? Let me guess. You knew I wouldn't find it 'til I made it home. By then, too late, right?"

My guilty smile gave me away. "Oh, come on, baby. I'm sorry, but I couldn't help myself. Besides, going didn't really help, anyway. I'm more worried about her now than I was before I talked to her crazy husband."

"Did I miss something? Myi, the woman said she hates you, she never wants to see you again, and she wishes you would've died too. She blames you for whatever pain she's going through. How can you say you're still worried about her? I mean, I know she was your friend and all, and you cared about her, but she clearly doesn't feel the same way about you anymore."

"I don't know that for sure."

"What do mean, you don't know it for sure? You just heard it straight from her husband's mouth."

"Exactly. And until I hear it from her mouth, I just can't believe it's true. I won't. I know Parrish. She wouldn't say anything like that to another human being, especially a close friend."

Ashton didn't reply right away, he just stared at me in wonderment, then said, "Wow, that's amazing."

"What is?"

"After all the times you tried to get in touch with her, she never once contacted you. Not once. Then after nearly a year you track her down, and her husband trashes you with all that garbage. And you're still concerned? You still care as much as you did before you talked to him? Damn, that's deep. I've got to admit, you're a better person than I am, 'cause I would've cussed him out at the door and erased them from my memory for good." Ashton walked over to the sofa where I sat and took me in his arms. After hugging and kissing me he said, "The way you love with your whole heart is one of the reasons I love you so much."

"I don't know about all that, but what I do know is it felt wrong. The way he insisted I leave her alone felt . . . I don't know, it felt desperate or something." I pulled away from Ashton and leaned back on the sofa.

"You mean her husband?"

"Yeah. It just didn't feel right. Even when he was saying all those mean things to me, it hurt, but at the same time I felt like it wasn't the truth."

"Maybe you didn't want it to be the truth. Look, I hate to bring this up, but keep in mind you had another friend you thought you knew. As close as the four of ya'll were to her, ya'll still didn't see it coming when she snapped. Including me."

I looked at him as he talked, then shifted myself to lay in his arms. I was now more vulnerable at the thought of Renalia, and realizing he was right.

He continued. "Baby, I can't tell you what to feel, and I know this is a hard situation. But you've already been to hell and back, and I can't stand to see you hurting anymore. Besides, it doesn't really matter much, anyhow. He's not gonna let you see her. And from what you say, she's too sick to do anything different than what he wants."

"Yeah, another fact based on his words." As strongly as I felt about the situation, I knew there was nothing more I could do about it. I had no choice but to drop it. But Parrish was never far from my thoughts.

Chapter Twenty-One

For a long time, Ashton and I had been the object of everybody's whispering and cowardly criticism. I say cowardly, because nobody ever said anything to our faces. Instead, they did it behind our backs, then showered us with phony smiles and fake greetings. Good thing we'd been living there long enough to know how things worked. Maybe it worked that way in every small town. I couldn't imagine it being much different anywhere else.

Ashton and I were glad that the shock of the tragedy had began subsiding sometime ago. Realistically, we knew the only way the whole scandal would die for good was if a much bigger scandal came along and took its place. And even then, it wouldn't really be dead, just buried for a while. People were always looking for somebody to blame. I refused to keep on being a *blame-mat* just because I'd survived. I had left the past in the past and moved on with my new life, but I would never forget my friends—I didn't want to. What I did want to do, was stop feeling guilty about the outcome, because I didn't choose it. God did. Ashton played a major part in helping me understand that. He promised to spend the rest of his life making me happy. He wasn't off to a bad start either.

One Thursday night he surprised me with dinner plans at this newly opened restaurant in town called Claire's Place. Most of the time when Ashton and I had dinner out, we'd end up at a restaurant somewhere in Hornlake or Southaven, about twenty-miles or so from where we lived. But the owners of Claire's Place had been advertising all over town, and Ashton really wanted to support them. Nobody knew more than him about wanting local support for a locally owned business.

We arrived at the restaurant around 7:00 P.M., to a nice sized crowd on the inside. After we were seated and placed our orders, I quickly warmed up to the place.

"Hey, it's nice in here," I told Ashton. "I like it."

Ashton nodded yes, while slowly looking over the restaurant. "Yeah, I like it too. I think they're gonna do well."

"It's about time we got a place like this in town. A nice sit-down-and-eat restaurant. Instead of so many 'pick up your order and get the hell out of here' places."

Ashton chuckled. "You're right. Wonder why I didn't think of doing this first?"

"Hey, you can't own everything, baby." I grinned.

"Why not? This would've been a new chall—"

"Good evening." A nicely spoken, middle-aged gentlemen had walked up with a woman and interrupted us. "Forgive our intrusion, I just wanted to come over and welcome you all to the restaurant and introduce myself and my wife. We're Mr. and Mrs. Peyton, the owners."

"Oh, good evening. It's a pleasure to meet you all, " Ashton replied, then gestured his hand at me. "My wife and I were just complimenting the nice establishment you have here. You've done a wonderful job with the place. We really like it."

"Well, thank you," Mr. Peyton said. "That's grand encouragement coming from such a successful business man as yourself, Mr. Drapers."

Ashton seemed humble. "I wish I could take all the credit for the success of Drapers Inc., but I can't. My father had a vision before I was even born, and he worked thirty years plus to build what I only took over."

"Yeah, but look how far you've brought it. It takes just as much hard work to keep a business successful as it does to make it successful. If you don't mind me saying, evidently, you've followed right in your father's footsteps by achieving just as much success. He must be very proud."

"Thank you, Mr. Peyton." Ashton smiled. "Daddy often brags a little when he approves of some of my decisions. On the other hand, when he thinks I should re-think certain ones, he doesn't have any problems letting me know."

"I'm sure he doesn't." Mr. Peyton laughed. "Well, for the record, let me just say when you led the family legacy into the new millennium with those Day Spas, that was a stroke of genius. Your father had to be proud of that one because my wife can't get enough of them."

The four of us laughed heartily, then Mr. Peyton said, "We're going to let you all get back to your evening. Have a good one." He and his wife started to walk away. She smiled and dipped her head at us as they left. Ashton nodded back, along with me.

"Thank you. We will," he told them.

"Aren't they nice?" I was impressed with the Peyton's hospitality. "I've seen them before, but I don't know them. Do you?"

"No, but my parents know them from back in the day. They live out west of town."

"How far?"

"If I'm not mistaken, quite a ways."

"So they've probably been out there a while, right?"

Ashton shrugged his shoulders. "Yeah, but I think they were kind of low-key before now."

"Well, they've got it going on now."

Our dinner came, and was more than delicious. The evening turned out to be wonderful. After leaving the restaurant, we stopped at Exxon in town square for Ashton to fill up. It was there that all the brand new drama in our lives would begin. I sat in the car while he went inside the gas station.

As I waited, I noticed this woman sitting in a silver Lexus across the parking lot from where we'd parked. It was hard to miss her, because she seemed to be staring since the moment we'd pulled up. I was used to people staring at me from time to time, so I didn't think much of it until she got out of her car and began walking in my direction.

The parking lot was lit fairly well, but I still wasn't able to focus on the woman's face and see exactly who she was. Although, she looked somewhat familiar in the distance, I didn't recognize her. I figured I'd made a mistake and maybe she hadn't been staring at me after all. Maybe she had been looking past me at the man in the car on the other side of ours, and now she was going over to talk to him. I stopped looking at her and began flicking through the radio stations.

A knock on my window came seconds later. "Excuse me, can I talk to you for a minute?"

When I heard her voice and looked up, it was then that I recognized her, but I couldn't imagine what she wanted with me. I opened my car door and stepped out. "Hi."

She just stood there staring at me for a brief moment like she had seen a ghost. Her forehead was filled with wrinkles of pain as she barely mumbled, "Why? Why did you take him away from me?" Tears filled her eyes and began dripping down her cheeks.

I knew immediately what she was talking about, but I was speechless. I had no idea what to say to her. She appeared too dignified and well-kept to be breaking down in front of me like that. I guess even a first lady can hurt. I figured her for her late forties, not that she looked it. As pitiful as she sounded, I was moved to tears by her.

I opened my mouth carefully, not knowing what was going to come out. "Ahh . . . Mrs. McCall? You are Mrs. McCall, right?"

She slowly nodded at me. "Yes."

"Mrs. McCall, I'm not sure I understand what you mean." I lied. I had no choice but to play dumb since I didn't know what else to do.

"Please, don't lie to me," she garbled, tears still running. "Just tell me the truth. Why did you want my husband? You already had one."

My bottom jaw dropped. Damn, did she have the wrong girl or what? I hurried to let her know that. "Wait a minute. Hold on, Mrs. McCall. You've got the wrong one. It wasn't me. I'm sorry, but I wasn't with your husband. I'm not the one who had a relationship with him."

"Don't you see? It doesn't matter if you were in the

bed with him or not, you were there. You saw all the wrong-doing going on and you condoned it. Sinner." She paused, shaking her head from side to side sorrowfully. "And in the end look what kind of disaster happened? God don't—"

"Mrs. McCall, I don't mean any disrespect, and I hope you don't take it as any, but your husband of all people knew right from wrong. He chose to be at that cottage, nobody forced him. I feel real bad for your loss, but I can't allow you to blame me for your grown husband's choice. So please don't judge me, or preach to me. I've had to live with this nightmare for almost a year, and believe me, you can't say anything to me that I haven't already tormented myself about."

"Torment? Did you say torment?" She suddenly composed herself, and began wiping her tears. "Chile, you don't know what torment is yet. But I guarantee you, you're gonna know soon enough. The day is coming when you're gonna wish you had died from that gunshot to your head right along with the rest of them. Mark my word."

Now I was offended. "Is that a threat? Are you threatening me?"

"Call it what you wanna call it, but you've got to pay for being a Jezebel like your friends did. Just because you lived to see a few more days don't mean you're getting away."

"So you are threatening me." I raised my voice and pointed my finger at her. "You know, you've really got some nerve, coming over here blaming me for your misery. If you wanna blame somebody, blame your husband, he was the one married to you. I was feeling sorry for—"

"What's going on?" Ashton had come out of the store and walked up on us without me even seeing him approach. That's how wound up Mrs. McCall had gotten me.

By her being an older lady and a so-called woman of God, I didn't want to disrespect her like that, but she gave me no choice. I had to put her in her place.

"This is Mrs. McCall, Zeke's wife," I told Ashton.

Ashton gave her an unfriendly look. "I know who she is. What I don't know is what's going on." He may not have heard the whole conversation, but his tone revealed he knew something wasn't right about her approaching me.

"Mrs. McCall, is there anything in particular you need with my wife? I'm Ash—"

"Oh please! I know who you are." She snapped, then jerked herself around and walked off.

"What in the hell is her problem?" Ashton asked me.

"You don't wanna know," I replied, opening the door to get back in the car.

On the way home I told him what she'd accused me of. He was pissed about it. He was even more pissed that she had threatened me.

Ten minutes after we were home the phone rang as I stood at the bar in the kitchen drinking a glass of water.

"Hello." I picked up.

"Hey, Mommy," Shad's sleepy voice came through the receiver.

"Shad?" I said, turning to look at the clock on the kitchen wall. "Little boy, it is fifteen minutes to ten. What are you doing still up and got school in the morning?"

He started laughing. "I know, I know. But I've been calling you to say goodnight and you didn't answer. You didn't answer your cellphone either."

"Oohh, I'm sorry, baby." I talked in my special little

boy's voice just for him, which he hated. "I accidentally left my phone at home. Why didn't you call Ashton's?"

"I did. He didn't answer either."

"Ohh, his ringer must've been turned down or off."

"Where ya'll been, Mommy?"

"Nosey Posey." I teased him. "We went to dinner at the new restaurant in town, Claire's Place."

"Aw, did ya'll like it?"

"Yes, Shad, we liked it very much. Does your daddy know you're up? Again?"

He hesitated. "Well . . . ahh . . . not exactly."

"Not exactly?" I sighed. "How about, no, he doesn't. This is the third time this week."

He laughed again. "No, he doesn't know."

"Okay, you called me to say goodnight, so say it and go straight to bed, now."

"Goodnight, Mommy, and tell Ashton goodnight too."

"Goodnight, baby. I'll tell him."

Ashton walked into the kitchen right after I hung the phone up. "Who was that, baby?" he asked.

"Guess."

"Shad?"

"And guess what he wanted?"

Ashton laughed. "To say goodnight, again."

"That's the third time this week. If he keeps it up, I'm gonna have to let Reginald know he's not getting in the bed on time."

"He'll be okay, he just misses his mother." Ashton put his arms around me. "I don't blame him. If I was away from you as often as he is, I'd miss you too." We kissed. When we retracted Ashton said, "You wanna know what I think?"

"What?"

"I think he really wants to come and live here with us permanently. He just don't wanna hurt his daddy."

"You think so? He hasn't said anything like that to me."

"I know so."

"How can you be so sure? Has he said something to you?"

"Not directly. He kind of suggested it."

"When?"

"I was working on the go-cart with him the last time he was here, and he asked me if I thought it would be cool for him to be over here all the time. I told him yeah, and asked if he wanted to stay with us all the time."

"What did he say? What did he say?" I was anxious for the answer.

"He said, 'nahh, I was just wondering about it. My daddy's gotta be with me sometimes too.' "

"That's music to my ears. But, Lord have mercy, if Reginald knew, he'd swear I was trying to replace him in Shad's life with you."

"Yeah, well, don't say anything to Shad about it. Let him mention it to you first."

"How can he? I never see him when he's here, unless I tie you down right next to me, then he'll stay put 'cause you're put." We laughed. Ashton flipped the kitchen light off on our way to the bedroom. We were in bed asleep inside an hour.

Chapter Twenty-Two

Shortly after 2:00 A.M., I woke up screaming from a terrible nightmare. "Nooooo! Nooooo! No! No! No!"

Ashton turned on the nightstand light near him and grabbed me, trying to hold me. I was tossing and turning as if I was fighting someone.

"Myi! Myi! It's okay." He struggled to calm me. "It's okay, Myi. Wake up. It's oka—"

"Stop it! Stop it!" I cried, covering my ears with both hands to keep from hearing him. "Stop it! Stop calling me that! Don't call me that anymore!"

He pulled away from me. "Okay! Okay, I'm stopping. I won't say it anymore."

I inhaled deep breaths at a slow pace to get a hold of myself. After a moment of calmness he reached over and stroked my shoulder. "You all right?"

"Yeah, I think so," I said softly, looking down at the covers as I sat in the middle of the bed with him right next to me.

"A nightmare?"

"Yeah," I leaned into his arms as he carefully pulled me close. "It was just a nightmare, that's all. Just a nightmare . . . just a nightmare." Repeating it many times, I was trying to convince myself, more-so than him, that it was only a nightmare and there were no other hidden fears about reality in my mind.

"Wanna talk about it?" He kissed my forehead.

"No," I whispered, hugging him back tightly.

"Hang on a minute." He turned around and fluffed the pillows in front of the headboard, then scooted back and propped himself against them and pulled me back into his arms. I lay on top of his chest stroking his abs, trying not to think about the bad dream I'd just had.

Ashton was everything I could've ever wanted in a man. A thirty-nine-year-old, strikingly handsome and very energetic guy. Extra fine, wealthy, and sensitive to my needs in everything he did. As I lay on his comforting chest, I began thinking about how wonderfully things had been going for us and how much I really loved him. I suddenly felt afraid that something bad was bound to happen and tear our world apart. I knew my "out of the blue" worries had plenty to do with the dream I'd just had, but I didn't want to talk about it at that moment. I just wanted it to go away.

Along with those same troubling thoughts came feelings of anxiousness, like I desperately needed him to prove to me that he really loved me as much as I loved him. I didn't understand it, but that was what I felt. As hard as he'd already worked to prove all of that to me, it wasn't enough at this moment. I needed to know that I was more important than anything or anybody else in his life, selfish but true. My heartbeat increased and a warmness came over me.

I started kissing over his chest softly and made my

way up to the bottom of his chin. He responded by gently caressing my back and trying to kiss my face as I moved at random over his neck. He smelled so good, I just wanted to eat him up. Ever since that night long ago when he came to see me at my apartment and we stripped down bare to make love and stopped in the middle of it, he had been going out of his way to put me in another world during sex. It had always been good with him, but since our courtship and marriage, it was phenomenal. Sort of like fireworks in paradise. He made every inch of my body come alive.

By now my breathing was heavy as I tried hard to control my huge passion for him. I had so much inside of me I thought I was going to explode.

"I want you, baby. I want you so . . . so bad," I whispered seductively. "Oohhh . . . I love you."

"I love you too, baby." He kissed over my face. "I love you so much."

He grasped my jaws in the palms of his hands firmly and pressed our mouths together in a fierce kiss. "Aahhh . . . aahhh, aahhh." At breathing intervals, we sounded out to let each other know how good it felt.

I pulled myself up and climbed astraddle him. He pulled my short nightie over my head and dropped it on the bed. One of the most intense things in our lovemaking was the way we held eye contact while in the process of doing it. We looked at each other so intensly, it was like our pupils would burn through each other's soul.

As I sat on him, he caressed both of my breasts gently, right before he began sucking them, one then the other. The wetness from his tongue was cool to my skin but hot to my core. My heartbeat had skipped all the way down past the bottom of my stomach, and now my pussy had a hankering thump going on.

"Oohhhh!" I didn't want to share his tongue with my tits anymore. I leaned over and stole the kisses of his mouth away from my titties. His tongue was so warm and tantalizing. I kissed him forcefully. He kissed me back the same. We worked each other's tongues over and over. I pulled at his tongue so vigorously it seemed like I was going to take it out of his mouth. I couldn't get enough of him. He was so in tune with my feelings, he sensed my extra high emotions. When I finally turned loose, and he was able to speak, he paused momentarily.

"Hey, you're okay, right?" he whispered.

"Yeah." I quickly started back to kissing him after answering. I didn't want our passionate action to stop, even though I knew he was only concerned. "I'm fine, baby. I just need you right now. I need you to make me feel good." After I told him that, our foreplay shot through the roof.

His dick was so hard, nearly busting through his underwear. I sat on top of it, but it wasn't in me yet. I wanted it in me. I raised up and hastily got out of my undies, then pulled down his shorts and clutched his dick tightly to ease it in me. Just as I felt the tip at my entrance, Ashton leaned away from me, motioning to reach over on his nightstand and do our usual thing, get a condom.

I grabbed his arm and stopped him. "No. I don't wanna use one. I want you naked. Just you . . . all the way."

He looked at me momentarily before replying. "Are you sure?"

"Yes. Don't you wanna?"

"Of course I do, but I want you to be sure."

"Baby, we've been careful and cautious and everything else all this time. Now I want you inside me . . . just you. I want my husband's bare dick inside me. Is that so wrong?" I kissed his lips. "Fuck me. Fuck me so good like I know you can. Let's lose it. Let's lose ourselves for this one time."

Without another word, he grasped the sides of my hips with both hands, lifted me up, and eased me back down on his dick. It felt good going in slowly. We had been playing it safe with condoms since forever. This was a nice change. Just to feel him inside me without being covered up gave me a sense of unmonitored intimacy. I thought we deserved it. By the sound of him, he did too.

"Oohhhh, yeah," he moaned pleasurably. "Oohhhh, yeah, yeah."

I rolled nonstop, working my ass up and down on top of him like I wasn't going to ever get anymore of his delicious dick again. At that moment, I gave the saying "giving him something he can feel" a whole new meaning. His growls told me so.

"Baby, it's so good. Oohhh, it's so good. Oohh, I love you so much. Please, don't stop. Ohhh, shit! Don't stop!" He sounded like he was about to cry. And he was working it from underneath as vigorously as I was on top. I thought it was a very tender time for both of us.

The more he talked to me, the more emotional I became. And the more emotional I became, the harder I wanted to fuck him. I began tonguing him as frantically as I had done earlier. Along with my tangy tongue technique, I sped into a vigorous ass roll that was so out of control it was almost vicious. I was turning into a madwoman. I knew all of these feelings were stemming from the nightmare. They were taking over my rational thinking. But I still didn't want to deal with any of it, so I continued expressing my feelings through our lovemaking.

"Is it good, baby," I asked him, letting up from the kiss. "Tell me if it's good."

"Oh, yeah, it's good. Oh, yeah, it's sooo good," he sang. "It's so good, I can't hold it anymore. I gotta cum. I gotta cum."

"Me too. Me too, baby. I gotta cum too."

He stuffed his mouth with one of my titties and sucked doggedly, while squeezing the other one extra tight. I held him firmly with both arms. From there we continued swerving and swinging 'til we were both satisfied. I rolled off him, panting from the workout. He panted just as much. I lay wrapped in his arms for a few minutes. Then out of the blue I began to cry. I tried hard to hold it in but I couldn't any longer.

"Baby, what's wrong?" he asked, trying to boost my head up from his chest to look in my face. "Why are you crying?"

"I'm not crying. I mean, I am crying, but I'm crying happy tears." I tried to cover up the truth. And damn, what a truth it was. It had everything to do with the bad dream I'd had. It hurt just remembering the details of the dream.

"Happy tears? Well, if they're happy tears, share some of them with me so I can cry too. You know I don't like it when you leave me out of stuff."

My sobbing didn't let me answer him right away. I began crying even harder.

"Baby, come on now. Tell me what's wrong? You're not crying like that 'cause you're happy. Something's wrong."

I still wasn't able to answer him. My tears were steadily increasing, but he didn't give up. He was determined to know what was wrong with me. "Come on, baby, does it have anything to do with that bad dream you had earlier?"

As bad as I wanted to keep the hurt and pain of the dream inside of me, he'd guessed what my tears were about whether he knew it or not. I reluctantly went ahead and told him the truth while still crying. It didn't come out quite as calmly as I wanted it to. In fact, I sounded down right angry through my tears.

"Yeah, it's about the dream, okay." I lifted myself off him and scooted to my side of the bed.

"Okay, so what's wrong? I mean, what was the dream about?" He looked confused.

"The damn dream was about you cheating on me. About you turning my fucking life upside down all over again. Once a cheat always a cheat, right?" I was downright hostile now. I snatched a wad of Kleenex tissues from my nightstand and began dabbing my tears.

"Tell me you're not serious?" He looked hurt. "I mean, tell me this is some kind of joke."

"Well, Mr. Ladies man, it's not a joke. It's real. And so is the life that you led all those years before I met you."

"Myi, you're—"

"I told you don't call me that, dammit!" I shouted. I completely lost it when he shortened my name like that again.

"Sorry." He stayed calm. "Look, I don't know what your dream was about, but you don't have the right to bring up my past. I haven't done anything to deserve it. We both had pasts when we got married and we agreed to bury them for the sake of having a real honest relationship this time around . . . together."

"Yeah, we did. And guess what? I'm not the one who's gonna break that agreement."

"Gonna break it? Did you say *gonna* break it? You mean you're going off on me 'cause of what you think I'm *gonna* do? What happened in the dream, huh? Did I do something in it to piss you off? And now you're trying to make it real? Myilana, that's not fair, and you know it."

I couldn't seem to stop shouting at him. I just felt so angry. "Not fair is me loving you with every breath I breathe, and you not being faithful to me after all the shit we've been through! And for what? A quick fuck with some ho you hardly know, just 'cause you look good enough to have it going on like that? Then surprise, surprise, we wake up one morning and gotta get tested all over again. No-fucking-thank-you! What the hell was I thinking? I divorced one cheating ass man just to marry another one. Men like you and Reginald don't change. Ya'll just change stupid ass wives to stay at home and take your bullshit 'til we wanna do it too. Fuck that! I'm never going through it again!"

He really looked hurt now. When he replied, he was almost whispering and very choked up. "Is that what you think of me? After everything we've been through, is that all you think of me? A cheating ass man, who's just like your ex-husband, and will never change? I've done everything in my power to prove to you, and to myself that I'm not the man I used to be. And I thought I was doing a pretty good job. Now, all of sudden you have some wild dream and it cancels out everything I've come to stand for." He exhaled a long breath and slumped his head over. "That's cool. If that dream was powerful enough to make you think you can't believe in me, then maybe you can't. But I know one thing for sure, it can't make *me* not believe in me.

All the shit I've done . . . and the changes I've made in my life, I didn't do it just for you. I did it for me too. Damn, a crazy ass woman shot me and I almost died. If that wasn't enough, I could've contracted a deadly disease. Either way, I would've been fucked. And you've got the nerve to sit here and tell me that wasn't enough bad shit to make a man wanna change his ways? I agree with you, Myilana. Why the hell did you marry me? I'm not even human. I'm a damn monster who's not afraid of anything." He flung the covers back, pulled up his underwear and left the room.

I felt bad. And with good reason. Here I was crucifying the man I had come to love so deeply, and believed he loved me the same, because of a dream. I knew he was right about everything he'd just said to me. He hadn't done anything to deserve my crazy accusations no matter how realistic the dream was. As I watched him leave, I felt two-feet-tall, but I just couldn't go behind him and apologize right now. We hadn't slept apart since getting married. Where was he going?

I snatched the cover up over me and stuffed myself down in the bed. *Damn, our first argument, and it's all my fault,* I thought. *I love him so much. Why am I doing this?*

It was true. Ashton's and my first argument was that night. And for no real good reason, other than my crazy insecurities, which had started from the dream. After crying for about thirty minutes or so, I drifted off to sleep, only to somehow pick back up with the same nightmare as before.

"Oh my God. Oh my God." I didn't scream when I woke up, but I sat straight up in the bed, exhaling out of breath. I grabbed my heart with one hand, it was beating extra fast. "Not again." I tossed the covers back and sprang from the bed to go find Ashton. He still hadn't come back to bed yet. I first checked the den, and there he was sitting middle-ways on the sofa with his eyes closed and his head lying on the back of the sofa. The only light in the room was from the muted TV. He must've dosed off after turning it on.

I walked over and slipped myself into his lap. He slightly jumped at my touch and opened his eyes. I lay my face against the side of his neck and felt his warm skin touching my lips and nose. He didn't push me away. He should have, but he didn't. I wrapped my arms around him and delicately mustered up a few regretful words. "Will *I'm sorry* make it better?"

There was a moment of silence before he answered, "I don't know. Say it and see."

"I'm sorry." I rubbed my lips over his neck and kissed him.

"Yeah, it made it better," he said softly, then wrapped his arms around me and squeezed me tightly.

"You're so easy." I teased him with gentleness.

He cupped my chin in his hand and raised my head up. "You're right, I am easy. But only for you. I need for you to know that." His seriousness came across plain and clear.

I slowly nodded. "I know. Me too." We kissed, then retracted. "I fell off to sleep for a little while and started dreaming that dream again."

"The same dream?" He slightly frowned.

"Yeah, the same one."

"Are you ready to tell me about it?"

"I need to . . . I want to. It's just so hard and so scary."

"If you don't wanna talk about it right now, that's fine. Maybe you'll feel more like it tomorrow."

I breathed out a long breath. "No. I need to go on and tell you. It was about that night. The night we got shot. I saw it all again, down to every last detail, only worse. It was almost like I was reliving it for the second time."

"Have you had any dreams about it before? 'Cause that's normal. I've had bad dreams about it too."

"No, not like this. I mean, I've had bad dreams about it many times, but this one was so much different. It was like I was there . . . back in the cottage, and everything was happening just like it happened when she started shooting us one by one." By now I was crying.

Ashton pulled me closer and hugged me. "Stop. Don't talk about it, baby. I don't want you to get upset again."

"I'm okay. I just wanna get it out."

"All right."

"I saw each one of their faces when they were dying. They were scared to death. It's like they were in this large amount of excruciating pain . . . and I could feel it with them. They were hurting so bad, Ashton. But the most painful part was when I saw Dhelione and Emberly's faces. I was screaming . . . I wanted to get out of there so bad." My heavy sniffling nearly took over the story. "And Renalia, oh, oh, the really scary part is . . . Renalia had killed everybody else and saved me for last. She started walking up on me saying all of these nasty, lowdown things."

"Like what, baby? What was she saying?"

I wiped my tears with the back of my hand. "At first she kept calling me a bitch over and over again, and telling me how she was glad I didn't die so I could suffer a real long time for betraying her with her man. She kept coming closer and closer . . . and the closer she came, that's when it got really weird. She stopped calling me bitch and started chanting my name. 'Myi, Myi, Myi, he's gonna break your heart. He's cheating on you just like he cheated on his first wife and you don't even know it. He's gonna make your life a living hell. Ha, ha, ha, ha! We might be dead, but you're no better off, 'cause you're gonna end up right back in the same situation like before, only this time you're gonna die even worse. Ha, ha, ha.' Then she started waving a gun in my face. I tried my best to get away from her, but I couldn't. I couldn't."

"Shh, shh, stop crying. It was just a nightmare, that's all."

"I'm sorry, Ashton. In the dream it just felt so real. I mean, all the stuff she was saying, it scared me pretty bad. It was like she knew what was gonna happen to me."

"Well, at least I know why you went off on me, and made me stop saying Myi. Look, I don't know why you dreamt that, but I hope you know it was *just* a dream. I wouldn't do anything like that to hurt you anymore."

"I know. Let's just try to forget about it, okay?"

"Okay."

Chapter Twenty-Three

The night I had the terrible nightmare was only the beginning of all the bad things awaiting Ashton and I. Late one afternoon I was home working in my office and a knock at the door interrupted me.

"Hi, can I help you?" I asked the police officer after I opened the door.

"Afternoon, Ma'am. Are you Mrs. Drapers?"

"Yes I am. What can I do for you?"

"Maam, I'm sorry to have to be the one to report this to you, but your husband has been in a car accident. I was one of the first officers on the scene, so I obtained his home address from his wallet, and came on out here to let you know he's been airlifted to Baptist Memorial South."

"What? No . . . that can't be. Car accident? Airlifted? Are you sure you have the right address, officer? I just talked to my husband a few hours ago." I wanted so badly for the officer to tell me he had the wrong address. I waited as patiently as I could as he looked down at a fold-over tablet in his hand.

"Is this 4261 Hickory Vine Road?"

I flung my hands to my mouth and mumbled, "Yes." Tears instantly surfaced in my eyes. "Oh my God. Please tell me he's all right? You said airlifted. Why did they hav—"

"Ma'am, try not to get too upset. Yes, he was airlifted. Now, I don't know his present condition, but his car flipped over at least six times, and when they took him from the scene he was still unconscious."

I fainted right there in the doorway while he was talking. The weirdest thing happened just before I passed out. The officer's mouth seemed to be moving very slowly and his words became distorted. Maybe I was in some kind of stupor or denial or something, but the last thing I remembered thinking was how much he reminded me of one of my senior classmates. This Caucasian guy named Brian Uterrman and his twin sister Lesley. The three of us were good friends in high school. I hadn't seen them in years. I wondered was the officer related to them, maybe a first or second cousin. I didn't have a clue why something like that was in my head at a critical time like this. The only explanation I could figure was that I just wigged out silently.

The officer was kind enough to carry me to the sofa and stay with me 'til I came to about ten minutes later. It didn't matter to me that I was lightheaded and off balance, the only thing on my mind when I woke up was getting to Ashton. The officer wouldn't let me drive myself to the hospital. He insisted I give him the number of a relative or close friend that could possibly come right over and drive me. I gave him my mother's number.

"Ma'am, believe me, I understand you wanna get to your husband as fast as you can, but driving while

you're crying and upset can cause serious disorienta-
tion. And that could land you in a bed right next to
him, or worse. He wouldn't want that, now would he?"

I knew the officer was right about me not driving,
because I couldn't stop crying long enough to see past
my own tears, so how would I see the road? It was
only about twenty minutes 'til my mother made it to
the house, but it seemed like forever. I locked up and
ran out the door the minute she pulled into the drive-
way.

Some twenty or twenty-five minutes later my mother
and I were standing in front of one of the emergency
room doctors with him explaining to me that Ashton
was still unconscious and being prepped for emergency surgery. One of his ribs had crushed and punc-
tured his lung on the left side. The moment I signed
the release papers they began operating on him.

Ashton's parents and sister and her husband arrived
at the hospital shortly after us. I filled them in on the
doctor's information, and from there we had no choice
but to sit and wait—and wait, and wait, and wait.
Those were the longest five-and-a-half-hours in the
world to me. It seemed like time had come to a complete stop while we sat in that waiting room. When
they finally gave me the okay to go into the recovery
room and see him some six hours later, I was only able
to stay a few minutes. Seeing him hooked up to all of
that equipment with tubes and chords everywhere was
a painful reminder of what I'd gone through when I
was in the coma. I needed to be strong for him, but I
didn't know if I was going to be able to.

I stood alongside his bed fighting the tears with
everything in me, and whispered in his ear, "Please
wake up, baby. Wake up for me and Shad. We need
you. I love you so much. You promised you would

never leave me. You promised." When he didn't respond, I couldn't hold the tears back any longer and had to leave right away.

With the exception of the one hour it took me to shower, change, and grab a few personal belongings when my sister-in-law drove me home the following day, I camped out for the next twenty-four to forty-eight hours in a somewhat smaller waiting room for family members of patients in recovery. Ashton's parents, my mother and sister were back and forth. Between the four of them, his sister and her husband, somebody was always there with me while I waited.

When I got up enough strength to not break down while talking about it, I told Shad what had happened. I made sure to sound strong and confident about his stepfather being okay, so he wouldn't worry. Finally, Ashton became stable enough for them to move him out of the intensive-care-unit into his own private room. One small miracle after the other came to pass, and he eventually opened his eyes and began talking to me.

Everyday he became stronger and stronger and on the fourth day he was able to sit up in the bed and talk. That was the day we found out the truth about the car wreck. Up until that time, we all had assumed that Ashton maybe lost control of the car, or some other kind of freak accident happened. He didn't. He told us somebody ran him off the road. It ended up not being an accident at all.

I immediately called the Coldwater police department and asked for officer Dary Ketchum, who was the officer that delivered me the news on the evening of the wreck. After I told him what Ashton remembered from the accident, he was dispatched to the hospital and sitting at Ashton's bedside within an hour or so to take a statement.

"All right Mr. Drapers, I think I've got everything down I need from you. Just a short recap if you don't mind."

"That's fine," Ashton replied.

I had already been through so many phases of emotions about the whole idea of some crazy person out there trying to injure my husband or maybe even kill him, but listening to Ashton tell the officer what happened again only reminded me that it was a harsh reality.

"Okay, the car first struck you multiple times in the rear of your car, then sped up evenly with you on the road and began side swiping your vehicle until you swerved to avoid a deep pothole and lost control, right?"

"Right." Ashton nodded. "But that pothole wouldn't have been a problem if the driver of that other car hadn't been side swiping me so hard. I travel that road at least once a week going to Hernando to this warehouse to pick up materials for the spa. So I'm very much familiar with the condition of the road, and those few construction issues haven't been a problem before."

"Got it." Officer Ketchum noted the information in his pad with his pen. "Okay, this other car was a tan Chevy, early model, maybe mid 80s, right?"

"That's right."

"And you first noticed this car when you passed it parked on the side of the road a few seconds before it caught up to you and rear-ended you?"

"Yes."

"And the tint on the car windows was too dark for you to tell whether it was a man or a woman, right?"

"Yes."

Mr. Drapers, do you know of anybody who would have reason to wanna harm you?"

"No," Ashton answered quickly.

"I mean, think real hard. Is there maybe a disgruntled employee, an angry friend, angry ex-friend, an angry ex-wife . . . maybe a—"

"An angry ex-girlfriend or present girlfriend?" Ashton interrupted him. "It's okay. You don't have to hesitate with your questioning officer Ketchum. I know you live in Coldwater just like we do. One of the downsides of living in a place that small is everybody thinks they know everybody whether they do or not. A business man, like me, who's not necessarily low-key gets it the hardest, now don't he?" Ashton paused, lightly smiling. "Look, the answer to your question is no. I don't have any ex-girlfriends. Not since I've been with my wife. Now, if you'd asked me that same question a year-and-a-half ago the answer wouldn't have been so simple."

Officer Ketchum slightly smiled back at Ashton with this humble look on his face. "I suppose, Mr. Drapers. So what about any past employees? Or your ex-wife? Or maybe even your wife's ex-husband? " He gestured his hand at me.

"No. I haven't had any employees to leave except by their own choosing. And my ex-wife, well, she's been a little bent out of shape since the divorce, but I've known her since high school and this type thing isn't her style. She's harmless. As far as Myilana's ex-husband, you're gonna have to ask her about him." Ashton turned his eyes to me, and so did Officer Ketchum.

"Ma'am, do you think your ex-husband is capable of something like this?"

"Honestly?" I furrowed my brows as I stared back at

the officer. "No I don't. I mean, he went along with the divorce surprisingly well, and I haven't heard much from him since. He's living with someone else and has been for a while now. The only time we interact is when it's concerning our son. We have one son to-gether."

Officer Ketchum flipped his tablet closed. "All right, Mr. and Mrs. Drapers, we'll start an investigation and see what we come up with. Thank you for your coop-eration. I'll be in touch." He left the room.

Ashton was well enough to be released from the hospital a few days after that. His upper abdomen area remained bandaged up tightly, and he told me it hurt a little when he breathed too hard or laughed. But his lung continued healing after the surgery, and he was in good spirits. That is, until I went to the mail box the day after we made it home and opened a letter addressed to me with no return address on it. It read:

YOU AND YOUR HUSBAND SHOULD HAVE DIED IN THAT COTTAGE WITH THE REST OF THEM GOD FORSAKEN, NO GOOD HYPO-CRITES AND SINNERS! DID YOU THINK YOU WOULD JUST WALK AWAY FROM THE WHOLE THING AND LIVE HAPPILY EVER AFTER FOR THE REST OF YOUR MISERABLE LIVES? YOU HAVE TO PAY JUST LIKE THEY DID! HOW DOES IT FEEL TO KNOW YOU'RE GOING TO JOIN THEM IN TEN DAYS? IN TEN DAYS, ON OCTOBER 17TH, THE ANNIVERSARY OF YOUR "NIGHT OF DEATH AND DESTRUCTION" WILL ARRIVE. TOO BAD YOU WON'T BE HERE TO SEE IT! BOTH OF YOU WILL BE IN HELL WITH THE REST OF YOUR FRIENDS! YOUR HUSBAND SURVIVED THE CAR WRECK, HE

WON'T BE SO LUCKY NEXT TIME. P.S. DIE!
DIE! DIE!

After I showed the letter to Ashton, we called the police and waited for them to arrive. Officer Ketchum
came out again since he was the one working on our
case. He immediately bagged the letter in a gallon-
sized Ziploc after reading it, then the three of us sat in
the den to go back over "the latest development" as he
called it.

"Well, at least we now know the incident with the
tan Chevy is directly related to what happened on October 17th of last year. Somebody's definitely out to get
the two of you, Mr. and Mrs. Drapers, and it seems to
be personal. Which means, it could be any member or
close friend of any one of the victims from last year's
murders. The person is very angry too, not just with
you all, but with the dead victims also."

"I don't understand." I frowned.

He turned the front of the letter toward the sofa
where Ashton and I were sitting and explained. "Look
how the person is referring to everybody as hypocrites
and sinners. Yeah, they're definitely pissed, pardon my
expression, at everybody who was involved, dead or
alive. Are you all sure nobody you know has been acting out of the ordinary lately? Maybe somebody related to one of the victims, and is also close to both of
you?"

"No," Ashton replied. "If it's a relative of somebody
that was killed last year, why do you think they would
be close to us?"

"Three reasons. Number one, either the person has
had you all under constant surveillance, or number
two, they've been doing a whole lot of checking up on

your private lives, or number three, they already know your daily routine."

Ashton and I stared at each other silently, perplexed about the whole thing. Then Officer Ketchum spoke up again.

"What I'm saying is the person in the tan Chevy who ran you off the road, Mr. Drapers, had to already know you were gonna be coming down that road at that particular time, so they parked on the shoulder and waited for you. You told me in the report I took that you make that trip at least once a week to pick up materials at a warehouse in Hernando, and you always go that route, right?"

"That's right," Ashton answered.

"Well, I think it's safe to assume everything I've already told you is a big possibility."

Ashton seemed dazed now. "Yeah, I guess it is safe to assume, huh? I just can't imagine who it could be, though."

Officer Ketchum slumped his head over for a moment then glumly said, "For what it's worth, I'm sorry about all of this. With everything you folks have already gone through not long ago, then for some crazy person to bring it up all back up again has got to be hard. But, I assure you, we'll do everything we can to make sure you folks are all right."

"Thank you, Officer Ketchum," I told him gratefully. Ashton continued staring down at the floor in silence.

"Look, I'm gonna go ahead and leave you folks to get some rest now." Officer Ketchum's abrupt decision to go told me he'd probably sensed how helpless Ashton felt, how helpless I felt. "But before I leave I want you to know I'm having this letter sent to the lab in Jackson to be tested for finger prints. In the meantime,

I wouldn't advise you to go out alone, Mrs. Drapers. You either, Mr. Drapers. At least, not 'til we can get this thing figured out, or get somebody in custody. Is there a relative or somebody who can go out with you when you need to go?"

"Yes. My mother or sister," I replied.

"Good. Call one of them when you have to go out," he said. "There's one more thing I need to ask you if it's all right, Mrs. drapers?"

"Sure."

"Three of you survived that night. You, your husband, and another woman, if I recall correctly from our reports. In light of this letter tying these circumstances to the circumstances back then, I'm gonna need her name and information on how to get in touch with her? We haven't heard anything from anybody else related to your case at the department, but since she was involved last year, it just occurred to me she may have gotten some kind of similar threat recently. I'll pay her a visit and see if she knows anything."

My head slumped over in sadness as I explained to him about Parrish being very sick with AIDS and how her husband had moved them to Memphis months ago, and refused to let me see her. Ketchum apologized to me about my friend, and told me he would still do some checking on her just to make sure. I gave him the address belonging to her that I'd visited not so long ago.

He took it down and headed toward the front door to leave. "I'll be in touch, Ma'am."

"Oh, my goodness!" I flung my hand to my mouth. "I just thought about something! Something that could help, Officer Ketchum. How could I not remember this?"

Ashton raised his head to look at me as Officer Ketchum walked back over and sat down again.

"All right, what is it, Mrs. Drapers?" he asked, taking his same notepad out.

"Well, at the time I didn't think this had anything to do with Ashton, but the more I think about some of the stuff written in the letter you have, it might somehow connect. I had a sort of unpleasant run in with a lady a few weeks ago, and she threatened me. At least, I took it as a threat." I saw Ashton frowning, he probably hadn't remembered the incident that I was talking about yet.

"What's her name?" Officer Ketchum asked me. "And what was the run in about?"

"Her name is Mrs. McCall," I said. "She approached me about her husband."

"What about him?" Ketchum furrowed his brows.

"Well, he's dead. He was one of the ones who died in the shooting at the cottage. He was the pastor at that big—"

"The big church on Elders Avenue," Ketchum took over my words. "You mean Mr. Zeke McCall?"

"Yeah."

"Well, what did Mrs. McCall want to know? What did she say?"

"She thought I was the one who'd had a relationship with her husband. I quickly explained to her that it wasn't me, but she told me it didn't matter whether I was with him or not, I was still guilty 'cause I was there when all of it was going on. And if I remember correctly, Officer Ketchum, she called me a sinner and told me I didn't know what torment was yet. But she could guarantee I was gonna know soon enough."

Ketchum looked uneasy as he hastily asked, "Anything else?"

"Yeah, she told me the day was coming when I was gonna wish I had died from the gunshot to my head. Mark her words."

"Is that all? Did she say anything about your husband?"

"No, she only talked about me. Maybe that's why I'm just now remembering the incident, 'cause it was me, not him. Anyway, just as I was telling her off, Ashton came out of the store and interrupted us. She sort of jerked away and walked off after that."

"Well, taking the contents of the letter into consideration, anything concerning one of you is undoubtedly meant for both of you. If she said everything you just told me, and in that manner, it certainly sounds like a threat." He seemed sure of the odds. "I can't promise you anything, but I'm gonna bring Mrs. McCall in for questioning."

"You really think she would be driving around trying to run somebody off the road? I mean, a lady like that?" I looked doubtful.

"Unfortunately, I can't rule out any possibilities. If not her, maybe a hired hand." Ketchum explained.

"Yeah." Ashton finally joined the conversation. "Doesn't she have adult children, baby?"

"I think so. Maybe it was her son," I answered him.

"Well, I can't say anything like that for sure," Ketchum admitted. "But in light of her confronting you and issuing threats, I can say it's a good place to start. So I'll follow up on it. You folks have a good evening." He rose to leave for the second time.

I walked him to the front door and opened it to see him out.

"Thank you for—"

The gunshot came out of nowhere. Blood splattered everywhere. All over my face, on my blouse, and on the outside of the front door. Officer Ketchum fell backwards on the floor, his eyes bugged out, and he began wheezing for air as if the bullet had cut off his wind supply. The bullet hit him in the chest. The only thing I was able to do was stand there in the doorway with his blood all over me and scream while looking down at him helpless.

I remember thinking within a matter of seconds, *Oh my God, they killed the police, I know they're gonna kill us.* Scared out of my senses, I couldn't move from that spot.

Then I heard Ashton yelling at the top of his voice, "Get down, Myilana! Get down on the floor! Quick!"

When I looked up at him, he was moving as fast as he could, even with his bandaged chest, to get over to the door where I was standing. It finally registered in my mind why Ashton was yelling for me to get down, so I dropped down on the floor in case the shooter decided to fire again. I was hysterical, shaking like trees in a hurricane.

"Myilana, calm down," Ashton said to me, while at the same time grabbing Ketchum by his shoulders. "Come on, baby, help me. We gotta pull him in the doorway so we can close it."

I grasped hold of Ketchum's arms to help Ashton. We stayed low on the floor as we managed to pull him all the way in the house and slam the door locked. Ashton's grunts told me he was straining his ribs and upper area, maybe even hurting himself from moving so much heavy weight.

"Call 911, baby. Hurry!" Ashton urged me as he checked Ketchum's pulse. By now Ketchum wasn't wheezing anymore, he was just lying there with his eyes closed.

I took a handful of tissues from the Kleenex box that

sat on the end table near the phone and wiped Ketchum's splattered blood off my face as I gave the 911 operator our address and told her a policeman had been shot. Before I even hung the phone up all the way, we heard glass breaking in the kitchen and what sounded like another gunshot through the window.

"Oh my God, they're still shooting, Ashton," I gasped.

"Grab that throw off the sofa and spread it over him. And stay down." Ashton took Ketchum's gun out of the holster and made his way to the kitchen, crouching down. After I placed the throw over Ketchum and put a sofa pillow under his head, I eased my way into the kitchen behind Ashton.

"What happened?" I asked, trembling all over, especially my voice.

Ashton sighed painfully, grabbing hold of the side of his chest. "Whoever's out there decided to shoot in here too . . . for whatever reason."

My tears hadn't stopped since the first shot was fired. "We're gonna die," I wept. "We didn't die last October 17th, but we will this one."

"Shhh, I don't wanna hear talk like that," Ashton whispered as he kneeled down in front of the bottom cabinets below the kitchen window. "We're not gonna die, but if the person out there decides they wanna break bad and come up in here, they're gonna die."

At that moment, what he said was my worst fear—the person outside doing the shooting deciding to force his way in and shoot us just to get it over with. I cringed at the thought. Our house sat on four acres of beautiful private property, and when I say private, I mean just that. Ashton was born and raised in the deep country parts of our town. Secluded living was the kind of living he was accustomed to, so he always invested and developed property outside the city limits. Except for the spas, of course. They were businesses in town.

The next closest residence to our place was about a half mile both ways. It was kind of like suburban living in a small town, ideal for peace and quiet. But one of the downsides was if somebody decided to hide in the many clusters of bushes and weeds and shoot at you, your neighbors wouldn't be able to help because they'd be too far away to see what's going on.

After what seemed like uncountable minutes of kneeling in front of the cabinets, I heard music to my ears. It was getting closer and closer.

"You hear that?" I asked Ashton.

"Yeah, sounds like the cops are here. Let's get up and let them in. Whoever was out there gotta be long gone by now."

The ambulance was right behind the police. Ketchum was rushed to the hospital, barely having a pulse. The other four police officers on site hoped we'd seen a car, a truck, or some kind of glimpse of the person who'd done the shooting. But after I desperately tried to explain how everything happened so fast, and the bullet just came out of nowhere, they were disappointed but understanding. They were also pissed about their fellow officer being gunned down for no apparent reason.

Among many unanswerable questions was whether or not the shooter was aiming for me. If so, he must've been a real lousy shot. Maybe he was trying to send some kind of deranged message by killing the officer who was working on catching him. That was just one, of the scenarios the police left us with. If only they had stayed ten minutes longer they would have gotten the chance to hear firsthand the answer to "why he shot Ketchum?" The maniac with the gun called our house shortly after they left.

Not knowing it was him, I picked up. "Hello."

"How did it feel watching him fall to the ground with a bullet in the same place yours is gonna be?" he said bluntly in a deep, scratchy, scary voice that I'd never heard in my life before.

My heartbeat increased instantly, and I became hot all over with fear. "Who are you? What do you want?" I could hear my own voice shaking like crazy.

"Who I am is not important, but what I'm gonna do to you and your good-for-nothing husband is. Your days are numbered, and I'm the one holding the counter, bitch."

"Why are you doing this to us? We've never done anything to you, we don't even know you."

"And just how the fuck would you know that, if you don't know who I am? I told you *why* in the letter, so cut the bullshitting small talk. When you two resilient bastards survived last year, I took it personal, seeing that both of ya'll took part in fucking up my family's lives. Now, I'm cleaning up the mess death made. See you in the A.M."

"Wait! We're not the only ones who survived! Parrish survived! What about her?" I deliberately raised my "still shaking" voice, so Ashton could hear me from the kitchen.

"What about her?" The caller uncaringly asked me the same question I'd asked him. "She's a dried up skeleton in pain with full blown AIDS. The bitch is already dead. To kill her and take her out of her misery would be doing her a favor. She needs to suffer every last one of the miserable days she's got left."

Ashton heard me, but by the time he realized I was

talking to the crazy man and made it to the kitchen phone and picked up, the guy had slammed his end down. All we could do was call the police and give them that information too. At least we now knew the crazy man had gunned down Ketchum on purpose. He'd murdered a cop just to make Ashton and I agonize over our upcoming turn. What kind of lunatic were we dealing with? This bastard seemed to be crazier than Renalia had become before she went off the deep end.

Chapter Twenty-Four

Repeated rings of the doorbell, along with count-less bangs on the door, woke us up about 11:40 P.M. a few nights after Ketchum was shot. I just knew it was the killer. *But why is he knocking on the front door?* I wondered, half terrified as I fumbled around in the dark trying to get a hold of myself. Ashton had told me not to turn any lights on. That way we wouldn't be easy targets in our own home for whatever commotion was about to happen after we made it to the front door. He was right. We already knew our way around our home in the dark, but whatever nut was at the door, didn't. I prayed that would give us a bigger advantage.

Even with our security system, I didn't feel very safe after that fool had shot clean through our windows. No security system could stop a bullet.

Bam! Bam! Bam! Ding-dong. Ding-dong.

"Open the damn door!" an angry male voice yelled inside to us between the bell ringing and door bang-

ing. "Ya'll hear me! I know you're in there! Open it up!
I ain't leaving 'til you open up!"

Ashton took the gun out of his nightstand drawer
and headed to the front door. "Stay here, Myilana," he
told me before he left the room.

"The hell I will," I mumbled, pulling out the baseball
bat that I'd put underneath the bed a few nights ago.

With so much madness going on lately, Ashton and I
had decided to take as many safety precautions as we
could. And it began with him getting the handgun out
of the closet and putting it closer to the bed at night.
From the sound of the lunatic at the door it seemed
we'd made the right decision. I eased up behind Ashton as he was peering through the peep-hole trying to
see who was causing the disturbance.

"You think it's the man who's trying to kill us?" I
asked him.

"I don't know who the hell it is, but he's about to get
his ass blown off. Right about now." Ashton unlocked
the front door and yanked it open before I could stop
him.

"No, Ashton. Why did you open this do—"

He was infuriated. He looked like he was going to
shoot first and ask questions later. I hadn't seen him
angry like this before.

"Who the fuck are you? And why are you banging on
my damn door in the middle of the night? You got
about a half-a-minute to answer me!" Ashton barked,
raising the gun up and pointing it at the tall, dark-
skinned, medium-built man standing there.

The man looked just as furious as Ashton. He appeared not to have a weapon, and even though a gun
was being held on him, he didn't back down one bit.

"Man, I don't care about that fucking gun you holding on me! You don't scare me, nigga! But if you keep fucking with my momma, you're gonna need to use that damn gun and a few more just like it to keep me from fucking you up!"

Ashton frowned. "Your momma? Who the fuck is your momma, you crazy ass fool? I don't know what the hell—"

"Ashton. Ashton." I interrupted because it hit me who the guy was. "That's Mrs. McCall's son."

I'd seen him around before, maybe when I worked at the mortgage company. Plus, he looked a lot like his father. *Is he the killer,* I wondered.

Ashton was so angry he snapped at me, and at the same time, didn't take his eyes off the guy, nor did he take the gun out of the guy's face.

"I don't give a shit who he is. His identity don't give him the right to come out here disrespecting my shit."

The guy shook his head aggressively. "Man, don't even let my momma's name come out ya'll's mouth! I'm the one you got to deal with! Tim, nigga! Tim!" He slapped his hand in his chest so hard it echoed. "Ya'll started this shit! Had the police picking up my momma over some trumped up shit! My momma's been through enough bullshit 'cause of ya'll scheming, whoring son-of-a-bitches as it is! She ain't got time to be trying to run your punk ass off no road!"

Ashton cocked the gun like he was getting ready to shoot Tim.

"No, Ashton!" I panicked. "He doesn't have a weapon! I'm calling the police on him, right now! Don't shoot him!"

That was the last thing we needed, Ashton shooting an unarmed man and facing a prison term.

Ashton spit at him. "Fuck you! And fuck your

momma! You got ten seconds to get off my property, and five of them are already gone."

The vicious look in Ashton's eyes, which I'd never seen before, clued me in that he wasn't fooling around with Tim. He was going to make good on his threat. But Tim didn't scare so easily. Brave fool. He wasn't moving away from our door fast enough for me. I thought for sure he was going to be shot when he fear-lessly peered back at Ashton and said in a calm way that raised the hairs on my arms, "I'll leave. But you damn sure ain't seen the last of me."

Ashton spit at him again as he walked off the porch, then barked, "Waterhead ass punk! Bring your ass on back so they can carry you away in a body bag next time!"

Tim McCall was picked up that same night after we reported what he'd done. And the two new officers as-signed to our case came out to see us about the inci-dent the next morning. They told us that Tim admitted he was angry about our implicating his mother, and when he came to our house it was only to insist that we leave her out of it because she was innocent.

Ashton and I confirmed what he told the officers, be-cause truly, he'd done no more than that. But we wanted to know why he waited 'til the middle of the night to come banging on our door if he wasn't guilty of something. Tim told the officers he hadn't planned on coming to our house, it was a snap decision out of anger. His mother had been crying all that day after being questioned at the police station, and when he woke up later that night and found her still sitting in the den crying he became very angry, and all he could think about was protecting her. So that was how he ended up at our front door in the late night.

The officers also told us that Tim denied having anything to do with running Ashton off the road or shooting Ketchum. They explained to us that he was no choir boy like his thirty-year-old brother, Zeke Jr., but he'd never been in any serious trouble like this before, only misdemeanor stuff. I wanted to know if they thought he was lying about his involvement, so I asked them, and they admitted they weren't really convinced it was him. Believing that, and the fact of him having an airtight alibi on the day of Ketchum's shooting, gave them no choice but to release him.

In all honesty, I didn't really think it was him either. I even understood him getting upset about his mother. And I could see where things could've happened the way he said they did, but I still felt he handled the whole thing all wrong. Officer Brown and Reid told us that Tim was two years younger than his brother Zeke, that would've made him twenty-eight. I recalled the man's voice from the horrible phonecall, Tim's voice didn't sound anything like it. Tim's voice was somewhat deep, but it was younger, not nearly as scratchy. The voice on the phone was almost senior-like, and much thicker. It belonged to somebody a lot older than twenty-eight.

Ashton and I must have talked about the whole thing for at least an hour after officers Brown and Reid left, and it was frustrating the hell out of us. Neither of us had been getting much sleep or eating very well, and we sure as hell weren't having any sex. If the slightest thing went bump, Ashton was grabbing for the gun. Our lives had pretty much turned into a nightmare, and none of our family members were taking the news about what was going on too well.

I had to all but tie my mother to a chair to keep her from racing over to the McCalls's residence like Tim

had done us, only she was going with her .45. She was
totally pissed about his surprise visit. She even told
Ashton he should've shot him since he was trespassing
on our property. It didn't take much for her to want to
shoot somebody over me and my sister and brothers.

There were times when I just went into the guest
bedroom by myself and cried 'til the tears dried on my
face. Many days I wondered if Ashton and I would
ever escape our awful past of '99. It was almost a year
later and people were still being hurt as a result of
what happened that night. I was glad when Officers
Brown and Reid gave us the good news of Ketchum
surviving and being in stable condition. The thought
of him dying while trying to help us, even if it was in
the line of duty, made me sad.

I missed Shad like crazy. We talked on the phone
pretty regular, but he had a hard time accepting not
being able to come home and stay like usual. He understood why, he just didn't want to accept it. Reginald
had been watching him like a hawk, and wouldn't even
entertain the notion of him coming to the house 'til the
whole mess was over. It wasn't often that he and I
agreed on anything, but I wholeheartedly agreed with
him about Shad's safety being first priority. If a fool
would shoot in our house without knowing who was
in there, it proved he didn't care if a child got caught in
the line of fire either.

Looking back over things as I often did, I never regretted meeting Dhelione, Emberly, Parrish, and even
Renalia, and developing such a tight friendship with
them because we were genuinely close from the beginning, and we were always supportive of each other's
problems. I just wished we'd made better choices, and
left the *revenge* clause out of our lives altogether. I felt
if we hadn't made those bad choices, things wouldn't

have happened the way they did. I cursed the day we came up with the idea of starting our so-called game. It was the biggest mistake of all. It not only cost them their lives, and hurt so many other family members in the process, it ripped my life to shreds and was still haunting me.

For the amount of fun we thought we were having over that five year period of doing what we did, not one ounce was worth the end result. As I sat in the guest bedroom alone, I closed my watery eyes and wished the girls were there to agree with me. When I opened them, they weren't.

Chapter Twenty-Five

"Hello," Ashton answered the phone groggily.
"Hey, baby. Were you asleep?" I asked him.

"Kind of dozing a little. Is everything all right?"

"Yeah, everything's fine. I'll be home in about an hour. Momma and Caron's going to Memphis to do some more shopping, but they're bringing me home first."

"You're not going up there with them?"

"No way. I've done all the shopping I need to do. We left home about 8:15 this morning to get groceries and some things for the house. It's six hours later and Momma and Caron have dragged me halfway across Mississippi the whole time. I'm not lying, Ashton, we've been in every store in every little town within fifty miles. Stores I didn't even know existed."

I heard Ashton laughing through the receiver. "Where'd they find all those places?"

"Hell if I know." I laughed with him. "I asked them the same thing. And I told them there's no way I'm going to Memphis with them. We probably wouldn't get back home 'til midnight."

"It's cool if you wanna go, baby. They love to shop and you need a break from being cooped up in this house anyway."

"What I need is a hot foot bath for my aching toes, and a court order forbidding Momma and Caron to ever do this to me again. I love to shop, but they don't know when to quit."

He laughed again. Where are they now?"

"Caron's putting her groceries up, then we're gonna take Momma's stuff by her house and put it up. After that, they're dropping me off on their way to Memphis."

"Okay, baby. I'll see you in a little bit. Love you."

"Love you too." I hung up.

Ashton had been staying home working out of my office since his release from the hospital. The sensitivity of his surgery required him not to move around a lot, so his doctor wanted him to take it slow while healing and not go back to a daily work schedule so quickly. I was surprised he'd been following the order so well. Other than a little complaining about not getting much exercise, he said he was enjoying the extra time with me. I felt some of his obedience had a lot to do with trying to be home and watch out for my safety. He didn't even want me going to the mail box alone, and it was right in front of the house. He walked out there with me every time.

It was a good thing he had a great staff in each one of the spas. All he had to do was call and check in with them every few days. He really didn't have to do that because the managers had been there for years and they could pretty much run the place with their eyes closed. I guess he just wanted to feel like he was doing something productive concerning his business.

Days passed and we hadn't heard anything else from the crazy man, not so much as a whimper. It almost seemed like the whole ordeal was over and things were back to normal, whatever normal meant for our family. I reminded Ashton that it was two days 'til the seventeenth and nothing bad had happened yet.

He sighed and said, "I don't know if that relieves me, or makes me even more uneasy."

In spite of his uncertain feelings, I had almost convinced myself that the drama was over and nothing else bad was going to happen. Shortly after Momma and Caron dropped me at home, Ashton put away all the groceries and household items, then made me a nice, hot footbath to soak my tortured feet in. He and I hadn't been able to unwind and make love in several days, so the cozy footbath turned out to be a good idea.

"Are they feeling any better?" he asked me as he caressed my toes with foot cream.

I lay back on the sofa wearing nothing but a thin and short, lavender wrap-around he'd bought me sometime ago. "Are they?" I whispered seductively. "If they start feeling any better, you're gonna have to stop rubbing my feet and start rubbing somewhere else."

He twitched his brows at me playfully without responding. Then he quietly slid down off the footstool that he was sitting on in front of me, and gently lay my feet in the seat of it. He then took the foot-bather away and returned in an instant.

"Rub you somewhere else, huh?" When he flashed me his famous bright smile, which I hadn't seen in a while, I thought I was going to cum instantly. He could still turn me on in a hot minute, not that I ever doubted he couldn't, we just hadn't been into it lately. We sure was about to now. First, he moved my feet off the stool and turned my legs around and placed them straight out on the sofa. Then he kneeled down and slid my big toe in his mouth and lavished a slurpy suck on it like I remembered oh so well. Each toe had it's turn inside his warm, succulent mouth.

His foot fetish was as powerful as ever. Wrapping my toes in his tongue one by one and caressing them seemed to give him an instant lift into total dynamism. He broke away from my feet only long enough to take off his shirt and sweat pants, leaving his underwear intact. The sensation I felt when he began gliding his tongue up the inside of my legs took my breath away. As he made his way further up my thighs, my pussy began hankering for the treat it was about to get.

He slid his hands under my ass and pulled me down further on the sofa, then opened my wrap all the way, exposing me naked. On the outside of my throbbing lips his tongue felt warm and pleasing, but when he moved to the inside and his tongue began sliding over the soft walls of my pussy, I screeched in pleasure.

"Oohhh, Ashton." I watched him slowly spread my legs and bury his face between, licking me from one side to the other. He was so gentle, yet so in control. I came almost immediately. He didn't really have enough time to enjoy his eat. After my orgasm I wanted his dick inside me.

"That was quick," he whispered, lifting his head and staring at me so lovingly.

"Yeah, I want you in me now," I whispered back, rubbing his shoulders.

"Okay, come here."

Within seconds he was lying on his back on the floor

with me astraddle him, easing down on his dick. It filled me up all the way. I slowly began to roll my ass. He lay underneath looking up at me, smiling sensuously while squeezing my breasts and stroking them.

"I love you." He pulled me down into a lip smacking, tongue teasing, hot kiss.

The kiss was so hot I couldn't stop rolling my ass on his dick. I ravished his mouth and began kissing him at random all over his face while we fucked.

"Ahhhh, I love you too." I swirled out of control.

"Oohhh." He reached down and grasped hold of my ass-cheeks and squeezed them ferociously as I rode him. His frowns deepened when he squinted his eyes and forehead into one big expression of pleasure. "I'm gonna cum, baby," he mumbled.

"Yeah, come on. I want you to cum so good."

We had a beautiful evening of lovemaking. Not only did he cum that time, but he and I came several more times afterward. We made up for lost time.

A few hours later we bombarded the kitchen in search of a quick meal. Along with our meal, we shared a pleasurable conversation, wine, and plenty of laughter, something we so dearly needed. The notion that all of our problems had disappeared into thin air made my heart beam happily. That evening couldn't have been more perfect if we had been planning it for weeks. It was one of the most romantic evenings I can remember. We ended our almost perfect night in the shower together. I say almost perfect because shortly after midnight is when tragedy struck, yet again.

Chapter Twenty-six

I sprang straight up in the bed. A couple of keen beeps, sounding like the alarm system was being tampered with woke me up.

"Ashton," I whispered. "Are you woke? Did you hear that?"

His sixth sense must have been on overtime too, he was already raising up in the bed, looking disturbed. The array of brightness from the moon shined through the sheer panels and gave us enough soft light to see plenty without having to turn on the lamp.

"Yeah, it sounded like the alarm. Stay here . . . and don't turn on the light." He made a motion to get up, but didn't get the chance.

Within seconds, our bedroom door flung open and a dark figure came rushing into our room. The figure stopped and stood just beneath the darker area in the room. Because the person wasn't close enough to the ray of moonlight that swept through the rest of the room, we weren't able to make out a face yet. While I was stuck to the bed like glue, Ashton quickly reached for his nightstand drawer to get the gun. Bang! A single shot was fired into the ceiling when the person abruptly raised the gun they were holding.

"Whatever you're trying to get out of that drawer, I'd leave it there if I were you. Trust me, the next shot won't be in the ceiling. It'll be in you."

It was at that moment when I completely lost rational thought. Tears plunged out of my eyes, and I thrust my hands to my mouth, scared screamless. This was it. Ashton and I would die tonight and there was nothing we or anybody else could do about it. I'd always heard people say, your past is never too far behind. It can catch up to you at the blink of an eye. This was ever so true in our case. Only thing was, I couldn't think straight enough to know who this person was that wanted, so badly, to do us harm because of our past.

To add to the list of puzzlement, how did the person manage to get around the alarm system and come into our home like that? If I had been standing up, my legs would have conked out on me instantly. I felt them weaken and tremble like jello under the covers. It wasn't until Ashton demanded to know who was there that it registered in my mind, *I know that voice. I've heard that voice before. But it can't be. How can—"*

"What are you doing in here? Who are you?" Ashton raised his voice louder, but the person didn't say anything, only pointed the gun in our direction. Then, without notice, the person slammed the bedroom door shut. I couldn't imagine why, maybe as a safety precaution that wasn't meant for us.

If the shadows on the opposite side of the room hadn't been shielding the person's face so well, maybe I could have made out who it was, not that it would've helped us any. Now that I could think at least one thought that made sense, I was pretty sure of the voice I'd heard. But how could it be? It seemed impossible for me to be right. As scared as I was, I couldn't keep quiet any longer. I had to know if my ears were fooling me.

"Tell me who you are? Come into the light or let me turn the lamp on so we can see better?" Each word slipped through my quivering lips like a two-edged sword. So many crazy thoughts and emotions were resting on that lone voice that I thought I knew. Why? I didn't know.

After a moment of silence, my question was answered when the person extended the gun outward, pointing to the lamp and gently whispered, "Turn it on."

Now I knew without a shadow of a doubt who the serene, but slightly nervous voice belonged to. The soft whisper gave it away. My throat sank to the pit of my belly, leaving me unable to reach over and turn on my light. Without hesitation, Ashton reached over on his nightstand and clicked his lamp on.

I gasped. Tears really raced down my cheeks now. The person was exactly who I'd figured on. "Parrish!"

Ashton sounded as shocked and perplexed as I. "You?"

Parrish just stood there, pointing the gun at us with this bizarre look on her face like she was lost. I didn't know what to think or what to believe. And I sure as hell didn't know what to do. The fact that she'd somehow broken into our house in the middle of the night, forced her way into our bedroom, fired a bullet into our ceiling, and was still standing there holding the gun on us, wasn't my first concern. It should have been, because it was plain as day what her motives were. She was there to kill us, which meant she was the one behind all of the threats and drama the whole

time. But how did the man's voice from the phone call
fit in? Maybe she'd convinced her husband to help her.

Somewhere in my unrealistic thinking, I totally disregarded all of the real issues. And during our brief
moment of silence, I managed to open my mouth and
say something that wasn't even remotely related to the
problem at hand.

"Oh my God, Parrish? You're well. I mean . . . you
look well. I thought you weren't well. I mean, I thought
you were sick. You're not sick? You're not dying?"
Tears continuously streamed down my face as I blun-
dered over my sentences, trying to hold it together.
"You look good. You look like the same Parrish. You
look like my same friend. How are—"

"Myilana! What the hell is wrong with you?" I must
have really confused Ashton, or gotten on his nerves
the way he yelled at me and cut me off. "Your friend?
Do you see the gun in her hand? She's the one behind
all this shit. She's here to kill us, and you wanna know
how she's doing? Damn, are you even woke, woman?"

I didn't mean to go overboard, but I was so glad to
see her, even in the midst of the devastating circumstances. Since the moment I'd found out about her
being sick, I had pictured her deathly ill, wishing I was
there to help her somehow. Now to see with my own
eyes that she was far from being real sick, I was glad. I
didn't know how to react or what issue to address first.

Ashton, on the other hand, knew exactly how he felt
about the situation. "What kind of crazy ass friends
were you involved with all those years, Myilana? Did
you even know what any of them were capable of?" He
exhaled a long breath. "The first one didn't get us, now
the other one's gone mad and is here to finish the job.
Shit."

Parrish still hadn't responded to either of us. She remained in the same spot with a look of uncertainty. Just as Ashton was about to say something else, she snapped at him. "Why don't you shut up!"

"Why don't you get the hell out of my house and take your damn problems with you! You obviously got plenty of them," he replied angrily.

"Not nearly as many as you've got. You're about to—"

"Why Parrish?" I sniveled in the middle of their bickering while wiping my tears away. "Why are you doing this?"

She turned her bizarre gaze to me. "You know why . . . you read the letter. Don't ask stupid questions like that. Everybody else died that night . . . by right, ya'll gotta die too. It's not fair for the two of you to get away scot-free while everybody else suffered in some way or another." She glanced over the bedroom begrudgingly. "Look how things wound up in ya'll's favor. A big pretty house. Married. No HIV. No early grave. No regrets."

I frowned. "No regrets? How can you say that? We have regrets everyday of our lives."

"Well, it doesn't look like you have any, does it? We played our game and lost, Myilana. Everybody except the two of you paid with their lives. Ya'll can't get away with that. You just can't."

"What about you?" I sniffled. "You didn't die. If it's so important for us to die, why isn't it important for you to die too?"

"I'm already dead. You just can't see it yet."

"How? How are you already dead? You look fine to me."

"I look fine to you. Ha, ha, ha, ha." She mocked me rudely. "Didn't Larry tell you I was HIV positive? Or were you too blissfully happy with your new husband to hear him?"

"Yeah, he told me. But he also told me you were deathly ill and couldn't get out of bed most of the time. He said you were practically hanging on by a thread. None of that looks true. You look just like you did the last time I saw you."

"Well, that was his exaggerated version of my sickness. After all, I'm the one to blame for ruining our family . . . so that's how he sees me whenever he bothers to look at me. The only reason I don't get out of bed sometimes is because I don't have anything left to get out for. My life is over. I figure if I stay there long enough I'll speed on my time. Who the hell wants to die with an incurable disease that everybody on the planet judges you for? Or better yet, who wants to live with it?"

"How can you say that, Parrish? What about Ti'ana? She's only twelve. She still needs her mother for as long as she can have you." I could hardly believe my ears. I didn't know who was rambling on through Parrish, but it wasn't her own words. Not the Parrish I knew, talking about leaving her daughter without putting up a fight. If I knew anything about her, she loved Ti'ana more than life.

"Shut up. Just shut up," Parrish snapped at me. I struck a nerve reminding her of her daughter. "Don't bring Ti'ana into this. My baby girl is being well taken care of with my sister, so you just shut up."

I heard the unpleasant words coming out of her mouth. I saw the gun in her hands, but something was missing. She seemed to be forcing herself to do what she was doing. Her overall routine came off as just that, a routine. As hard as she was trying to convince us of wanting to harm us, I wasn't buying it. I didn't sense that same coldhearted, killer instinct from Parrish like I'd done with Renalia when she snapped. Parrish's angry face looked pasted on, and her uncaring words sounded like some kind of recital, a front. She looked too nervous and unsure for any of it to be real.

Another unexplained thing was how she constantly glanced back at the bedroom door like she was afraid of something in the next room? Ashton had been quiet and patient during the time I was talking to her. Maybe he was hoping I could say something to change her mind about what she was doing. Now he was on edge again.

"Look, Parrish, it doesn't have to end like this. The stuff that happened back then is over. Why can't we just leave it in the past? We'll never forget about the ones who died 'cause they shouldn't have died like that. What happened can always be a lesson for us."

Parrish poured out this sorrowful look, then pointed the gun directly at Ashton and extended her arm, indicating she was about to fire.

I instantly freaked out, crying like crazy. I couldn't bear to sit by again and watch another person that I loved be shot in front of me, even if I was going to be next. Before I realized it I had dived in front of Ashton to block the shot.

"No, Myilana!" Ashton yelled, pushing me out of the way. He flipped our positions and wrapped me in his arms with his back to the gun, protecting me from the inevitable bullet. This meant he was going to be shot in the back, and still die before me. I struggled hard to remove his grip, so it wouldn't go down like that this time. But he held onto me as tight as he could, rendering me powerless.

All I could do was scream through my tears and wait for him to collapse. "Nooo, Ashton! Noo! No! No!"

With all of my struggling and weeping he wouldn't

let go. He had slid his mouth directly on top of my ear and continuously whispered, "Shhh, shhh. I love you, baby. Shhh, it's okay. I love you, shhh." His helpless murmuring only made my heart hurt worse, because I knew in a moment he wouldn't be able to say anything else.

Seconds passed. Nothing. That fatal shot we were awaiting hadn't come yet. By now I'd lowered my loud weeping a notch, and instead of hearing the gun go off, we heard desperate crying that wasn't mine. Ashton loosened his grip on me only enough for both of us to turn around and see what was going on.

Parrish had dropped the gun, fell to her knees on the floor, and was crying just as hard as I was. Her river of tears and earsplitting chants filled the room with mourning. "I can't! I can't! I just can't! I can't do it! I'm sorry, I can't!"

Without having a second thought, I broke free of Ashton's hold and dashed to her side. Kneeling down, I wrapped my arms around her to comfort her. "It's okay, Parrish, don't cry."

Ashton wasted no time going into the nightstand drawer for his gun. I was glad he kept the gun on the bed next to him, instead of holding it on her 'til he called the police. She was obviously confused and sorry for what she'd done. I tried my best to console her. "You don't have to cry, Parrish. It's all—"

"Myilana!" She yelled, only hugging me for a moment, then abruptly pulled away. She was freaking out like something else was wrong. "Myilana! He's—"

Slam bam! The bedroom door suddenly flung open before she could tell me whatever it was she was trying to tell me. All eyes turned to the person that entered the room so fiercely. Parrish's eyes had widened so big, she almost looked traumatized. And with good reason. His expression and presence alone was petrifying as he stood before us. She instantly began pleading with him.

"Please, Larry, I can't do it. I can't hurt her, she's my friend. I love her. Don't hurt them? They haven't done anything to you. I'm beg—"

"Shut up, bitch!" he barked viciously, looking down at her like she was nothing. "I should've known you were too weak to follow through and do the job. You're pathetic. You're willing to trade your own child's life for these two worthless bastards. What kind of mother are you?" He spit at her.

"No! Don't you touch her! Don't you touch Ti'ana!" Parrish shouted through tears.

I grabbed her and held her back from trying to jump at Larry with no weapon in her hands. The second he mentioned their daughter, she made an attempt to get up and get at him. I knew by the look on his face he would have shot her without so much as twitching.

"Parrish calm down," I said. "Just calm down and tell me what you're talking about? What's wrong with Ti'ana?"

"He's gonna kill her. His own daughter. He threatened me . . . told me if I didn't agree to be a part of his plan to kill ya'll, he would kill Ti'ana and make it look like an accident. His own child, Myilana!" Parrish was tearing hard while explaining. "I didn't wanna shoot ya'll, but I couldn't let anything happen to my baby girl. He wrote all of that stuff down for me to memorize and say to ya'll . . . he made me do it. What kind of coldhearted man would threaten to kill his own child?"

Larry glanced over at Ashton, who was standing alongside the bed watching patiently. Larry then raised

the gun he was holding higher, maybe to make sure
Ashton didn't try anything.

"Didn't I tell you to shut up!" he growled. "How do I
know she's my child? All the fucking around you've
been doing, how do I really know, huh? She may not
even belong to me. That's how I can do it, because
she's your daughter, not mine!"

"Larry, this child has been in your life for thirteen
years. Long before any of this mess, or the mess from
last year ever happened. You used to treat her like roy-
alty. I told you before, I never slept with anybody else
when we first got married. I was always faithful to you
back then. She's yours! You know she's yours! Do whatever you want to me, but leave Ti'ana out of it!"

He ignored Parrish's pleas. I, on the other hand,
breathed a sigh of relief even in the midst of the bad
predicament. I felt relief because my gut feeling about
my friend wasn't wrong, after all. The minute I saw
Parrish's face when the light was turned on I knew
deep down that she didn't really want to do what she
was doing. I didn't know why I knew, I just did.

Now all of it made sense. She had no choice, because she felt her daughter's life was in danger. No way
I could've blamed her for doing what she'd done.
Given the same circumstances with Shad, I would've
done it to protect my baby too. Ashton hadn't said anything, but I believed he understood her reason also.
Now we just needed to get the gun away from her
crazy husband.

Larry's bitterness was unbending. He peered at us
through those black pit holes he called eyes, reminding me of my visit to their place in Memphis when he'd
told me all those lies about Parrish's illness. My unset-
tled feelings about that crap had come full-circle. Finally.

"All three of you fuckers took part in messing up my life! And now you've gotta pay! If I'm gonna die, ya'll will die too." Tiny spit-beads shot out of his mouth as he snarled at us.

"Larry, it's not their fault. Nobody told you to go jump in the bed with Renalia when she invited you. You made that choice. We're both sick because of what you did, not what I did. She infected us through you, not me. Why can't you understand that? Renalia couldn't have given me a virus by being my friend. Be mad at yourself." Parrish's hurt reminded me of my own pain when she turned and looked at me.

"Are you okay?" I asked her softly.

"He blames ya'll for everything, Myilana." She sobbed. "He's been planning a way to kill you and Ashton since we moved to Memphis . . . even before then. I didn't wanna move way up there, but he made me go. When I first got out of the hospital he took all the phones away and wouldn't let me talk to anybody. Not even you or my own sister. He kept telling everybody I didn't feel like being bothered. When I finally got well enough, I told him me and Ti'ana were leaving. That's when he swore he'd kill her and make me watch if I didn't do what he said. When you came to the house to see me, I heard you. I was listening in the hallway. I wanted to talk to you so bad, but he was obsessed then, and he still is. I knew he would've hurt her. He even borrowed his brother's tan Chevrolet to run Ashton off the road. I didn't wanna do any of this, you've got to believe me. You've got to believe me, I didn't."

I put my arms around her and held her tightly. "Shhh, it's all right. I knew something was wrong when I came to see you, I just didn't know what. It's not your fault."

"All right, cut the crap!" he shouted. "Ya'll have had your little catch up moment, now it's time to go bye-bye. And guess what little wifey? I want you to know you really fucked things up by not going ahead and shooting them. Now, I've got to shoot all three of you."

Parrish gasped. "You were gonna kill me all along, weren't you? You were just using me to do your dirty work. What about Ti'ana?"

He pitched her a nasty sneer. "What about her? She don't need you."

"She does need me, I'm her mother," Parrish cried.

"I know you didn't think I was gonna let you live after all the shit you did. I numbered your days the same time I numbered theirs, bitch." He slightly waved the gun. "It wasn't supposed to go down in this order, but it'll work out just the same. Three filthy cheaters in one night. I'm not the only one who wants ya'll dead. Plenty of folks do, they just won't admit it."

"You're sick, Larry," I said with disgust. "You're not gonna get away with this."

"Oh really? Well, I beg to differ. I'd say I've gotten away with plenty. For one thing, I got in your house and turned the alarm off with no problem, didn't I?"

I pitched him a look, demanding to know how he'd managed to disarm our alarm.

He read me like a book, still smirking while he answered, "It's amazing what kind of information you can get when you give two-hundred dollars to a functioning caine-head who works at IBT Home Security. By the way, isn't that your alarm company? And aren't they based in Memphis? I've got a little tip for you. The next time ya'll go shopping for an alarm system, you might wanna go with a national company like ADT or Brinks. That way you won't have to worry about any local jokers knowing your private information and selling it. Oh, I forgot, there won't be a next time. Ha, ha, ha, ha." Now he was mocking us.

But unfortunately, he was right about the security company. Ashton and I made a bad choice to let one of his "out-of-town" friends do our alarm system because he was bringing his business to Memphis from Nashville and needed more subscribers from our area. Now that we knew the truth about how Larry got in, we would have to deal with the issue later. It didn't matter though, Larry's time was almost over, and for some reason I wasn't afraid to say it.

"You're still not getting away with this shit, you evil bastard." I snarled at him.

His smirk quickly disappeared as he jumped down my throat. "Your husband's a lot smarter than you are. He knows how to keep his mouth shut when he's staring down the barrel of a gun fixi—"

"TONIGHT ON CNN OUR TOP STORY IS!!"

Bang! Bang! Bang!

"Oohhhh, Myilana!" Parrish yelled, grabbing hold of me as I fell over on the floor.

Everything happened within seconds. Like Larry said, Ashton had been deathly quiet for quite a while. But what Larry didn't know was that Ashton was fixing to take him down. Ashton had signaled me a quick nod, letting me know he was getting ready to do something. I didn't know what he was going to do, but I did know I needed to keep Larry's attention focused on me.

Provoking him by repeatedly telling him he wasn't going to get away with what he was doing rubbed him the wrong way and kept him talking. Then after Ashton pressed the power button on the extra small remote control that he was holding, the sudden noise from the television snatched Larry's attention to the screen across the room. The second he turned his head to look, Ashton grabbed the gun off the bed and shot him.

As he fell backwards to the floor, he didn't drop the gun he was holding, that's how he managed to get a random shot off before Ashton put another bullet in him. Three shots fired. Two hit Larry. And the one I received from Larry's gun, well, at least it didn't leave me unconscious this time. I saw when Ashton ran over to make sure Larry was dead, then he immediately came to my rescue. I was still alert when the ambulance and police arrived.

Chapter Twenty-Seven

The weeks fled. It was already just a few days before Thanksgiving. The anniversary of October 17th, '99 had finally come and gone. We were ever so glad to see it leave too. Ashton and I did take the time to light a candle and say a prayer in remembrance of our friends. As far as the second night of tragedy, which could've ended a lot worse than it did, the angels must have been watching over me that night. The bullet from Larry's gun only grazed me. One of the paramedics who arrived with the ambulance examined me. He had to work overtime convincing Ashton that I was going to be all right.

"How is she?" Ashton asked him.

"Oh, she's fine, sir," he replied as he bandaged up my arm. "She's very lucky. It was just a flesh wound. The bullet only grazed her shoulder. I cleaned it up and put some antibiotic ointment on it before I wrapped it. She'll be just fine."

"You sure she don't need to go to the emergency room for that? I mean, whether it went in or not, it was still a bullet, man." Ashton paced back and forth over the floor.

The paramedic shook his head. "No sir. It's just like falling down and getting a scrape. The worst that could happen is it could get infected if it's not properly medicated and covered. I'm going to leave her a package of antibiotic cream and a few bandages. Other than that, she's great. That is, considering what you folks went through tonight."

"Infected? How—"

"Ashton, honey, I'm fine. I don't even feel it. Stop making a big deal. It could've been worse."

He eventually settled down after everybody left, including Parrish. I hated that the police had to take her in for questioning until the details of the whole thing were straightened out, but they did. Ashton and I stood by her side as she cooperated with the authorities in every possible way. At the informal hearing she retold the story of Larry's plan from the day he'd mentioned it to her. She told it to the judge the same way she'd told the police the night they grilled her at our house, then took her in.

Everything down to the rifle that shot officer Ketchum, the threatening letter we received, the phone call, and the tan Chevrolet that belonged to Larry's cousin, trailed back to Larry. The only thing that Parrish's fingerprints were on was the handgun she held that night. Ashton and I answered for that when we explained the details of Larry confessing to everything he'd plotted in front of us. Bottom line, he'd forced her to do what she'd done.

She was soon released, finally able to get on with her life. Considering she'd been held prisoner by Larry for nearly a year, she was finally free in more ways than one. Now that she no longer had any of that to worry about, she hurriedly moved back home to Cold-water and rented an apartment for her and Ti'ana at the same place I'd stayed before Ashton and I got married. Her place was only fifteen minutes from our house. Larry's life insurance policy, plus benefits she still received from her past job, left her and Ti'ana pretty well off. So even though she did have the virus, she was able to focus on staying well instead of worrying about a job or how to make money.

We visited each other often. And when we weren't at each other's house, we were on the phone chatting almost like back in the day before October '99 ever happened. We were still in the healing process, but everything we were experiencing was a part of it. Shad and Ti'ana had always enjoyed playing with each other over the years, so now they kept us busy taking them places too. I felt so blessed. It was good to have a friend again. A real friend. Somebody who really understood things. Momma and Caron loved me, and they had been wonderfully supportive, but there was no way for them to truly relate to the way I felt sometimes. They hadn't been through what I had.

Parrish knew firsthand about the hurt 'cause she'd been there too. She'd been to hell and back same as I. We could talk about things that others could only imagine feeling. Ashton, of course, understood because he'd been apart of the darker side also. He was happy that Parrish and I were moving forward with our friendship, trying to stay positive.

A few days before Thanksgiving, we decided to go out to the public cemetery and put flowers on Dhe-lione and Emberly's grave. Neither of us could bring ourselves to make a special trip out to Renalia's yet. We found out her parents had gone out of their way to have her buried at a different cemetery. A private one, way out in another county. For them to do that, it almost sounded like they knew she had turned evil and was trying to get her as far away from Coldwater as they could. It would've been a lot less trouble for them to bury her at Oak Hill where the girls were.

Cemeteries always looked peaceful to me, but there was something extra serene about Oak Hill. Maybe its visual loveliness gave it the plus. The day Parrish and I went out there with the flowers to put on the graves, it seemed more beautiful than usual. The sun shined bright in the sky, and the weather was pleasant for that time of year. Southern Mississippi's weird that way. Here we were in the Thanksgiving season, and still able to wear short sleeves and short pants without catching a chill.

"I think we picked the perfect colors, don't you?" Parrish asked as we were leaving Emberly's gravesite. We had already placed the flowers for Dhelione on her grave.

"Yeah, Emberly liked wearing every color except . . ."

We looked at each other and said, "Green," at the same time, then laughed.

"And why didn't she like green?" I asked playfully, remembering what Emberly always told us about wearing green.

"When she was ten her momma made her wear a little green dress to school every Friday, and the kids always teased her with a rhyme. 'Green, green, your booty ain't clean.'" Parrish and I giggled heartily.

"Oh, man. Remember the first time she told us about that. We almost popped a gut laughing, didn't we?" I flung my hand to my chest trying to control my laughter.

"Yeah, and then she told us the day she turned eighteen and started buying her own clothes, she never wore green again."

Parrish and I had already had our sad tears when we first arrived at the cemetery. Now it felt good to reminisce about fond memories of our friends, and laugh about how much fun we'd had when they were with us. We were so into it, we didn't notice the woman that was waiting near the gate until we got close up on her.

"Afternoon, ladies," Mrs. McCall said. "Flowering your friends' graves?"

"Hello, Mrs. McCall."

"Hi there." Parrish and I spoke to her simultaneously.

"Yes, we took flowers to our friends' graves." My response wasn't too vigorous, but I didn't want to be rude and not answer at all.

By now she was eyeballing my dear friend up and down. "Did you get a chance to put any flowers on Zeke's grave yet?" she asked Parrish blatantly. It was at this moment I was glad I'd already told Parrish about Mrs. McCall's and my past run-in. My girl knew what was up with this old grudge-holding heifer, so she could handle her business.

Parrish sighed. "Look, lady, why don't you get over it. He's dead and gone, he can't have either one of us now. And for the record, I wasn't the only one your husband was sleeping with. Can you handle the truth?"

She didn't break a sweat while peering at Parrish intently, then she uttered, "Try me."

"Fine," Parrish replied angrily. "He was a big ol' freak, and he had plenty of women on the side. But I